THAT GIRL

THAT GIRL

JILLIAN DODD

Editor: Jovana Shirley, Unforeseen Editing
Photo: © Regina Wamba
Cover Design: Mae I Design

Jillian Dodd Inc.
Seminole, FL

Jillian Dodd is a Registered Trademark of Jillian Dodd Inc.

ISBN: 978-1-962549-54-7

Books by Jillian Dodd

Eastbrooke Academy®
Best Friends Aren't Forever
Popularity Isn't Easy
Kisses Don't Stay Secret
First Loves Are Hard To Forget

London Prep®
The Exchange
The Boys' Club
The Kiss
The Key
The Party
The Country House
The Choice
The Club
The Match

The Keatyn Chronicles®
Stalk Me
Kiss Me
Date Me
Love Me
Adore Me
Hate Me
Get Me
Fame
Power
Money
Sex
Love
A Very Keatyn Christmas
Keatyn Unscripted
Aiden

That Boy®
That Boy
That Wedding
That Baby

That Love
That Ring
That Summer
That Promise
That Forever
That Crush
That Girl
That Someday

Dating in the City
Writing Mr. Right
Heart Stopper
Crazy For You
Catching Feelings
Party Of One
Save The Date
Urban Cowboy
Check, Please
Happily Ever After

Crawford Brothers
Vegas Love
Broken Love
Fake Love

Spy Girl®
The Prince
The Eagle
The Society
The Valiant
The Dauntless
The Phoenix
The Echelon

Girl off the Grid

SATURDAY, JUNE 20TH

Twelve days.

Ainsley

I WAKE UP and look at the clock. It's nearly nine. I can't believe I slept in so late.

I touch my abdomen and think about my call with Damon last night. The decision I made not to tell him that I'm pregnant.

My questions this morning are: *Was it the right thing to do? And what are the consequences of my decision?*

It does mean I'm going to have to go through pregnancy alone. But I believe it will be worth it. I care for him. Love him. Want his first season of college football to be everything he's ever dreamed of. For him to be able to focus on those goals and experiences. To have nothing to distract him. For the press to talk only of his accomplishments and not on the fact that a less-than-two-week summer fling resulted in an unplanned pregnancy.

Which is the other big issue.

We have been together for all of twelve days.

Day one was just harmless flirting.

Day three, the night of Chase and Dani's wedding, I found out about my dad's gambling addiction, drank too much, and tried to seduce Damon.

Day four, I woke up mostly naked with him in my bed. And later that day, we shared our first kiss.

Day six was our first date, when we spent a fun night in a tent he had set up for us.

On day seven, after making sand angels, we were naked together in the shower, and the physical side of our relationship progressed past kissing.

Day eight was our butterfly picnic, where we first said *I love you.* Where we spoke of how fast things were moving between us and how we believed we were soulmates.

On day nine, we watched fireworks together, and later, I fell asleep on his shoulder.

On day ten—the night of his birthday party—he wished for birthday sex, took me to his suite, and asked me to be his girlfriend. And when he blew out the candles just after midnight on his actual birthday, he said, *I wish Ainsley would love me forever.*

On the eleventh day, we shared a long night filled with passion and love, ending my sexual drought.

And on the twelfth day, our last day together, we agreed I would visit him whenever I could. We discussed how we would label our relationship and ultimately decided he would call me what he'd called me since the first day he saw me—his future wife.

I look down at the charm-filled bracelet on my wrist. The charms he gave me to remind me of each of those days. Days spent falling in love with him.

I told him I truly believed he was my first *real* love. And that I wanted to support him in football, life, and beyond.

And that's what I'm doing—supporting him in football so that he can enjoy it in his life and beyond.

I smile when I think about what else we said that day. How he asked me to move to Lincoln with him. Since I have to work this summer and then finish my degree at a different school this fall and get a job, we decided to do the long-distance thing until after I graduated and then reevaluate things at Christmastime.

Christmastime.

That's when I'll tell him.

I grab my phone and look up his season schedule. Their last game is Thanksgiving weekend. If they have a good enough record, they will go to the conference championship game the following weekend.

There's another reason why this makes sense.

Damon is the ultimate in big gestures. If I told him now, he'd want to get married. I know he would.

And although we're in love and we're going to have a baby, there's no need to rush that kind of commitment.

It would be too much, too soon. I mean, take my parents, for example. They got pregnant and married after only knowing each other for a few months. And even though they are now just getting a divorce, honestly, as soon as my mother found out Dad had lied to her about all the money he'd lost, she should have left him then.

And I don't want to go through that.

I think Damon's wonderful. But by not telling him, I can keep the focus on our relationship. We'll have time to figure out if there's more than just love there. If we could have not only a loving and healthy relationship, but one filled with mutual respect.

And I know Damon is nothing like my ex, Brad. I don't believe he will cheat on me. But I don't know that for sure. I don't know how he will react if he doesn't end up starting. Or how he will behave when he becomes the star I know he will be. And how he will handle the attention he's bound to get from everyone—from journalists to girls.

The only thing I don't like about this plan is that I'm going to have to—well, not lie to him exactly, but I won't really be telling him the truth.

And somehow, I'm going to have to hide this pregnancy from him.

From Sammy.

From everyone.

To be honest, it might not be that hard. Other than being a little tired, I really don't *feel* pregnant.

I pop out of bed and go into the bathroom.

Look at the tests on the counter, double-checking that they're still showing positive.

I close my eyes.

"Remember in Haley's wedding toast, how she talked about our first summer here? How we call it that summer? *The summer we will never forget?" he said.*

"Yeah."

"Being here with you today is like that. I'll never forget the way you look, what you say, how you kiss me, and how you make me feel. I know we've been flirting and kissing, but today feels like one of those moments. The start of something we'll never forget."

Tears filled my eyes as I clinked my glass against his. "To us."

We sealed the toast with a kiss, and then he held my gaze and said, "I love you, Ainsley."

I was shocked he had said it so soon and asked if he was serious.

"I've always been serious about you."

"I mean, I thought the whole future wifey was, like, just a flirty thing."

He shook his head. "I wouldn't joke about that."

And I could barely believe it.

"You really are in love with me? Like, it's not just some crush?"

"Most definitely not," he said, sliding his finger across my cheek. "I am in love with you."

I press my eyes shut tighter as I'm overcome with emotion. I so clearly remember locking eyes with him the first time I saw him, feeling like I was starring in a romance movie and had just met my true love.

"I want you to know how I feel. How I've felt since I first saw you. Tell me what you're thinking." He pulled me onto his lap. "Actually, don't tell me what you're thinking. Tell me how you're feeling."

"That day, we, um … like, our eyes met …" I stuttered out.

"I knew then," he said.

Tears filled my eyes as I cradled his handsome face in my hands. And then I said what was truly in my heart.

"I love you too, Damon."

And I knew I meant it.

Which is why I'm doing this.

MONDAY, JUNE 22ND

A contented sigh.

Ainsley

"WOW," JADYN SAYS, pointing to one of the two design boards I set in front of her. "This design is quite unique."

And I'm trying to figure out if that's like someone saying you look *nice* when you think your outfit should elicit a word like *fantastic* or *gorgeous*.

I swallow and hope she doesn't hate it because I am obsessed with the way it turned out. The other board is nice. It's just that it's way safer. Standard. Typical.

But I feel like Uncle Tripp has never played anything safe in his life.

She looks at the other board, nods approvingly, then goes back to the first one. "Tell me about your inspiration for this."

"Um, well," I stutter out, because I know this is going to sound silly the second I say it, "I imagined the kind of home Uncle Tripp would have if he were a cowboy. Thought the lobby of the hotel should look like that."

She starts laughing.

Shit.

But then she says, "That's exactly what this is. He's going to love it. The massive copper-covered fireplace is truly an incredible idea. It's very much a mix of the rustic vibe of Cowtown with a touch of Dallas bling."

I heard Fort Worth was called Cowtown, but I sorta thought it had to do with cowboys—which I guess, in a way, it kind of does. It got the name because of the cattle drives that had started in the Midwest and ended at the Fort Worth Stockyards.

"And these coffee tables—are they honed marble?"

"No, they're concrete," I tell her.

"And gives it sparkle? A glitter finish?"

I shake my head. "They're actually made from Unimin white quartz sand, which glimmers. I like the juxtaposition of the rough stone with the smooth copper. Plus, you can put your boots up on it and never hurt it. Same goes for cocktails."

"I really like the rich color of these chairs," she says, studying the other board. "Do you think you could work them into this design?"

"Yeah, I think that would look—" I start to say, but then a coworker sets a steaming bowl of refried rice with some kind of fish in front of Jadyn, and I immediately feel sick. "Oh, um, can you give me a minute?" I say to her, quickly leaving the room and heading straight to the bathroom.

I take a deep, cleansing breath.

The smell made me feel like I could throw up, but now that I'm away from it, I'm completely fine.

Oh my gosh. Do I have morning sickness? But then I laugh at myself because it's not morning. It's nearly one.

I probably need to look up pregnancy symptoms. What's normal and not. And see a doctor to get confirmation.

Although I did take a pregnancy test again this morning, just to be doubly sure. Because other than being tired—which, considering the number of hours we've been working, isn't a surprise—I feel good.

And I'm glad. I need whatever symptoms I might have to wait until I'm done with this project.

Because now, more than ever, I really need to do well. I need Jadyn to give me the most amazing referral letter ever so that I can get a good job when I graduate.

"ARE YOU FEELING okay?" Jadyn asks when I return.

"Yeah, sorry. Just a little tired. But I'm fine."

"I feel ya. I've been exhausted too," she says. "This is a big project to try to make perfect in a short amount of time. Are both designs within budget?"

"They are. The only variable is that copper prices change often, but right now, we're good."

She looks out into the main office space and yells, "Claire, can you come in here?"

Claire, who is just under Jadyn in the design pecking order for this project, gets up from her desk and joins us.

Jadyn says, "How far along are you"—I start to panic. *How could she possibly know I'm pregnant when I just found out myself? I'm sure I look guilty when I glance down at my belly*—"on the bathroom plans?"

And I realize she isn't talking to me, but rather to Claire.

I let out a deep breath.

"We have some mood boards and a bunch of ideas," Claire replies. "But we're waiting for the exterior and lobby plans to get approved so that everything will be cohesive."

"Excellent. Look at this concrete," Jadyn says. "I would love to make bathtubs out of it, but I think they would weigh too much. Don't you think that it would make amazing sinks though? Almost a trough-style with the counters and sink all in one piece."

"That would be very cool," Claire says. "Hang on." She rushes back out, stands in front of the big bulletin board with all our random inspiration, and then comes back in and sets photos and tiles in front of us. "It'd be a splurge, but when I was in Scotland, I stayed at a beautiful inn that had this modern copper tub, lined with stainless steel. We could add polished chrome fixtures. Wood paneling on the wall behind it maybe? And look at these classic green-and-white marble floor tiles. I was thinking we'd do them in a diamond checkered pattern."

"Yes to the tubs if we can get them in time," Jadyn says with a grin. "I love them, and the stainless steel interior is great for hygiene. Start with the tubs and the sinks and see what else you come up with." She grabs the tiles and swaps their positions around the photo of the tub. "What if, instead of wood on the wall, we use wood-looking tiles on the floor and do the marble tiles on the walls? Maybe mock it up both ways."

Claire nods, looks excited, and quickly exits with the samples, eager to get started.

"You did a really nice job on this, Ainsley. Obviously, your uncle made sure you got this internship," Jadyn says, tapping on my board, "but this design proves that's not the only reason you were chosen."

And I swear, I have a smile plastered on my face for the rest of the day.

I'M JUST GETTING home from the office when my phone buzzes. I smile as I see Damon's adorable face on my screen.

"Hey, gorgeous," he says.

"Hey, you," I reply, dropping my tote on the coffee table, plopping down on the couch, and putting my feet up.

"How was your day?" he asks.

"It was awesome. Jadyn loved my lobby design. Hang on. I'll text you a picture of it."

I do, and when he gets it, I watch him break out in a wide grin.

"This is amazing. The fireplace—is it copper? It's so bold. How did you come up with something like that?"

I shrug. "I don't know. I just was inspired. It's a weird combination of this town, its heritage, and my uncle Tripp."

"You're very creative. I'm impressed," he says, but then his mouth forms a naughty smirk. "Although, if you're alone, I know a way you could impress me more."

"You go first," I say, knowing exactly what he's thinking.

He quickly pulls his shirt up over his head, revealing tan muscles.

Two can play at that game, I think, slowly unbuttoning my blouse.

"I miss you," he says with a sigh.

"I miss you too. How was your night out with your teammates? We didn't get a chance to talk yesterday."

"It was pretty good. Last year, Treyvon and Chase were roommates. And it sounds like Treyvon partied a lot. Got a lot of girls. But apparently, Chase and I are a bad influence on him. He only had a couple of beers when we were out, is focused on eating healthy, and has started drinking hydrogen water for faster workout recovery."

"And the girls?" I tease.

"Oh, he says that's healthy for him," Damon says with a laugh.

"And what about you?" I ask.

"What about me?" he wonders, legitimately looking confused. But then he goes, "You know I'm pretty strict with my diet."

"I was referring to the girls. I'm sure there were some at the party."

"There were, but—are you questioning things with us already?" he asks.

I shrug and bite my lower lip. Because I don't know. *Am I?* Yes, kind of. Maybe. Sorta.

"Well, if you are, you shouldn't be. And anytime you think otherwise, take a look at that bracelet on your wrist and know that whether I'm with you or not, you're always wrapped up in my love."

"Do you think it's a little crazy that we fell in love in, like, twelve days?"

"Actually, it was just eight days when I told you I loved you. And don't forget, you said it back," he says seriously, pointing his finger in my direction.

"Is that better or worse?" I ask with a laugh while I'm shaking my head.

"Better or worse? Sounds like wedding vows to me. What do you think? Christmas wedding? Then you move to Lincoln with me and get a job here?"

My mouth drops open. Especially since I know what he'll learn at Christmastime this year.

"Don't worry," he says with an adorable wink. "That wasn't a proposal. You'll know for sure when it is. And with that, I bid you adieu, Champ."

"Good night, Damon."

"Good night, my future wife."

I hang up, then let out a contented sigh as I imagine a holiday wedding. I think back to the New Year's Eve party my parents had one year when I was still young enough to play with dolls. Barbie and Ken got married under the sparkling gold decor, and Ken kissed the bride at midnight to the cheers of the partygoers.

It's been my dream wedding ever since.

MONDAY, JUNE 29TH

Continues to impress.

Ainsley

TODAY, WE ARE presenting our final design plans, along with their corresponding budgets. I'm surprised when I see the exterior design has been updated to include copper drainpipes and eaves. The modern black metal window frames that have been part of the design from the beginning are still there, but the exterior is now the color of the deep green velvet chairs in the lobby I designed, and there are what look like cognac leather awnings over the first-floor windows and doors. A big Texas star, made from the green-and-white marble that will be featured in the bathrooms, is inlaid in the concrete in front of the main entrance, giving off a welcome-rug type vibe.

I'm up next with my presentation of the lobby and reception spaces, and I manage to get through it with confidence I didn't know I had. We continue to go through boards for everything—from the on-site restaurants, the rooftop bar, spa, offices, and hotel back end to the laid-back luxe of the guest rooms and suites.

And it's all really beautiful.

Uncle Tripp is here, seeing everything for the first time.

When all the boards have been presented, he stands up and claps. "Wow. This team continues to impress me. I don't know how you did it, but it feels like a place I'd be happy to live in every day. Thank you. And thank you for upholding our budget. I feel like you were all very creative in splurging on big impacts while being conservative on other design choices. Congratulations on another job well done. To those of you who are working with us for the first time, we hope it's not the last. And I promise, you all will be invited to our grand opening next year."

The team has been looking a little frazzled during the last few days, but I think we all feel energized and happy right now.

As we're dispersing, Jadyn asks me to stop into her office. Uncle Tripp joins us, and we all take a seat.

"You may have noticed that many of the final details for the hotel were based off your lobby design," Jadyn says.

"I wasn't sure if it was just a coincidence," I tell her.

"It wasn't. At all. Thank you for your hard work. And for leaving the family reunion with us."

"I'm glad I did. I learned so much. I'm really grateful for my time here."

"I think you taught us all a thing or two," Tripp says. "Great job, Ainsley. And since we stole you away from the resort early, that means tomorrow will be the official end of your internship. I'm heading to the Archibald Lodge on Wednesday. If you'd like, you can fly with me there. I know you aren't officially supposed to start for another week, but the 4th of July weekend is one of our busiest times of the year. You're welcome to take a couple of days off down there and work the holiday, or you can fly back home, take a well-deserved break, and report as planned."

"I'd love to fly down with you. Mostly because my car is still there. And I think I'd like to do just what you suggested. A few days off but work the holiday weekend."

"Excellent," he says.

"And speaking of excellent," Jadyn says. "I'm sure you'll start interviewing for jobs later this fall. Know you will get excellent references from us."

"Thank you so much," I tell her.

"I'll pick you up in front of your building around ten. Sound good?" Uncle Tripp says.

"Yeah, that's great. I figured I'd have to rent a car and drive there. This will be so much nicer."

I LEAVE JADYN'S office and immediately call Damon, wanting to tell him everything.

But he doesn't answer.

WEDNESDAY, JULY 1ST

Keeps on giving.

Ainsley

UPON MY ARRIVAL at the resort, I'm ecstatic when given the key to one of the guest cottages. The bellman takes my bags while I take a golf cart to visit the resort doctor.

Fortunately, he's not busy, so I get in right away.

"Hello, Ainsley. What brings you here today?" he asks me.

"Doctor, my seeing you is confidential, right?"

"Oh dear," he says, "is it itchy?"

"Is what itchy?" I wonder, but then I realize he's talking about a common problem at the hotel. I don't know why people don't read the signs, stay on the paths, and out of the woods. "Oh, no. I didn't come in contact with any poison ivy. This is something else."

"The *something else* is what I meant," he says. "It seems some of the crew have been having unprotected sex, and there have been some unexpected consequences."

As in other people are getting pregnant too? "Um—" I start to say.

"To answer your question, it is confidential."

"Even from my uncle?" Because I need to verify this.

"Of course," he says, looking concerned.

"I'm pregnant," I blurt out.

"Oh. That is not what's going around," he says, looking surprised. And then I realize he was referring to a sexually transmitted disease.

He recovers quickly.

"You did a test, and it turned positive, I take it?" he asks.

"Yes, sir."

"How far along are you?"

"I think, like, seven weeks," I reply.

"Well, congratulations. Why don't you give me a urine sample?"

He hands me a cup, and I go use the restroom.

A few minutes later, he confirms what I already knew.

"When was the first day of your last period?" he asks.

After I tell him, he looks at a chart and says, "That will put your due date on February the twenty-second."

My mind goes back to Damon telling me about his number eleven being an angel number. And I know that twenty-two is considered a double angel number. Which makes me feel like it was meant to be.

Just like I'm meant to be with Damon.

I think.

"That means conception would have occurred around June the first," he says.

"I know you're not an obstetrician, but I'm hoping I can see you while I'm here for the summer."

"I have a better idea. I'll consult with one of my colleagues and have him come here for your appointments. And I can refer you to an OB-GYN for when you're back at school."

"Thank you. I really appreciate it."

"A few more things. With you working outside, it's going to be very important that you're careful. Drink lots of water. Stay hydrated. Try to stay in the shade as much as possible. Have you had any morning sickness?"

"I felt nauseous based on a strong smell one time, but I haven't gotten sick. I've been a little tired, but other than that, I'm doing well."

"All right. Let me get in contact with my colleague, and I'll let you know when he will be here."

"Thank you," I tell him, then head to my cottage.

SINCE I'M GOING to be here for almost two months, I unpack fully and get settled. Then I go to the kitchen and open the refrigerator, hoping to find a bottle of water while thinking that I should run to the grocery store.

I'm pleasantly surprised to find it fully stocked with a bunch of my favorite foods. There are prepared meals, fruit and veggies, and a variety of drinks.

I grab a bottle of water and an apple and decide to eat it on the screened porch and take in the view of the lake.

I'm shocked to discover that I'm in the cottage closest to where Damon and I had our picnic. Where we shared *I love yous*.

Which means I have to call him.

"You'll never guess where I am," I say when he answers.

"Fort Worth still, I assume?"

"No, my internship is over. I tried to call you the other day, but you didn't answer, and you didn't call or text me back. What's up with that?"

"Yeah, sorry. I literally just left the store with a new phone. No calls or texts were coming through. You know though, if you're ever worried, just text Chase."

"And seem like a jealous girlfriend?"

"Girlfriend?" he says. "I thought you decided that was too juvenile, *my future wife.*"

"Fine. I didn't want to seem like a jealous future wife."

"So, where are you?" he asks.

I press the video button on my phone. "Why don't I show you?"

"Look at you, all sunny and bright," he says when he sees me. Then his voice softens. "You look gorgeous, Ainsley."

"That's because I'm having a moment. Look!" I flip the phone around so he can see the spot. "The butterflies are here!"

"I bet they showed up because of you," he counters with a grin.

"Well, if they did, they're going to be disappointed that you aren't here with me."

"I miss you," he says.

"I miss you too. But guess what else. Usually, when I'm here all summer, I live in the staff accommodations. And I don't know if it's because my schedule was different coming mid-season or if Uncle Tripp set it up, but I'm staying in one of the guest cottages. By myself. And the fact that I'm in the one closest to *our* spot has me feeling all romantic and happy. I'm really sorry that I had to leave early, Damon."

"I know you are. And it wasn't the same without you. Do you start work today?"

"No, I'm going to take a few days off, then work on the Fourth since that's a huge day here and the resort is always sold out. What are you doing for the holiday weekend? Are you staying at school or going home?"

"Chase and I are driving home this afternoon. The lake we live on always does a golf cart and bike parade, an ice cream social, and a fireworks show. And since Chase's dad retired, he's really gotten into smoking meat, so we're looking forward to ribs and pork butts. I wish my phone had been working. I didn't realize you were done with your internship so soon."

"The end date got moved up because I started early. And the lake with your family and fireworks sounds fun. You'll have to tell everyone hi for me."

"I will. Dani's flight from LA lands tomorrow afternoon, so the whole family will be there."

"How did her internship go?"

"She absolutely loved it. She'll spend the weekend in Kansas City, fly to Connecticut on Monday, then finish the internship at their corporate headquarters."

"I bet Chase can't wait to see her."

"It's all he's been talking about. Speaking of that, I need to see *you* soon."

"Any chance you have a break in your schedule and could come down here?"

He grins at me. "Yeah, maybe later this month."

"I'm going to hold you to that," I tease.

After we say goodbye, I think about the first time we had sex. Being with Damon was amazing. I felt so loved. So cared for. And he made me feel really beautiful. I mean, it doesn't hurt that he's smoking hot, but I just love his tender side. And I will admit, watching the way he handled my dad, with both confidence in his ability and respect for my dad, was … well, kinda hot.

It's also crazy that we probably conceived on his birthday.

Talk about the gift that keeps on giving.

I have a moment of doubt, wondering if I'm doing the right thing by not telling him.

But when a butterfly flits in front of me, I know it will all be okay.

MY PHONE RINGS in my hand, and I answer quickly, assuming it's Damon calling me back.

But when a voice from the past says, "Ainsley," I realize I shouldn't have just deleted his number. I should have blocked it too.

"Hey, Brad," I say, rolling my eyes.

"Can we talk?" he asks.

"About what?"

"My engagement."

"What about it?"

"I'm just sort of freaking out, I guess. Seeing you again, um … it affected me. You looked so beautiful. And happy. Does that Damon guy make you happy?"

He's made me more than happy, I think, then chuckle to myself. "Yeah, he does, Brad."

"How long have you been dating?"

"A little over a month. Why?"

"I've been dating my girlfriend—"

"You mean your fiancée," I correct.

"Yeah, Bailey. I'm … we broke up. Sorta."

"Sorta?" I wonder aloud.

"My mom told me that you told her why we broke up," he says, changing the subject.

"I'm sorry about that. It just sort of slipped out. But I can't fault you for it. I hadn't told my mom why either. I was too embarrassed that I hadn't known you were cheating."

"Where are you at—like, right now?"

"At my uncle's resort in the Ozarks. Why?"

"Can I come see you?" he asks.

"Why would you do that?"

"Because you were my best friend for so long," he says. "I miss you."

"Oh, Brad. I can tell," I say with mock sincerity. "After all, it's only been three years since we've spoken, but quite honestly, had we not run into each other, it hopefully would have been longer than that."

"You're mad," he says.

Which is something he always used to say. Anytime I questioned him, he would turn it around on me.

"I'm not mad. I'm actually thankful that you did what you did. It forced me to make decisions about what *I* wanted out of life. And I couldn't be happier. And you should be too. Bailey seemed like a lovely girl."

"I can't get you out of my head," he says. "I think there's a reason why we ran into each other. I think—no, *I want* us to get back together."

To this, I let out a laugh. "And have you told Bailey that? Did you actually break up with her?"

"Not exactly. I wanted to see how you felt first."

"Oh, okay. Well, here goes. How I felt was betrayed. Disgusted. Devastated. We'd dreamed of a life together. You said you'd always love me. I was angry. Hurt. And sad. Really, really sad. I also was incredibly embarrassed that I wasn't smart enough to know that you weren't faithful. And the crazy thing is, had you told me you wanted to see other people, I would have been open to that. We'd discussed it before we went to college. It wouldn't have been a surprise. But you chose to go behind my back instead. That's how I felt."

He lets out a sigh. "I actually meant, how do you feel about us getting back together? Giving it another shot."

"I think you should stick with the girl you bought the engagement ring for, the one that looked like the ring I always dreamed of."

"So, if I were in the lobby of the resort right now, you wouldn't come talk to me?"

"You're here?" I'm shocked.

"Yeah, I am. My mom called your mom to find out where you were."

"I feel really bad for your fiancée. If you don't plan on being faithful to her, I hope you let her go. Goodbye, Brad. And please, don't call me again."

"Oh, so you're all hot for the Diamond kid because he's rich—is that it?"

"Money has nothing to do with why I love him. He's honest, transparent, and a really good man."

"Man? Please. He just graduated high school."

"He's more mature than you have *ever* been, Brad."

"Yeah, right," he says. "I remember what that was like. Sex is a lot different when you have experience."

"You know though," I say with a grin on my face, "you might be right about one thing."

"And what's that?"

"I *am* all hot for the Diamond kid. Bye, Brad." I hang up and immediately call my mother.

"Mom! What were you thinking?!" I say the second she answers. "Why in the world did you tell Brad's mom where I was?"

"Uh, I—did I?" she asks, sounding confused. "I guess when we went to lunch the other day, I did mention you were working at the resort again this summer."

"So, she didn't call you specifically to ask?"

"No. Just small talk at lunch. But I don't think we'll be having lunch again."

"Why not?" I ask.

"She made excuses for why Brad cheated on you."

"He showed up here. Thank goodness no one told him where I was staying. He wanted me to meet him in the lobby."

"What for?"

"To talk about getting back together."

"No!" she says, sounding a little like Sammy when I tell him the gossip.

Speaking of Sammy, I should call and tell him.

"Yes. He called me. I said no."

"Good. I'm proud of you. Um, there's something I should probably tell you."

"Have you heard from Dad?"

"Oh, no, not yet, but I kinda maybe met someone," she says.

"Someone—oh, wait. Like, a guy someone?"

"A man, but yes. He's a colleague of Van's. He lost his wife to cancer about ten years ago and has two grown children. I mean, we've only been on a couple of dates, but he's nice. I'm seeing him this weekend, and we're going together to Van and Lori's housewarming next weekend."

"The kid in me wonders if it's too soon, but the adult in me wants you to be happy."

"Thank you," she says sincerely.

"I'm still really worried about Dad. Isn't there anything we can do?"

"There really isn't," Mom says. "Your uncles have had a private investigator looking for him, but he hasn't used any of his credit cards or his phone. They think maybe he's using an assumed name. Basically said we'll have to wait till he contacts us."

"That sucks," I say.

"I know it does, honey."

When we end our call, I say a quick prayer for my dad. That he's okay. That he's not living on the streets. That he's safe. And that he will call me.

I also think about the fact that Mom is going on dates. I know she filed for a divorce, but still …

Then I call Sammy.

"You're never going to believe what just happened," I say when he picks up.

"You heard that Roman is going to ask me to marry him?" he asks.

"Wait. Is he?"

"I think so! I'm so in love with him."

"Does that seem—I don't know—like, too soon? Like, have you worked through your issues?"

"What issues?" he asks in a singsong voice. "He's perfect. *We're* perfect."

"Since when?"

"Since he came back into my life. I'm deliriously happy. Be happy for me."

"I am happy for you," I say, trying not to sound tentative even though that's how I'm feeling.

"I can hear it in your voice. You don't approve."

And he's right. I don't know if I do.

"Well, I just had something similar happen, and I did not want to go back to the ex who cheated on me."

"What do you mean, you had something similar happen? Spill."

"I'm done with my internship. It went amazingly. I want you to come with me to the grand opening next year so you can see my design. I did the lobby. And they even changed the exterior and hotel rooms to go with it."

"That's really cool, and I'd love to. But are you saying you talked to Brad?"

"He just called me. Was in the hotel lobby. Said he wants me back."

"Ohmigawd, girl! What did you say?"

"I said no. He asked how I felt. He was really asking if I still had feelings for him, but I went off and told him *exactly* how I'd felt when he cheated on me."

"What did you say?!"

"Actually, you would have been proud of me. I told him I felt betrayed, hurt, lied to, embarrassed, and sad."

"That's how I felt with Roman," he says softly.

"I know you did. And I'll be honest, you suggesting you want to marry him worries me a little."

He sighs. "He said he wouldn't ever again. And he was very sincere. People change sometimes, right? Although what your mom said that night when we chatted has stuck with me. And it does scare me a bit. So, tell me the rest."

"Oh, get this. He said he had kinda, sorta broken up with his fiancée."

"Which means he's stringing her along," Sammy says.

"Exactly. And when I said no, he acted like the dick he is and said, *Oh, so you're all hot for the Diamond kid because he's rich—is that it?* And I told him money had nothing to do with it."

"Then what did he say?" Sammy asks, seemingly enthralled.

"He suggested Damon wasn't good in bed because he's younger."

"He didn't?! What an ass."

"Right," I agree. "But guess what I said back. Well, first, I said he's more mature at eighteen than Brad will ever be. That I love him because he's honest and transparent. Then I told him he might be correct about one thing."

"Ohhhh, what was Brad right about?"

"That I *am* hot for the Diamond kid."

"Ahhh! Amazing comeback! I love it! And how are things with Damon? Like, how did you leave it? Are you in a relationship? A situationship? Friends with benefits?"

"Things are good. He's sweet. We're exclusive. He wants me to move to Lincoln after graduation. And he's going to try to come see me this summer."

"That's great, but what if you can't find the kind of job you want there?"

"Well, we actually said we would talk about it at Christmas-time."

"Not to be a pain, but our lease is up here a few days after graduation."

"I forgot about that. Gosh, I feel like so much is up in the air," I say with a sigh, feeling overwhelmed.

"Don't freak out," Sammy says. "My backup plan is that I

move all my stuff to my parents' house until I figure it out. You can do the same."

"You're right," I agree.

"Now, back to Roman. Please be happy for me," he says.

"If Roman truly makes you happy, Sammy, I promise I will be."

"I love you. Maybe Roman and I should come down one weekend to visit you. Wouldn't that be fun? I do have a break between my summer classes. Maybe I will suggest it."

"That would be great. I'd love it."

"Hang on. Let me look up the dates. Um, okay, it's the week of July twentieth."

"Perfect. My cottage has three bedrooms, so you can just stay with me."

"Sounds like a plan. Love you lots!" Sammy says, ending the call.

THURSDAY, JULY 2ND

Couldn't resist.

Ainsley

I'M LYING ON a blanket in the grass, reading while getting some sun, when I hear someone call my name.

I turn around to see Damon standing next to my cottage. His hair is pushed back in the front, and his eyes are sparkling.

A wide smile forms on my face. *I can't believe he's here!*

I stand up and rush toward him, tears blurring my vision.

He runs toward me.

When we meet in the middle of the meadow, I leap into his arms, wrap my legs around his waist, and kiss him.

And this kiss …

It kills me. Destroys me.

I've been going along fine. Doing fine. Working.

But his kiss makes me realize that whatever doubts I had about us not being meant for each other were wrong.

I belong with him.

Literally forever.

I don't care how long it's been.

I just know it—feel it—in my heart.

All of a sudden, we are at the door to my cottage, Damon carrying me inside.

It's then that he finally stops kissing me to speak. "Which way to the bedroom?"

I nod my head to the right and put my lips back on his.

When he lays me down on the bed, he says, "Are you crying?"

I sniffle. "I'm so happy you're here. What a wonderful surprise."

He pulls off my shirt, undoes my shorts, and says, "What's next is going to be even more wonderful."

Our lovemaking is fast and fervent, and we both collapse on the bed after.

"You're right," I say with a smirk. "It was wonderful."

He rolls to his side and leans up on his elbow while his other hand gently glides from my neck down to my abdomen.

My abdomen. And I want to tell him so badly.

I consider it briefly, but when his hand slides lower, I'm back in the throes of ecstasy.

"You look gorgeous," he says, caressing my face.

"You're sweet, and I can't believe I'm actually lying here with you. How did that happen to come about?"

"You mean, how did I happen to come?" he says with a smirk.

I give him a playful little shove. "It's just, after talking to you, it sounded like you had your weekend all planned out with your family."

"Because I thought you would still be in Fort Worth. And as soon as I heard you were here, I couldn't *not* show up. This is our place. Plus, I needed to see you. Touch you. Love you." He grins. "In fact, I may not let you out of this bed until you have to work on Saturday."

"Are you staying all weekend?" I ask, hoping the answer is yes.

"That's the plan. If you'll have me," he teases.

"I'm pretty sure I already have," I joke back. "Is your family okay with you missing the holiday?"

"They know I'm obsessed with you. I don't think it was a big surprise."

"I'm very glad about that. With me being so busy, I feel like our conversations have been rushed. And I can't wait to lie in your arms and just talk—"

"Talk?" he asks.

"Okay, maybe not *just* talk. But, like, I want to get to know you better. I don't even know what your major is."

"You'd think we were at a frat party and you were trying to pick me up," he teases.

"Actually, it was *you* who picked me up—*and* carried me in here."

"And I'm *so* glad I did," he flirts. "We're good together."

"We are compatible sexually, for sure, but what about in other ways? That's why I'm excited to spend more time with you."

"I think we can figure that out. In bed," he says.

"You can't just stay in bed the whole time. I do know that about you. I assume you're going to need to work out?"

"I feel like I just got in a pretty good workout," he says.

And I swear, the way he looks at me makes me blush. I bite on the edge of my lip because I want more. In fact, I've never felt sexier in my life.

"But you're right. And I know just what I want to do."

"What's that?" I ask.

"Beat you in a round of golf."

"And if I beat you?"

"I could make a naughty comment about that, but I won't," he says. "Obviously, if you are victorious, it will destroy my ego once more. But I think I will be able to pick up the pieces. And then challenge you to a game of mini golf to try to redeem myself."

"You're silly."

He leans in and gives me a hard kiss. "Actually, I am quite serious about you."

Things get more heated from there.

"I HAVE TO admit, I've never …" I start to say, but then realize I might sound lame. *Also, how is it that the sun is already starting to set?*

"Never what?" he asks.

"Spent so much time in bed with someone."

"Me neither."

"Really?" I ask, sitting up.

"Why does that surprise you?" he asks.

I run my fingers down his buff chest, across his tight abs. "You're hot, Damon. Obviously in excellent physical condition. I just thought, maybe …" I say, suddenly feeling tongue-tied, possibly because he's kissing my neck again.

He stops and looks up at me dreamily. "I've never felt this way before. I've also realized that Champ is a good nickname for you, not just because you're a boss at golf, but because you make me feel like a champion whenever I'm with you. Like I've won the game of life." He smiles coyly. "For sure the sex game of life."

What he says causes tears to fill my eyes. "I'm trying to take you at your word, but I find that hard to believe."

He grins at me, moves my hand down to something hard, and says, "You had better believe it."

"Damon! I was talking about—"

"I know," he says, giving me a sweet kiss. "I couldn't resist."

I pull him closer because … we can talk later. "And I don't want you to."

FRIDAY, JULY 3RD

A strong jawline.

Ainsley

A SINGLE BEAM of sunlight shines through the space between the window trim and the curtain, hitting me square in the eyes. I blink a few times. I'm not sure what time we finally fell asleep, but it doesn't matter. Damon makes me feel like I'm the sexiest thing on earth, and that is something I've never felt before. I look at him happily and smile, remembering how I woke up in a panic the morning after his sister's wedding because he was naked in my bed.

Now, I just feel happy, content, satiated.

I take a moment to study him. His arm is draped across my body, keeping me close. His hair is mussed, probably from me running my hands through it. Damon has really beautiful hair. It's thick but silky soft. Blond with natural highlights. I know his hair bleaches out with the sun, but it's more like he has strands of different colors. Some almost platinum, others blond, some that are a darker blond, and a few that are more of a strawberry blond.

Half of his face is buried in my pillow, and I can't help but reach out to touch it, my fingers caressing a high cheekbone before gliding down across a strong jawline, then running across his pale pink lips.

"Mmm." He lets out a contented sigh as one eye flutters open, revealing a beautiful brown color, flecked with gold.

If he were a Greek god, he would probably be Apollo with his golden hair—a god associated with radiant light, sun, and beauty. But then you'd have to combine that with Hermes, the god of sports and athletes, who was known for his speed and agility.

And it makes me wonder, "How come you're not a quarterback like your dad?"

He snuggles his face against my shoulder. "Shouldn't we be talking about last night? Which was incredible, by the way."

"It most definitely was, but answer my question."

Instead of using his lips to speak, he decides to kiss my neck.

Which makes me giggle and squirm.

"I love your laugh," he says when he stops kissing me and starts tickling me.

"I love him," I say, just going for it and grabbing his crotch because it's pretty clear the direction this playfulness is heading.

WE SHOWER TOGETHER, and then he goes out to make breakfast while I blow-dry my hair.

I hurry through it, wanting to look nice, but at the same time, I don't want to be away from him for even a moment. In the end, I partially dry it, put on some mascara and bronzer, and throw on a bikini, pulling a flirty little dress on over it.

When I step out of my bedroom and into the living room, I stand there for a second and observe him. It's obviously not the first breakfast he's ever cooked, I think, as I watch him move effortlessly around the kitchen.

He's barefoot, wearing nothing but a pair of swim trunks. But the best part is that tall, buff, and hot Damon is also sporting a floral apron.

And there's something so sexy about it. And I'm such a bad person, but if Brad had ever put that apron on in front of me, I would have laughed him right out of the room.

It's small on Damon, the bottom of the apron hitting like my miniskirt does—high on the thigh. He's such a juxtaposition. Is that the word for it? Or maybe he's a walking contradiction. Like when a guy says a girl is a lady in the street but a freak in the bed. Damon is this crazy combination of sweet but fiercely protective. He's serious about most things, but affable and fun. Always cracking jokes.

And I love all of it. All of him.

"Too bad you have on those shorts," I say, flipping up the hem of the apron with a smirk.

"I'm pretty sure you could wave a wand or just kiss me, and they would magically vanish. Only problem is, I'm starved."

"Whatcha cooking?"

"Everything," he says with a laugh. "Bacon, hash browns, chocolate chip waffles, and although it's kinda runny and not quite up to Mimi's standards, her caramel sauce."

And although my stomach felt slightly queasy when I smelled the bacon cooking earlier, I'm suddenly ravenous.

Lick it off.

Damon

I SPREAD THE food out on the counter, and then we fill up our plates.

"Wanna eat outside?" she asks me. "The porch is screened, so it's not buggy, and it's probably not too hot yet. Plus, the view."

"The view is pretty good right here." I give her ass a little slap as I walk past her and open the door.

"You're obsessed with my ass," she says in a singsong voice, a smile plastered on her face.

"I sure am. Of course, that's all your fault," I tell her as we take our seats.

She rolls her eyes, then drags a piece of her waffle through some caramel sauce. Her eyes move again, this time practically rolling to the back of her head. She likes it. *A lot.* And now, all I can think about is her licking it off my body.

"This is like a bite of ecstasy."

"Ecstasy, huh? I'll be sure to tell Mimi that," I tease.

"If she likes sweets, she will totally understand. Now, back to our original broadcast," she says.

"I don't know what you mean."

"When you arrived, I told you I was excited to hang out and learn more about you. So, I will ask again. You already know that my major is interior design. And while I know your goal is playing pro, are you planning on getting a degree?" she asks.

"For sure. In fact, I'll be taking higher class loads in the spring and summer so that I can graduate in December of my junior year, before the draft."

"That's awesome. And what's your major going to be?"

"Business. Finance, specifically. Ultimately, I would like to get a law degree."

"That surprises me," she says.

"You asked me before if I was smart," I tease.

"I know you're smart. Why law?"

"A couple of reasons. My dad's agent, Carter Crawford, was a star quarterback in college. He got hurt and couldn't play anymore, so he got his law degree and stayed in the game that way. If something like that ever happened to me, it would be a fun way to still be a part of the process. And in general, I'd like to understand the intricacies of contracts. All the legal jargon." I laugh. "Although when Chase and I were young, we used to joke that our backup plan was to be rock stars."

"I can see you being drawn to that. And you do have a nice voice," she says with a smile on her face before polishing off everything on her plate.

"You must have been hungry," I tell her. "I don't think I've ever seen you eat that much."

"I'm starving," she says. "And you're a good cook."

"Thank you."

"Although I can think of something that would have made seeing you in the kitchen even better."

She's wearing a naughty grin, and I am hoping she is ready for breakfast in bed.

"What?" I ask.

"It would've been fun if you'd cooked with *just* the apron on."

"We would not be sitting out here right now," I say as she

crosses her long legs. I stop speaking to watch.

"True." She laughs.

And although I know being a rock star is not in my future, I feel like I could write a song about that laugh. Those legs. Her perfect curves. Long brown hair. Big green eyes. And a smile that brightens my world.

"And back to my question. Why aren't you a quarterback like your dad?"

"Oh, that's easy," I start to say, but then she touches my hand and says, "Hold please," then gets up. "I think I need one more little square of waffle. And some more milk. Do you want anything?"

"Just you," I say. Although the second it comes out of my mouth, I realize it sounds kinda cheesy, but I don't care. I'm crazy about this girl.

She's back a few moments later with more food, and I watch as she slathers butter into the waffle's indentations, then picks it up and dips it directly into a bowl of caramel before taking a big bite. "Okay, keep going."

And I can't even remember what I'm supposed to keep going with because she has a little drop of caramel on the corner of her lips. I stare at it.

"What?" she says self-consciously, looking down at herself. "Did I spill?"

I lean over, rub my thumb across the offending caramel, and then lick it off my finger.

"Why is you simply sucking that off your thumb so damn sexy?" she asks me.

"Probably because you're thinking about other things I can suck on," I say in a deep, aroused tone, motioning with my head toward the door.

"One, I have to finish eating. And two, I don't think I can … you know, on a full belly. Isn't sex like swimming? You should wait an hour before you get back in the water?"

That makes me laugh. "Probably. Okay then. Why I'm not a QB is because as a kid—well, still, even now—I liked to run. Fast. So, when Chase and I played ball in the backyard, I'd want him to throw it to me so that I could run and catch it. And I'm glad I did. I still love the freedom of running as fast as I can to get to the spot where the ball appears to just drop into my hands. And it helps that I ended up with physical traits suited for the position—good speed and agility. Good hands and good length."

"Good length." She glances toward my crotch and raises an eyebrow at me as she polishes off her second helping. "That you do."

Then she gets up, strips off her shirt, tosses it at me, and saunters inside. It doesn't matter that she still has a bikini top on.

I get the hint.

As I follow her inside, a conversation I had with Chase earlier this summer replays in my head.

"I'm a little worried, to be honest," Chase said. "I know you really like her, and I just don't want—"

"Me to get hurt?"

"When Dani and I were struggling at school last semester, it affected me."

"I thought it was the guys calling you Hype *that affected your relationship with her."*

"I think it goes both ways. I want you to be happy, but at the same time, I'm worried about what happens if you aren't."

"I can keep my personal life separate from football," I stated, grinning at him. "Always have. Champion mindset right here."

"How can I say this so that I won't offend you?" Chase stopped the treadmill and just looked at me.

I held up my hands, letting him know that I had no clue, especially when he knew that I was not easily offended. Shit like that rolled off my back, mostly because I didn't care what other people thought.

"I think I know the answer to this, but humor me," he said. "Have you ever felt like this about anyone before?"

"No, I have not. And why would that offend me?"

"That's not the possibly offensive part. It's that you don't know what you will do or how you will react because you have never felt this way. Shit rolls off your back because you don't care what most people think. You care about what your friends and family think. But what happens when she is mad at you? When there is a misunderstanding? Or what if, to her, this is just a vacation fling with a guy who crushes on her?"

When I go into the bedroom and find her sprawled out on the bed, fully naked, I don't care if I end up getting hurt.

I know in my heart that she's the girl for me, but I also know that if we don't work out for some reason, the pain, as well as the pleasure, will have been worth it.

And after the last twenty-four hours with her, I'm even more sure of that.

This list.

Ainsley

I WAKE UP from a blissful sleep, finding myself alone in bed. I take a deep breath and exhale with a dreamy sigh. I'm literally in heaven right now. So happy that I can hardly believe it. And I love that Damon surprised me by showing up.

He's so amazing. So caring.

So good in bed.

Like, I can't even.

I close my eyes and smile, then get up, pick my bikini off the floor, put it and my dress back on, and go in search of Damon.

I find him sitting on the front porch, talking on the phone.

He smiles at me and holds his screen in my direction. "Ainsley is up!"

"Hey!" His sister waves at me. "I heard from Auntie Jay that your internship went really well."

"And Damon said you loved yours too," I reply.

"It was really cool to see all the work that goes on behind the scenes. The production of live television. I'm so excited to go to their headquarters."

"You're supposed to at least pretend that you missed me," Chase says, coming onto the screen, but I can tell by his light-hearted tone that he's just teasing her.

"How was the rest of your honeymoon?" I ask. "Was the location as amazing as it sounded?"

"It was even better!" Dani says. "The staff was attentive. The food was amazing. The view to die for. It was wonderful."

"But we did learn one thing the hard way," Chase says.

"What was that?" Damon asks as he and I share a confused glance.

"Sex on the beach is … well, just say no, if it's ever on the table," Chase says seriously. "Actually, you'd be much smarter to do it on a table."

"Chase!" Dani screeches. "Don't tell them that."

"I'm saving them from possible future disappointment," he jokes. "And chafing."

"I'll be honest," Damon says, giving me a wink. "It's always been on my sexual bucket list."

I need to see this list. Now.

"Cross that shit off," Dani says with a laugh.

"Exactly," Chase agrees. "Even if you try to stay on the towel, sand still gets everywhere. And I mean, everywhere. And it sticks to … well, things that are wet."

"I can't believe we are talking about this," Dani says, briefly covering her eyes, "but he is correct. And sand is … well, rough. Especially on the more sensitive areas of your body."

"And let's not forget about overtly friendly crabs and their little pinchers," Chase adds.

Dani starts laughing hysterically. "That was funny though. He was …" She laughs some more. "Let's just say that things were already going badly when he screamed like a little girl and jumped off me."

"The damn crab bit me!" Chase says dramatically.

Damon's eyes get huge, and he goes, "Do we want to know where?"

"It was his toe," Dani says.

"I'm just glad the little fucker didn't attack me somewhere else!" Chase exclaims, looking very serious and causing me and Damon to laugh.

"You can't be talking to them without me," Haley says, popping her head into view.

"There's my Hay Girl," Damon says. "Well?"

Haley steals the phone from Dani's hand and shows us her leg, sans boot. "It's off! I go back in two weeks for one more X-ray, and if all still looks good, I'll be able to start rehab."

"That's amazing!" Damon says. "Congrats."

"I couldn't have done it without you," Haley says seriously just as their little sister, Emersyn, jumps on Chase's lap.

"I want to do the pretty colors, but Mama won't let me do it myself."

"Because fire is hot and can be dangerous," Chase says to her.

"And the boys are naughty," she says. I assume she's referring to Chase's younger brothers, Ryder and Madden. "So, Chase make Emmy pretty colors."

"What are pretty colors?" Damon asks.

"Smoke bombs," Dani says. "I was obsessed with the colors when I was a kid too. We'd better go help her."

We exchange goodbyes, and then I say to Damon, "I'm going to need to see this sexual bucket list of yours."

Damon chuckles. "There's not a literal list. But I think most people think sex on the beach in the moonlight sounds like something romantic they'd like to do."

"I will admit that I've always thought the same, but after the sand angels, I had my concerns."

"All I can remember is loving getting the sand off you in the shower," he says, his voice deep and sexy.

"That was fun," I agree.

"And I would like to point out that it was *you* who ended our getting-to-know-each-other session today."

I grin. "Whoops."

He pulls me onto his lap and gives me a kiss. "Do you want to try to get in a round of golf?"

I look at the sky, noticing the clouds rolling in. "Have you checked the weather? It sort of looks like it could rain."

"Chance of it later this afternoon, but the cloud cover is keeping it cool."

"I wonder if we can get a tee time," I say.

He looks at his watch. "I already got one. Can you be ready in about ten minutes?"

I jump off his lap and say, "I can."

At your service.

Damon

WE'RE IN THE golf club, ordering a late lunch when we hear a burst of thunder and rain starts coming down in buckets.

"Glad we finished when we did."

"Should we discuss the game?" she asks smugly.

I lean over the table, making a circular motion with my hand and lower my head in reference. "Your Highness and Great Champion, I am at your service."

"Oh, really?" she says as I lift my head and give her a playful smirk. "Does that mean you are ready for round two?"

Hell yeah, I am. Except …

"I haven't been keeping an exact count, but I'd say we're *well* beyond the second round."

What I say causes her to blush as the waiter delivers our food—her opting for a cheeseburger, fries, and lemonade while I ordered a Cobb salad with grilled chicken and sparkling water.

"We are," she says, "but I was actually referring to the fact that you told me if you lost at golf, you were going to have to challenge me to mini golf."

"I think I'd like to challenge you to a different kind of round first," I tell her, sliding my hand up her thigh under the table and staring into her green eyes.

"We could have them package our food to go, but we'd get really wet."

I can't help but chuckle, my mind going to sexy places involving … well, I think you know.

"Damon!" she says, her eyes getting big. "I meant the *rain*."

"The rain that ended the drought?" I tease.

I love getting her worked up. In all sorts of ways.

She sits there with her lips pressed shut, trying not to smile. But finally, she can't hold it any longer and breaks out in laughter. "Let's eat first—don't you dare make a naughty comment about that—and then maybe we can discuss the rain."

"Fine," I say. "So, what else do you want to know?"

"What's your favorite meal?"

"Like, ever or everyday type thing?"

"Oh," she says, looking intrigued. "Tell me both."

"Favorite meal ever in my life is our picnic. My dad says that food tastes better when the company is good."

"I will admit," she says, "that's definitely high on my list, but I also loved … although technically not a meal, the champagne and cake on your birthday."

"That was a fun night," I say with a sigh, remembering.

"It was."

"As far as favorite things to eat, I love a medium-rare grilled steak, roasted broccoli, mashed potatoes made with cream—gotta be made with cream—almond butter smoothies, and tacos, any kind. What about you?"

"I've always thought there is something to be said about food tasting better depending on who you are sharing it with. So, there are meals I remember that stand out. Like my mom saved up, and the two of us went to France for my high-school graduation. I had taken French class in school and could sort of speak it. But we went to this little town called Annecy. I really didn't want to go there, but Mom insisted. It was gorgeous, set in the French Alps. There were cobbled streets and old historic buildings built around picturesque canals. We sat on a rooftop restaurant overlooking one of the canals and ate cheese fondue with roasted potatoes and bread with white wine. It was amazing."

"I love that story," I tell her. "Have you traveled much? Do you want to?"

"We used to do summer road trips in the States as a family, growing up, so I've been to almost every state except for a few on the upper East Coast. The trip to France and my study abroad in Italy are the only places I've been internationally. The food in Italy and the architecture are incredible. It's hard not to be inspired there. What about you?"

"Dani used to do competitive cheer, so we traveled a lot for that, and I've been all over to different football camps. Internationally, we've done trips to Germany and England for a few of my dad's football games. Some winter break trips to Caribbean islands. That kind of thing. I've not been to Italy, and I'd really like to go. You can be my tour guide."

"I'd love that. We were based in Florence and did see some other beautiful small towns in Tuscany, but there are so many more places there I want to visit. As for my favorite food, I do love me some pasta. Any kind, really. And bread. I ate so much when I was there, but never gained a pound because we did so much walking." Her eyes brighten, and she grins. "I even learned to make homemade pasta. Maybe if you're good, I'll make it for you sometime."

"Haven't I been pretty good already?" I ask, raising my eyebrows and smirking at her.

"You know, it's really hard to keep your mind on track. And believe it or not, I'm still hungry. I was thinking of getting another order of fries."

"As long as you eat them in bed."

"No, 'fraid not," she says as she motions to our server. "Do you not want to get to know each other?"

"I know everything I need to know. I know how to get you—"

"Damon!" she scolds, her voice quiet. "There are children present."

I just grin at her. "You know I'm right."

"No, actually, you aren't. Because I'm not dating you for your body."

I flex a bicep at her.

"I'm not saying that I don't like it very much," she says, scrunching up her face and looking a little distressed. "Like, you haven't even asked me about my internship yet."

"You haven't asked about football yet either. But we have had conversations about both on the phone."

"I know. It's just that—never mind," she says, her focus now solely on dipping a fry into ranch dressing, then gliding it through the ketchup on her plate.

And I know I've messed up. Because now, if I ask her about it, she isn't going to want to tell me. My sister and Haley are the same way.

I reach out and slide my hand across her arm and say seriously, "I'm sorry. I want to know every single thing about you. About your internship. About your life."

She looks up at me, tears shimmering, and gives me a shrug. *Shit.*

"Are we having our first fight?" I ask her.

"Is it wrong of me to want to learn more, um … about you?"

Mood swings.

Ainsley

I ALMOST JUST said, *Is it wrong of me to want to learn more about the father of my child?*

And why am I suddenly feeling sad? And why am I pushing this when I want to drag him back to the cottage and have my way with him just as much as he does?

The waiter drops off a basket of fresh fries.

But I've lost my appetite.

I shake my head. I'm being ridiculous. And I know it.

"I'm not really hungry anymore," I tell him. "Let's just go

back home."

"Okay," he says, quickly flagging down the waiter and signing for our bill.

As soon as he does, I stand up and walk outside, needing some air.

But then the heat hits me, and I sort of feel like I could faint. I stop and steady myself on a nearby bench.

"Are you okay?" Damon asks. "You looked like you were going to pass out."

"Yeah, I kind of felt that way. It was hot on the golf course. I might be a little dehydrated."

He takes my hand and leads me to our golf cart and helps me get seated.

"Do you think you need to see the doctor?" he asks me.

I panic. *No, that is not at all what I need.*

He'll find out that I'm pregnant. And although I wish he could know now, that I could talk to him about it, I can't.

Won't do that to him.

It's only a few months. They will fly by, and once his season is over, I'll tell him. I don't want to change the trajectory of his career. And the fact that I haven't really had any of the symptoms I'm supposed to have has me kinda worried.

Which makes me feel teary again. *Shit.* Maybe I do have symptoms—like those hormonal changes that can cause crying and mood swings. But that's good, right? When the hormones go up, it means the baby is growing.

I close my eyes and take a deep breath. "No, I'm fine. Probably just tired. We didn't get a lot of sleep last night."

"That's true," he says seriously.

Usually, he'd be grinning about that fact. And I can tell that he's truly concerned about me.

"I'll be fine," I say with a smile. "Honestly, I'm feeling better already."

"Well, let's get you out of the heat. Have some water at home and watch a movie or something."

"What about some ice cream first?" I ask.

He grins. "Your wish is my command, Champ."

And I can't help but smile.

It Turns me on.

Damon

WHILE WE'RE EATING our ice cream, I decide to test the waters. "I heard from Auntie Jay that your internship went well and that you are amazing, but I haven't heard what specific things made it really good."

Her face lights up. Thankfully.

"So, you already know that I was in charge of the design for the lobby and you saw a picture of it, but what you don't know is, that design was so well liked that it changed elements in many other spaces in the hotel. Which really is how good design often works. While some prefer each room have a separate, unique vibe, it's widely believed that a cohesive color palette is more calming. It makes us feel like it's all one big, soothing space. Each room isn't the same though because you use the colors in each space but in different ways and in varying degrees," she says as she takes a bite of the praline pecan ice cream she ordered, topped with hot fudge.

I watch her savor it. The pleased smile that crosses her face is the same one she makes in bed. And it turns me on.

But I proceed.

"Growing up, our house was like that. Rooms were tastefully done but very formal, and each room was a different color completely. It felt a little, um, less approachable, I would say. But our house now was done with the same colors in different ways. Did you know that Jadyn actually designed the whole thing based off my dad's favorite pieces from his wardrobe?"

"I didn't know that. I have heard of designers doing that when they have a client who seems to not know what they want. You can go in their closet and usually see all their favorite colors. Do you know what your dad chose?"

"Believe it or not, I do. There was a navy pin-striped suit with a tie that was gray, purple, and teal. A brown leather jacket and brown suede shoes."

"Now, I need to see your house!" she says.

"It's crazy to think you've never been there. Although home is becoming my condo. And that's a place you will be visiting soon. When do you think you can come up?"

I look at the calendar on my phone. "The Monday before school starts. I'll probably be there late in the day, and I can stay for your game."

"Oh, about that. I don't know if you looked at the schedule, but the game is an away game. In Ohio."

"That sucks. I don't think I can get there and get back to school in time to get settled before classes start."

"I figured so. The next weekend then? For my first home game?"

"Of course. But the real question is, are you going to start? If I recall correctly, I agreed to go to the first game you started, not just played in."

"I've only been there for a few weeks, so it's too early to tell, but that's the plan."

"Either way," she says, "I will be there. I'm so excited!"

"And you'll stay with me. Dad just told me that they upgraded our suite to a much bigger one to accommodate all our families. Your uncle Tripp, my mom and Van, Dad and Jennifer, and Chase's family. I'm sure the condo building will be bustling with activity."

"I can't wait to see the condos, yours specifically," she says, giving me the kind of look that lets me know that *specifically* refers to my bedroom. "Also, I've never been to Lincoln, so you're going to have to show me around."

"I will. But back to your design. Tell me what changed in the rest of the hotel."

"Oh gosh. Overall, they added touches of copper, shades of green, and a rich cognac color from my design and integrated it everywhere. Like the exterior design got updated to include copper drainpipes and eaves to go with the copper fireplace in the entry. They added copper pots hanging in the flagship restaurant and copper tubs in the guest bathrooms. The cognac color was featured on glazed tiles in the bar, leather awnings on the outside, and suede chairs in the hotel rooms. The green showed up on a marble feature bathroom wall, in a Texas star at the front entry, and the walls of most of the biggest suites. And then there was this sparkly white concrete color I found for a custom coffee table. It ended up being used to make sinks for all the bathrooms in the hotel. It's cool because concrete is really durable and the white color is timeless, but it has a cool, somewhat-rustic, natural appearance."

"I know how Jadyn came up with the colors for our house. Where did you get your inspiration? You told me it was just a weird combination of the town, its heritage, and your uncle Tripp. But, to be honest, I didn't really follow that."

"You remember what I said?" she asks, looking shocked.

"Of course I do. I practically hang off your every word." I grin.

She pats my forearm and goes, "Now, you're just being silly." But then she stops and stares into my eyes. "Seriously, Damon, you have no idea how much that means to me. That you actually listen and not just let it go in one ear and out the other."

I lean across the table and kiss her. "That's because I care about the things important to you. It's like every piece of information I get from you just adds to me understanding the tapestry of your life."

"Huh. Well then, you'd better hurry up and finish your ice cream so I can show you more of my tapestry."

"I'm already full," I say, standing up, leaving the rest of my sundae and grabbing her hand.

She doesn't have to ask twice—that's for sure.

When we're in the golf cart, she says, "Oh, and to answer your question, I pictured Uncle Tripp as a cowboy."

Which causes me to laugh.

SATURDAY, JULY 4TH

Simple Things.

Damon

MY DAD ALWAYS says it's the simple things in life. And I finally understand. It's waking up with the person you love sleeping next to you. Smiling at the clothes scattered on the floor from last night. Recalling the way her lips felt against yours. And how a kiss can convey so much without a word.

I think about yesterday and how I sort of upset her. I've always had a plan for my life. I set goals and achieve them, but my mind is always on the endgame. I keep pushing and driving. And I realize that while that might work for getting to the pinnacle of your career, it might not work in a relationship.

I've been pushing. Because I know what I want. I can visualize it—us married. A bunch of kids. A happy life together.

Which is the keyword. *Together.* My dad says it's important that your teammates are all on the same page. That your goals align if you want to win. And what I have to remember is that while she's been my goal for three years, I just finally showed up on her radar. That we've only spent a total of two weeks together in person. And although I've gotten to know her body quite well during that time, she's right. I don't know how she likes her coffee. Or if she even likes it. Now that I think about it, I don't think I've ever seen her drink it.

And I need to know those things.

She stirs next to me, making a sweet little moan and moving her hand across my chest, which instantly turns me on. I pick her hand up and kiss it. Her eyes then flutter open, revealing gorgeous green irises.

"Mmm." She looks up at me through her lashes. "What time is it?"

"Six thirty. What time do you have to work today?"

Her eyes fly open, and she leaps out of bed. Naked. "Seven!"

She rushes into the bathroom and slams the door shut in a panic.

I decide to get up and make her breakfast. I throw on a pair of shorts and go survey the fridge, pulling out eggs, leftover bacon, and some cheese. Then pop some bread in the toaster.

She comes out of the bathroom about the time I have it all put on a paper plate.

"Oh gosh," she says, glancing at her watch, "that looks amazing. I just don't have time to eat."

"I'll drive. You eat," I tell her.

"You're going to drive me to work?"

"Is that okay?"

She smiles. "Yeah, it's great. Let's go."

I hand her the plate and a fork and grab the keys, and we go hop in the golf cart.

On the way there, I tell her, "You look cute. Very sporty."

She's got on her uniform, consisting of a white resort-branded ball cap and polo, paired with a white athletic skort.

"Thanks. When they redid the resort, they updated the uniforms as well. And I'm thankful. Last year, they were mostly black and way too hot in the summer," she says in between shoveling food in her mouth. "This is really good. Thank you so much for making it for me. I woke up starving."

"You're welcome. Although we need to discuss what foods you like and don't like. I was considering making you an omelet with peppers and onions, but wasn't sure."

"I love the scrambled eggs and toast, but the omelet sounds amazing too. I'm not a huge fan of anchovies, eggplant, or oysters. That's about all I can think of."

"Good to know," I reply. "And what does your day look like? Could we have lunch together? Can I help? I don't really have anything to do other than work out this morning."

"I have lunch break from eleven to noon and am off at four. Why don't you come pick me up at eleven? And I'll ask my manager if you can tag along with me this afternoon. It's going to be extra busy."

We pull up to the golf club area.

She glances at her watch. "Record time," she says. "Which means I still have time to kiss you."

And it's a very good kiss.

What I want.

Ainsley

DAMON MEETS ME at eleven, and I take him to the employee

dining room inside the golf club. The air-conditioning is always cranked up, and it's a wonderful reprieve from being out in the sun. The room sits under the club's main restaurant and actually has a decent view of the eighteenth hole.

"How was your workout this morning?" I ask him as we grab food from the buffet. "Did you go to the gym?"

"Yeah, I did. I expected it to be packed, but it wasn't. And that was really nice."

"They were all here," I say with a laugh. "Everyone's wanting to get in a round of golf before the family festivities start this afternoon."

"What do the family festivities consist of, and when do they start?" Damon asks.

"It kicks off at noon with the chefs outside cooking up burgers, hot dogs, and fried chicken along with lots of side dishes and patriotic desserts. They'll have water-gun fights, bounce houses, blow-up waterslides, splash pads, and a foam party, which the kids will love. We have a small group tournament—just twenty guys—that starts teeing off at noon. I heard from some of the waitstaff that they were pretty rowdy last night. Lots of alcohol was consumed—big bar tab, great tips. Anyway, once the last foursome has teed off, the course will be shut down to set up for tonight's carnival. It's always a big hit. There will be wheelbarrow and sack races, lawn games, face painting, carnival games, and lots of food. We should go," I say with a grin. "One of my little known talents is that I'm very good at the ring toss. Maybe I can win you a prize."

Damon puts his hand on mine. "I'd love that actually."

"After that, everyone will move down to the *Big Top*—that's what everyone has started calling the screened area where Chase and Dani had their after-party—for the dinner buffet that follows. The chefs have been smoking meat since last night in preparation for today. Big barbecue spread with all the fixings, ice cream sundaes and s'mores, live music, followed by fireworks at sundown. And if you aren't worn out after that, a stars-and-stripes music festival that is scheduled to go until dawn."

"Wow!" Damon says. "That's a lot to do. You up for that?"

"Definitely the fireworks. And it would be fun to dance with you."

"I'd like to dance with you again too," he says, looking into my eyes.

"In bed?" I say with a smirk.

His eyes crease at the corners, and a wide smile forms on his face. "Chase and I used to do that—hell, we still do. Say, *In bed.* We started doing it after we learned about sex. We thought we were so cool. Now, it's just funny."

I stare at him for a beat. "It wasn't supposed to be a funny comment."

He swallows, nods, and slides his hand across the top of my thigh. "Even better."

"All right, lover boy. I have a surprise for you." I whip a polo shirt that matches mine out of my tote bag. "I will definitely take your help this afternoon. I might even split my tips with you."

"I'd rather you owe me," he teases.

"Let me guess. In bed."

He laughs. "Exactly."

"I'm amiable to that. Now, finish up your food. We have work to do. And I need to restock my cart before I go back out there."

Once my cart is restocked, he asks, "What do you want me to

do?"

"I'll make the drinks. You can hand them out. And let's bring our cart out, too, in case I need you to run back for something. Normally, I drive around all day, but because we're so busy, they have us set up every three holes. I start on the ninth for this shift."

THE AFTERNOON IS busy but going fast. Everyone has been in good spirits today—pun intended—probably because it's actually a really pretty day. After a storm rolled through last night, there's a cool breeze, and today's high is only going to be eighty-two. They also seem really excited about the festivities tonight and are all looking forward to the fireworks. Many are decked out in patriotic colors in honor of the day.

There's a noticeable difference when the last foursome of the guys in the tournament get here. You'd think they'd be having a ball, but based off their chatter, they are all hungover as well as highly competitive. And aren't playing up to their standards.

One guy is getting teased about not being able to get it in the hole. On and off the course. Apparently, he's newly divorced.

"Another round of shots?" one of the guys says.

"Bro, we shouldn't," another says.

"Since when has that ever stopped us?" Another slaps him on the back and grins.

Guy Four says to me, "Guess we're doing more shots. Doubles, please."

"Sure. What would you like?"

"Well, we did vodka to start, whiskey at the third whole, rum at six"—he turns to look at his buddies—"so tequila?"

Damon and I share a glance.

"Hell yeah!" they all cheer.

I pour the shots, and Damon delivers them.

"You're a big guy," one of them says, looking up at him. "You play ball?"

"Sure do," Damon says.

"You look familiar," another says. "How come?"

I can tell by Damon's look, he doesn't want to get into it.

"People always say that to me," he says easily.

"Cool," the guy says.

They take their shots, down them, hand Damon a hundred-dollar bill, and then off they go.

"Wow," Damon says, handing me the folded-up bill. "Nice tip."

"It is. And that's the last group. I'm supposed to move to the fifteenth hole now since the server there started his day earlier than I did." I glance at my watch. "Should be done right around four if they don't dally too much."

We hop in the cart, drive to the assigned hole, and relieve a guy named Paul, who has been doing this job with me for the last few years.

"That's quite the group," he says, shaking his head. "It's just like last night at the bar. They were handing out hundred-dollar bills like it was all they carried." He laughs. "Actually, it might *be* pocket change to them."

I introduce him to Damon.

"They've had a lot of shots already, it sounds like," I tell Paul. "At what point do we cut them off?"

"We didn't cut them off last night, and they had way more. They were drunk, for sure, but those guys can handle their liquor. I think they are trained professionals."

"All right, good, because I don't want to have to be the one to tell them the cart is closed."

"You'll be good," Paul says. "You guys coming to watch the fireworks tonight?"

"Wouldn't miss it! I hear it's supposed to be the biggest one ever," I reply.

"All right. I'll see you there!" he says, then takes off.

I HAVE FUN working with Damon. He seems to be enjoying it and most definitely has the gift of gab. He's chatting and asking about their games while I ask about what they are looking forward to tonight.

One thing I've learned from working here is to talk about everything *but* their golf game. Because they will do one of two things—not move on to the next hole fast enough or get more irritated over their play. And irritated people don't tend to tip well.

But thankfully, that doesn't seem to be the case so far today.

"Can you hold down the fort?" Damon says after the golfers we just served move on. "I need to hit the head. I was trying to wait since there's only two more foursomes left to come through, but I can't."

"That's okay," I tell him. "There's a restroom back just a hole, by the fourteenth tee box."

He gives me a kiss and says, "I'll miss you."

"You're silly," I say, but a smile is plastered on my face.

The second-to-last foursome comes through. They are happy and possibly a little tipsy.

"You guys look like you could use some waters," I offer, which is our standard line in this case.

And they all take me up on it and move on.

The next group is moving quickly because they are on the green as soon as the others leave.

The hundred-dollar tipper sinks a putt, then saunters over toward me. He gives me a once-over, his eyes drifting slowly down, and I can tell he's specifically looking at my legs.

A few steps, and he is at my side.

"You look like you could use a water," I say. "It's getting pretty hot."

I get a smirk in return.

"You're pretty hot."

"Thank you," I say politely. "Can I get you anything?"

He moves closer, his eyes boring into mine. "What I want is you."

I smile. After years of working here, I've gotten used to those guys who drink too much and think they have a chance.

"I'm afraid I'm not on the menu," I say with a stern voice as I hand him the actual menu.

"When do you get off?" he asks.

"Very late. After the fireworks," I lie.

He slides the back of his hand down my forearm.

"Please, don't touch me," I say sternly, backing away. "If you do it again, I'll be calling security, and you won't ever play here again."

His next move is to grip my arm tightly, so much that it hurts. "I can do whatever the fuck I want," he says. "And what I want is you."

I want to grab the walkie-talkie on the side of my skirt, but I can't because he pushes me up against the side of the golf cart.

And suddenly, I'm scared, my heart beating wildly, but I yell out, "Let go of me—now!" just as the guy goes flying backward and onto the ground, Damon standing over him.

By now, the rest of the foursome seems to realize something's going on, and they rush over to join in the fray, acting like Damon just attacked their friend. The guy on the ground is yelling about how he's going to sue the resort.

"Why'd you do that to him?" one of the bros asks Damon.

"He assaulted her. She told him to back off, and he didn't listen. So, I made him do it."

I quickly radio in an SOS with a specific code that lets the clubhouse know what's happening.

The guy pops up off the ground and lunges at Damon, telling his friends, "Don't worry, I can handle a punk like this."

The guy is barely six foot with a dad bod, but he's had enough to drink to think he's some kind of pit bull.

He takes two steps toward Damon and throws a punch at him.

Damon simply sidesteps, much like he probably does to would-be tacklers, causing the guy to miss and fall to the ground again, inertia getting the best of him. At the same time, a security golf cart pulls up with both a hotel guard and a police officer.

They don't ask many questions since they already know what happened.

I point to the guy, so they grab him, put him in cuffs, tell him he's under arrest, and read him his rights.

One of the bros decides to be a hero and throws a punch at the security guard, who was leaning down to help the sheriff.

He gets tased, which is something I've never seen before, and it doesn't look pleasant.

The guy who attacked me turns to me and yells, spittle flying out of his mouth, "I'm going to sue you. Sue this hotel and get your skinny ass fired. Do you know who I am?"

"No, I don't, sir," I say.

Damon steps between us and says to the guy, "The question you should be asking yourself is, do you know who *she* is?"

"Who the hell cares? She's just some dumb bitch. I suppose you two are having a thing."

Damon moves closer to the guy, who is being held back by the cop, then turns to me and says, "Tell him who you are."

I stand up straight and look him in the eye. "I'm Ainsley Archibald."

"As in the *Archibald Lodge* Archibald," Damon says. "You should never treat a woman like that, and in this case, you definitely messed with the wrong girl."

Two more security golf carts show up with more guards.

"Get in," they tell the other bros. "We're taking you back to the hotel to gather up your and your friends' belongings. Your entire group has been officially banned from ever coming back to this establishment. Just a few moments ago, two of the waitresses came to our office to report how disrespectful your group was. This is a family resort, and if you can't behave yourselves, you get kicked out with no refunds. Your friends are being retrieved from the club as we speak, and you will all be escorted out together."

They take off. The guy who wouldn't take no for an answer and the Tased one are loaded into a golf cart.

By this time, the hotel manager, Buck Boone, has arrived.

He shakes his head at the guys and tells them that not only are they banned, but that their friend could be facing charges.

Then he comes over to me.

He is in his fifties, has been friends with my uncles since they were kids, and has had the nickname Big Boone for as long as anyone can remember. He's a mountain of a man—six-five with hardened muscles. He retired after a decorated career as a Marine and was recruited to run this place. Everyone here respects him, and we all know that despite his hard exterior, he has a heart of gold and always treats his employees with great regard.

"Are you okay, Ainsley?" he asks me.

"Yeah, I'm fine."

"Do you need to be looked at by the doctor?"

I look at my arm. It still has red marks where the guy's fingers dug into my skin. But other than that, I'm okay. Sort of.

Both Boone and the officer take their phones out and take photos of my arm. Then they take official statements from Damon and me, separately, regarding the events that transpired.

Which leaves me feeling rattled.

Once that's over and they leave, Damon wraps his arms around me, and I practically fall into them.

"Let's go home," he says, walking me to our golf cart.

"I need to take the serving cart back up to the club."

"Someone else can get it," he says, putting me in the cart and taking off.

I don't say anything to him the whole way there.

When we get inside, I tell him I'm going to shower.

He nods.

I go into the bathroom and strip off my clothes, turn the water on, and get in.

Yes, I'm a sweaty mess from being outside all day, but I also feel like I need to get any remnant of that man off me. Cleanse myself.

I'm scrubbing my body with soap when Damon steps in the shower with me.

And it's then that I start crying.

Damon hugs me tightly, and we stand that way under the water for a really long time.

you look like an angel.

Damon

I SQUEEZE HER tightly when all her emotions finally come out. Once her crying slows down, I kiss her forehead, then turn off the shower. I grab a big, fluffy towel and hand it to her. She dries herself off, and then I help her into a robe.

I kiss her cheek, dry myself off quickly, put on a matching robe, then lead her into the bedroom and pull back the covers.

I get in and hold my arm out so she can snuggle up.

She lies on her side, lays her head on my chest, and curls up next to me. "I'm glad you were there today," she says softly.

"I am too," I say, gently running my hand from her forehead and then down the length of her hair.

Pretty soon, I can tell by her breathing that she's asleep. But I don't stop caressing her. Instead, I'm thinking about my fierce desire to protect her.

I remember a night when Chase and I were in eighth grade. My sister called him. She was at a party and drunk. Was going to get driven home by a senior who had been drinking. Chase was freaking out, worried. But because we didn't want her to get in trouble, we decided to go get her ourselves, which meant taking Chase's dad's car without his permission. And there was the pesky fact that neither of us had our license yet.

Of course, we got caught by his dad before we left, but once we confessed about the situation, he took us to the party. Both his dad and I wanted to go inside with Chase, but he said no. It was just a few minutes later when he texted his dad, told him to call the cops, to pull up as close to the door as possible, and that he'd be out in sixty seconds.

I smile, thinking about how I timed him. He actually was out in forty-seven.

When we got back to Chase's house, my sister was pissed at Chase, drunk, and bawling. There was some family drama—my dad getting all upset before Jennifer got Dani calmed down and Dad took her home. I was spending the night there, but was sent downstairs while Chase got reprimanded by his mom, after which, he got sent up to his room.

No surprise that once they went to sleep, I snuck up there.

Chase was a wreck. Mostly because my sister had said she hated him. That everything was his fault. I distracted him, asking about what had happened inside because I was dying to know.

He told me that when he got there, Dalton, our school's senior quarterback, was all over my sister. He was kissing her, his arms tightly around her, feeling her up. He said it was like a flip switched inside of him—an almost-animalistic reaction to a perceived threat. Like when the hair on the back of a dog stands up. He told me he never understood how someone could kill another person, but that night, he felt like he could have. His need to protect her overtaking rational thought.

That's how I felt today. I wanted to kill that guy for touching Ainsley the way he did. For hurting her, scaring her.

I think about the world. How some people think they have

the right to do whatever they want with no regard to how it will affect others. How others are just downright evil. I've always worried about my sisters, especially my little ones.

I chuckle to myself, imagining how I will feel when I have children of my own. And it's scary, but I know that I would protect Ainsley and my future children till my last dying breath.

Part of me is afraid to have kids—if for no other reason than them having to possibly face something like what happened today or something much worse.

Ainsley stirs, squints her eyes, and then looks up at me. "Sorry I fell asleep on you. Have I been sleeping long?"

"Just about forty minutes. How are you feeling?"

She presses her cheek against my chest, sort of rubbing it like a cat would do. "I'm here with you. I'm all good. Have you been just lying here, or did you sleep too?"

"I was content with just rubbing your hair," I tell her, planting my lips on the top of her head and giving it a kiss.

"You must be tired of me falling asleep on you," she says. "Did you at least get to, like, read on your phone or something so you weren't bored?"

"No, I couldn't reach it, but it's okay. I was sort of reminiscing."

"About what?"

I smile, then tell her about the party.

"Afterward, Chase told me that his need to protect her overtook his rational thought. That he wanted to kill the guy. I felt that way today."

"I tried to defuse the situation. I was trained on how to handle it, and over the years, I've gotten pretty good at avoiding anything like that. But this guy took it a step further than any time before.

And I went from pissed off at the asshole to scared."

"I'm glad I was there," I tell her, kissing the side of her face. "You told me yesterday that you wanted to learn more about me. The night of the party I just told you about had quite the aftereffects for both me and Chase."

"What happened?" she asks, sliding her hand down my arm and intertwining her fingers with mine.

"After our high-school team lost Dalton, the starting quarterback, because he had a broken hand, a series of unfortunate events occurred. The third-string quarterback got kicked off the team for drug use, and right before the state championship semifinal, the second-string quarterback was messing around on the gymnastics equipment during PE, landed wrong, and broke his ankle. Which meant that Chase, an eighth grader at the time, was brought up to play—to lead the team." I smile. "Of course, I talked my way onto the team as well."

"Of course you did," she says with a laugh.

Which makes me happy to hear. It means she's not thinking about the events of today.

"So, it was a crazy game. They'd score. We'd score. Chase was throwing really well, but at the end of the game, with little time left, we were down by three and too far away for a field goal that could tie the game and send it into overtime. Right before the last play of the game, I told the coach to put me in. Told him that Chase had been throwing to me his whole life. That he needed me on the field because Chase always knew exactly where I was going to be. And that if he wanted to win this game, that's what he needed to do."

"A crazy game for a guy with a crazy amount of confidence. How were you so confident at such a young age?"

"The thing is, it didn't feel like confidence. It was just … what I knew to be true. I could envision exactly how the game would be won. I see a problem, and I try to fix it. Sometimes, I get into a little trouble for that."

"How so?"

"Like with Haley when she was recovering. I knew what she needed to do. To get better. To heal. And I pushed her to do so."

"But she pushed back?" she asks.

"On some things. From a workout standpoint, it motivated her. But there were times when she was feeling upset or down about it all, and I would ask her how I could fix it. But she told me that I needed to stop trying to fix everything. That she just wanted me to listen so that she could talk through what she already knew was right. That it was okay to sometimes just listen and not solve. It was eye-opening for me."

"It's nice that you want to try to fix things, Damon. But I could see me feeling that way too. Sometimes, I just need to talk through things. So, what happened in the game?"

"Let me set the stage," I say, smiling. "The stadium is packed, fans cheering loudly as both teams lined up. Chase went under center, took the snap, and stepped back into the pocket. Our offensive line held while I raced down the field. I was wide open because not only was I fast, I ran the perfect route. It also didn't hurt that they'd double-teamed our best receiver. Although I didn't see it until I watched the replays, Chase stepped to the side to avoid a sack, then launched the ball downfield. I knew before I turned around that it was a perfect throw based on the cheers of the crowd."

"So, you caught the ball and won the game? Became the heroes?"

"Not exactly," I say with a sardonic chuckle. "Just as I was about to catch the ball, one of my teammates cut me off and tried to catch it himself. I guess he thought he could catch better than me."

"Was he right?"

"No, he dropped the ball. Boom. We lost. I was pissed. Chase was pissed. The whole team was. The fans too. They couldn't believe he'd tried to intercept the ball from his own teammate. The poor guy felt horrible about it. But Chase handled it like a pro. I actually still have the video on my phone because what he said has stuck with me. Want to see it?"

"I would love to," she says.

I scroll to find the video, then press play. We watch as Chase stands up on a bench and starts speaking.

"We all heard the chatter on the field when the game was over. There was a lot of emotion. Some of you blamed me. Some of you blamed Damon. Some of you blamed Joshua. Actually, most of you blamed him. But basically, it was someone else's fault.

"Should Joshua have gone after the pass when his teammate was wide open? Probably not. He tried to intercept the ball from his own wide-open teammate, Damon. He failed, making them both miss.

"But what if things had happened the other way? What if Damon had missed it? And even though it came down to one play that didn't go our way, no single person is to blame for our loss.

"As a team, we never should have been in that position to begin with. How many guys missed passes in the game? What about missed blocks? Missed tackles? Fumbles? Our team lost tonight. That means, we all are at fault for the game's outcome.

"I'd also like to take a moment to thank the seniors for their leadership and for all of you giving me a chance to prove myself. I hope

I'll be good enough to lead this team onto the field next fall."

One by one, the guys who are sitting with towels over their heads stand up. And eventually, they start clapping, ending the video with a standing ovation.

"That's actually a really beautiful moment," Ainsley says. "I can see why you kept it."

"Want to see something else?" I ask.

"Of course."

I pull up another video. "This is all of us at the Mackenzies' that night."

We watch as I yell out, *"Holy guacamole! We made ESPN!"*

I grab the remote and turn on the TV. On the bottom of the screen is the headline—Eighth-grade phenom quarterback throws for over 550 yards for high-school team in the Missouri state playoffs.

"They also showed the last play. Over and over. Mentioning what not to do."

I look over at Ainsley. She's in tears.

"What?" I ask her.

"It's just really—this is exactly what I was talking about yesterday. I want to know about all these moments in your life. Defining moments. The things that make you who you are. Thank you so much for sharing it with me. Also, did I mention that there is a new trope now that fits you perfectly."

"Do I want to know?" I say with a chuckle.

"The golden retriever hero. It's been made popular by a current professional athlete who plays here in KC and dates a pop star."

"Oh, I know who you are talking about. But what does it mean?"

"The guy is energetic, friendly, and crazy loyal. Has a playful side, which makes him fun to be around. And is happy and secure in his relationship.”

“I bet he likes to be pet too.” I break out into a wide grin, feeling happy.

And when she takes off her robe and moves on top of me, I get even more so.

WE'RE LYING IN bed, snuggling, when her phone rings.

“It's my uncle,” she says. “I should probably take it.”

“Of course,” I say. “Put it on speaker.”

“Hey, Uncle Tripp,” she says. “You have me and Damon on speaker.”

“It sounds like you two had quite the afternoon,” he says. “Ainsley, I know you were trained to handle these situations, but I'm sure it was scary. And, Damon, I'm glad you were there.”

“Thank you,” she says. “The guy was holding my arm, so I couldn't reach my walkie. I'm glad Damon was there too.”

“Hmm,” Tripp says. “I suggested upgrading that technology, but everyone said they were used to the walkie-talkies. I'm going to reconsider that with this sort of situation in mind. Come up with a new plan. Are you sure you're okay?”

“Yeah, I'm fine now. Thank you.”

“Good to hear. You excited for the fireworks tonight?” he asks, changing the subject.

“Yeah, I'm sure they will be spectacular.”

“That's the plan. I just arrived and wondered if you two would like to join me and a few special guests out on the yacht to watch the festivities.”

“Oh, that would be really nice,” she says.

“Remember the dinner we had on it? Tonight will be a redo of that."

"We'll be there," she says with a grin. "What time are you departing?"

"In an hour. That work?"

"Yes, it will. I can't wait. That was one of the best dinners of my life!"

She hangs up and smiles at me. "You're going to love this."

I lean over and kiss her. "I think the only thing I love now is you."

Our kisses turn passionate, but she says, "I can't go with wet, scraggly hair and no makeup."

"You'd better get up then," I tell her, giving her thigh a couple of little taps.

She hops out of bed just as her phone rings again. She picks it up, glances at it, and tosses it in my direction.

"It's Sammy. You talk to him. I have to get ready."

"Hey, Sammy," I say when I answer. "It's Damon. Ainsley's here, but she's got to get ready for an event tonight."

Sammy goes, "Well, I'm glad you answered because I have news! Put her on speaker."

I do, then say, "Okay, she can hear you now."

"Ahhhhhhhh!! Guess what. And this is B-I-G!"

"What?" Ainsley and I ask simultaneously.

"Roman and I are taking a trip! Together! To the Ozarks. To visit you! Do you know what a big deal this is? A family event is what broke us up last time. And now, he's agreed to come there to meet you, which is almost the same. It's such a big turn of events."

"But last time we talked, you said you thought he was going to propose. Why is this bigger than that?" Ainsley asks.

"He's going to propose?" I say, confused. I hadn't heard about this.

"It's a new development," Sammy says. "And, yes, we have actually talked marriage. Did I tell you why? I can't remember. But he's going to move to Manhattan for his job. It will make it easier for him to travel his territory. When he's in town, he doesn't bother with a hotel, just stays with me. Add that to the fact that he's ready to meet my friends, and it just confirms everything. And I'm ecstatic. Blissful. And all the other dreamily-in-love words."

"When are you coming?" Ainsley yells out.

"Every time I'm with him. Multiple times, if you want to know the truth," Sammy says. "That's the other word we could use to describe the relationship. It's orgasmic."

I chuckle while Ainsley goes, "That's not what I meant."

"Fine," he says in a mopey tone. "Remember how I have a break between summer classes? I thought Roman and I could get up early on Friday the twenty-fourth and drive down. We'd leave that Monday morning."

"That sounds great, but I have to dry my hair. I'm shutting the door. Bye, Sammy!"

"Well, I never," Sammy says to me. "She's impossible."

"I haven't experienced that yet," I say in her defense.

"She's not really impossible," he says. "I'm just excited. So, you're down there now. That means you get some weekends off. You should come too. I'd love to meet you. I'd love for you to meet Roman. We would have so much fun."

Although I don't know what I'm getting myself into, the thought of coming back in a few weeks does sound very appealing. Mostly because of the girl in the bathroom, frantically getting ready.

"I'll be here," I tell him and end the call.

Then I get myself up, get dressed, go into one of the other bathrooms, wet my hair down, comb it back, and throw on some deodorant.

Done.

I'm sitting on the couch in the living room, reading on my phone, when she comes out, looking gorgeous in a long, flowing orange sundress. The color takes me back to the first night of the family reunion earlier this summer. To the flirty sundress she had on—the one with little flowers all over it. I thought of her as my Garden of Eden.

And I still do.

Tonight's dress also features a floral print, but the flowers are large, and the dress falls almost to the floor. She looks elegant. And I love that the heels on her feet bring her lips up closer to mine.

I whistle at her, causing her to blush. And I love it.

"You are a vision," I tell her. "You look like an angel."

"That was exactly the look I was going for," she teases, then lowers her voice. "Although I don't think they typically wear orange."

What's meant to be.

Ainsley

DINNER ON THE yacht is the same menu as when we were here for the family reunion and equally fantastic.

The special guests that Tripp invited are a group of his biggest investors. He gives them an update on the Fort Worth renovations, and then makes an announcement. That with the upcoming renovations of Kansas City's iconic football stadium, he sees a big opportunity. That he's already purchased a beautiful plot of land on which to build a brand-new hotel that would serve fans for both the football and baseball stadiums as well as the concerts and events hosted in the area.

Everyone is surprised by this since his thing is taking historic hotels and bringing them back to greatness. But they love the idea.

When a single firework is launched into the sky to indicate the forthcoming show, we all move out to the sundeck.

Damon sits in a chaise, then spreads his legs to allow me to sit with my back against his chest.

He whispers in my ear, "You know how on your birthday, you're supposed to reflect on your year. I don't really do that, but I guess there's been something about the fireworks since we started coming down here that makes me think. About where we've been. What's transpired over the year. And I look ahead to the future. What the year will hold. I talk a lot about the power of our mindset, but I also know that the divine is mixed in there. What's meant to be. What's not.

"How we've grown, changed, and matured has been a big focus for me. Watching fireworks with you, twice during our time here this summer and again tonight, has me thinking a lot more about me, personally. And about us." He slides his hands down the sides of my arms. "All the things that I picture for us. For our life together. It sucks, being apart, but I know it will be okay because I can imagine our future."

"And what do you see in that future?" I ask him.

"It's mostly snippets of life. Moments. You cheering me on at games this fall. You in my bed. You graduating and moving to

Lincoln to be with me. A bunch more winning. A national championship or two.

"Talk to me about kids," he says, changing the subject. "I don't want to wait for them. Do you?"

I can't do anything but nod my head.

Because I'm afraid if I speak, the truth will tumble out of my mouth.

"Good," he says, putting his lips on my shoulder. "Chase and I were talking the other day about our future kids. How not only do we want them to grow up together and be close like we were, but also how we might achieve that when we end up on separate teams, in separate cities. So, we're thinking of doing something with our NIL money."

"That stands for Name, Image, and Likeness, right?"

"That's right. And the community where Mom and Van built their new house has acreages available. Dad and Jennifer just bought a plot there. She wants to have a place where all her stuff is together." He chuckles. "In other words, she needs a bunch of garages to house her car collection and a big closet for all her clothes."

"It's cool how she's able to balance living where she does, having what I'd call a normal life, but then you see her on a red carpet, and she looks so glamorous."

"She's just thrilled that the tabloids seem to avoid the Midwest. Anyway, Chase and I want to buy land there too. That way, no matter where we play football, we'll have a home base to live in the offseason. I already told you that I want you to design my house, but in this case, it wouldn't be just my house. It would be our house. You'd be designing our future. Like, would you be cool with that, living there?"

"I haven't seen the house or the land yet, but I'm assuming my uncle wouldn't move there if it wasn't really lovely. And he always says that real estate can be a good investment."

"So, you're cool with me spending our money on that?"

"Damon, it's your money."

"True, but as soon as you agree to marry me, it will be our money. For our life. Our future. Our children's future."

Tears fill my eyes. "I think it's a great idea, Damon."

SUNDAY, JULY 5TH

Ainsley

I WAKE UP slowly, happy I don't have to work today. I roll over, looking for Damon but find his side of the bed empty.

His side of the bed.

And he actually does have a side. He always chooses the left side of the bed, which means I'm able to snuggle up in my favorite spot, tucked under his right shoulder with my head on his chest. Even though not directly above his heart, I can still feel his heartbeat. And something I've noticed is that Damon's resting heart rate must be quite low because his always beats much slower than mine. And its gentle rhythm is quite soothing.

A quick glance at the clock on the nightstand causes my eyes to go wide. It's a little after ten. I can't believe I slept in this long. One thing I've noticed about being pregnant is that I sleep so hard. And even with my little nap yesterday, I was exhausted by the time we got back from the fireworks. I remember Damon kissing me as my head hit the pillow.

I hear a noise come from the other side of the bedroom door and then suddenly smell the wonderful scent of food cooking.

Something fried. And I don't know what is going on, but I love fried food right now—which is weird because it's something I normally avoid.

My tummy immediately growls. I've also been hungrier than usual. Well, for the most part. Sometimes, I can't get enough food. Other times, nothing sounds good.

I stretch out my body and then get up, donning a robe, and patter out to the kitchen.

Damon is again shirtless, wearing the apron. And it makes me smile.

"Morning," he says. "Sleep well?"

"Obviously," I tease. "How long have you been up?"

"Believe it or not, I slept in too. Which is not something I usually do. I got up about an hour ago and decided to whip up breakfast."

I sit down at the breakfast bar and say, "It smells good. Whatcha cooking?"

"Gravy," he says. "I asked Mimi to teach me how to make it during the family reunion. It's one of my favorite things. Everyone says gravy is so hard to make, but it's really pretty simple. I've got the biscuits in the oven, and the hash browns are cooked and waiting in the pan."

"That sounds really good," I tell him.

He smiles. "Since I'm in the Ozarks, I thought I'd make chicken fried steak too. Although you didn't have any steak, so I made chicken fried chicken instead. I had to pound it out thin and everything. My batter," he says, pulling some tin foil off a platter on the island and showing me the chicken cutlets, "leaves a little to be desired, but it tastes good even if it doesn't look too pretty."

Just then, the timer dings, and he goes, "Oh, the biscuits

should be ready."

And when he turns around and bends over to open the oven door, I get a shock and start laughing.

"You're cooking naked!" I hoot.

His sexy, naked butt is clearly visible.

He pulls the golden-brown biscuits from the oven, sets them on the stovetop, and then turns around to face me. Cue the big grin.

"You're naughty," I tell him, still laughing.

"Hey, you're not supposed to laugh about that. Me naked around you is very serious."

"I'm sorry," I say. "I thought you had on shorts, like the other day, but then you turned around."

"*Butt* being the keyword," he says with a chuckle.

"I mean, you saw my naked butt on my wild night—only fitting I see yours as often as possible."

He comes around to my side of the counter, pulls me to my feet, undoes my robe, then sets me up on the counter.

Very quickly, my legs are wrapped around his waist, and he's kissing me hard.

But hunger gets the best of me. "Do you mind if we eat first?"

He reluctantly nods and lets go of me.

We fill our plates and then sit at the kitchen table and eat.

"I'm not ready for you to leave," I tell him, feeling emotional. "This weekend was so much fun."

"It was, and thanks to Sammy, I'll be back down here in just a few weeks."

"That should be interesting. Thankfully, the other bedrooms are upstairs, above the kitchen, on the opposite side of the house from our room."

"Our room," he says, looking at me dreamily. "I can't wait until we can live together. Be together all the time."

"I can't wait for that either," I tell him. "I know our goal is for me to move to Lincoln with you after graduation, but I'm worried about finding a job there."

"Whatever happens, we'll make it work," he says reassuringly.

Which makes me feel good. Like we're a team.

"By the way, Mimi taught you right. This is all delicious. In fact, I'm going in for seconds."

He smiles and says, "Me too," then surprises me when he picks me up and carries me into the bedroom.

DAMON SLOWLY EXPLORES my body, looking at it like he'll never see it again or maybe just tucking away the memories for when we're apart. And when he kisses down my belly, tears form in my eyes, and I think about the fact that he's sort of kissing his baby. Our baby.

I run my fingers through his hair, and the words almost form on my lips. But I know I can't tell him. Not yet. I have to be strong.

AND A FEW hours later, I'm teary again when he gets loaded up in his car and kisses me goodbye.

"I wish you didn't have to go," I tell him.

"I wish I didn't have to either. I keep thinking the last time I saw you was the best time of my life, but things just keep getting better. I love you, Champ."

"I love you too, Damon," I say.

THURSDAY, JULY 23RD

I told you so.

Ainsley

I'M OUT ON the golf course, driving the beverage cart to the next hole, thankful that my shift is almost over. I'm making a mental list of the things I want to do tonight—most revolving around ordering a few groceries since Damon as well as Sammy and Roman will be here tomorrow—when my phone rings. The caller ID says it's hotel security.

I answer. "This is Ainsley."

"It's Larry from up at the guard shack."

"Hey, Larry. What's up?"

Larry is an older gentleman who is rumored to be a retired CIA operative. I don't know if he plays the role of hick very convincingly or if he really is one. No one does.

"We got a guy up here at the gate that says he's fixin' to be stayin' with you. Are you expectin' a visitor today?"

"Um, no, but I am tomorrow. Who is it?"

"Name on his ID is Samuel. Says I can call him Sammy. And he's been sputtering on about a disastrous final exam and a devastatin' breakup. Guy seems a little unhinged, if you want my professional opinion."

"A breakup," I fume. "I swear, I'm going to kill Roman."

"You're not actually fixin' to, are ya?" Larry says. "Because if so, I will pretend I didn't hear those words, for they would indicate premeditation."

"Uh, no, I don't mean it. I'm just upset that Sammy's ex came back into his life, only to upend it again. Please let him in and—actually, let him in but keep him there with you. I'll drive back to the club, find someone to cover for me, and then I'll come get him."

"Oh Lord, help me," Larry says. "There's boo-hooin' going on again. He's definitely off his rocker."

"You got any alcohol in the guard shack, Larry?" I ask him.

"Only for medicinal purposes," he replies.

"I think Sammy may need some medication."

"Roger Wilco on that," he says before hanging up.

"Ahhhhh!" I yell, getting my frustration out.

I can't believe Roman did this to Sammy. AGAIN!

I'm also upset Sammy had gone back to the asshole to begin with. But I can't say that.

I drop the beverage cart off at the club, beg my manager to finish the last fifteen minutes of my shift, and drive to the resort's entrance.

I can see Sammy sitting in the guard shack, holding a drink and seemingly shooting the breeze with Larry. There are currently no tears, and he doesn't look the least bit unhinged.

But the second I pull up, he comes rushing out of the shack and throws his arms around me before I even get the golf cart stopped. I press the brake and stand up, hugging him back.

"Don't even say it," he says to me.

"Say what?" I ask.

"I told you so."

"I'm not going to say that. You did what you felt was right for you. But what happened?"

"I've been telling Larry here all about it." He turns around. "Haven't I, Larry?"

"Yes, you have." Larry's wearing a strained smile. "And while I'm sorry for the *tragedy that has descended upon your life*"—Larry looks at me—"his words, not mine"—he turns back to Sammy—"I'm gonna need you to get the hell outta my shack. I got work to do."

"Come on, Sammy," I tell him. "Let's get you settled."

Sammy tosses Larry his keys. "Can you take care of—" he starts to say, but Larry tosses them back and goes, "I ain't no damn valet, son."

"Follow me," I tell Sammy. "I'll show you where to park."

ONCE WE GET his car situated and I get him and his bag loaded onto my golf cart, I head toward my cottage.

"It's real purdy up in here," Sammy says, trying to mimic Larry's accent. "I ain't been to the Ozarks since I was knee-high to a grasshopper."

"You seriously are not going to talk like that all weekend."

"I don't know," he says, shrugging his shoulders. "I reckon it'd be kinda fun."

"I reckon it would be even funner if you slept in a tent."

"Whatever," he says, holding the plastic cup in his hand. "Cheers to the Ozarks. And to probably failing my final."

"Do you want to tell me what happened?" I ask gently.

"I literally couldn't concentrate during the test."

"I meant with Roman."

He downs the rest of whatever Larry gave him. "This stuff tastes like straight-up gasoline," he says, shaking his head.

"If I had to guess, it's moonshine. And a strong one."

"Well, when in France—I, er, mean, the Ozarks. Oh, bloody hell, you know what I mean."

"Yes, I do. You've gone British," I tease.

Sammy does a little smile. "So, here's the skinny. I wanted to get packed before my final so that I could relax with Roman tonight, as we had planned an early morning start to our trip tomorrow. I had just finished when he called. He told me—literally almost word for word what he had the last time I tried to get him to meet my family—that it's too much because I'm not the only person he's seeing."

"But you were in a relationship, I thought."

"I thought too!" he says, starting to blubber. "I don't know what I'm going to do."

"What did you do last time?" I ask him, even though I know the answer.

"I let the misery take over my life. Questioned if I was a lovable person. Wallowed in sorrow and self-doubt."

"And what should you do this time?"

"Drink," he says, holding up the empty glass. When I tilt my head and squint my eyes at him, he says, "Although I am well endowed, clearly, I need to grow a set."

Not what I was expecting him to say, but it suffices.

"I'm sorry," I say again.

I SHOW HIM the cottage and get him settled in his room upstairs. It has a pretty view of the water and a balcony set with a table and comfy chair.

"This is adorable," he tells me. "I'm calling it elevated rustic luxury. Very nice."

"Why don't you get unpacked while I shower off and change? Then if you want, I can show you around the resort. Are you hungry?"

"Part of me says that I'll never eat again. The other part of me wants nothing but decadent food and drink."

"Lucky for you, I know exactly where we can get that. But only tonight. He doesn't really deserve your tears."

"I know he doesn't. And I'm certainly glad I learned all of this now. I can be over him forever and move the eff on with my life. You know, when you came here, I put it out to the universe that you would meet a man, and you did." He smiles at me. "Damon's going to be here tomorrow, right?"

"Right," I state.

"I'm so excited to meet him in person. At least there's one bright thing about this weekend."

"I'm excited for you to meet him too," I say.

I'M FEELING REFRESHED after my shower, so I slip on a breezy sundress. And when I do, my hand falls to my belly. I'm definitely not showing yet, but it looks—no, it just feels a little different.

And I realize I may have to adjust my plan. That I might not be able to wait until the end of the season. I look up on my phone when it becomes obvious to others that you're pregnant. It says it varies, but typically by the end of the second trimester, which would get me to mid-October, depending on how much I'm showing.

I go out into the living room and find Sammy on the couch,

flipping through a magazine.

"You look lovely," he says. "Am I dressed okay?"

"Yes. You look nice." And I mean it. Sammy is handsome.

"The place I'm taking you for dinner is the resort's nicest restaurant. They are booked full, but the staff is holding us a spot at the bar. The food is so incredibly good. In fact, I took the liberty of preordering us some starters. Let's get going."

NOT ONLY IS Sammy nice to look at, but he's also the kind of person who has never met a stranger. People love him. And tonight is no exception. He's spoken to all the patrons around us, and he's on a first-name basis with the staff. He's sipping champagne to celebrate his new life—or at least, that's what he's telling everyone.

When I refuse a glass for the second time, he goes, "What's up? You love champagne. You should splurge with me."

"I really don't drink much when I'm working here in the summer. I'm out in the sun all day, and I really have to focus on not getting dehydrated."

"That means there's a story," he says, narrowing his eyes at me and grinning.

"Not a story. I just learned my lesson after going out one night. To be honest, I didn't even drink all that much. It's just that I had already been dehydrated from working out in the sun all day and threw in the alcohol. The next day was my worst day ever on the job. I felt horrible. And since then, I make sure that no matter how busy I am, I take care of myself."

"That's what I have to do," Sammy says. "Start taking care of myself. I let myself get so wrapped up in Roman. I've done nothing but eat a lot and work out very little." He looks down at his now-empty dinner plate. "Obviously, not starting tonight."

"Tell me about your classes. What are you taking this summer?"

"Art Appreciation is the final that I probably failed. Monday, I start History of Design."

"Oh, I loved that class. It's crazy how what people wear is such a clear indicator of what's going on in their life. As you're living it, you think they're just trends, but they really are often dictated by things like war and peace. Good times and bad. Religion. Politics. You're a history buff, so you'll love it."

"At least I'll love something." He pouts.

"You have one more semester of school, and then you'll be getting a job and moving. You have a lot to look forward to."

"We both do," he says, holding his flute up.

I pick up my water glass and clink it against his. "To us."

"To us," he agrees. "And I'm hoping to get a job in the Kansas City area so I can be closer to my big, crazy family."

Sammy's mom had two children, and his dad had three when they married. Together, they had three more children, Sammy being the youngest.

"Especially since Mom and Dad are getting older. It's crazy that some of my siblings are old enough to be my parents and that I have nieces and nephews who are almost my age. We sure have a good time together though." He rolls his eyes. "Although there's always a little drama. Just last week, during a family barbecue, my sister Suzie and her husband got into a fight over something stupid."

"What was it?"

"In this case, it was because he had left the corn dish she'd made to share sitting on top of the car and drove off. It fell off on the highway and broke her favorite casserole dish."

"That's kind of funny."

"Well, luckily, we all do get along for the most part. Speaking of family, how are your parents?"

"Mom is doing well, likes where she's living, and she's dating someone. Neither of us has heard from Dad since he left rehab. It's one thing if he's mad at Mom or whatever, but not to call me is just kinda mean."

"Addictions wreak havoc on families. I know I'm sitting here, drinking champagne, but I've been considering cutting out alcohol. Did you know that a lot of professional athletes don't drink? Or they do, like, just on special occasions or during their offseason?"

"Is this your offseason?" I tease, but what I'm really thinking is, this will be great. I won't have to explain why I'm not drinking. "Seriously though, I would do it with you. We can come up with some fun mocktails for our dinners this fall."

"I feel like we've always eaten pretty healthy, but we should work on that too. When we graduate and start new jobs, we'll be lean, mean, working machines! Speaking of jobs, what are you hoping for?"

"Something that I will love in the town with the man I love."

I try to stifle a yawn, but Sammy notices.

He glances at his watch. "What time did you get up this morning?"

"Up at six and working by seven."

"And when does Damon get here?"

"Around eleven. I guess he's flying down this time."

"Must be nice," Sammy says.

"He'd spend all day driving otherwise," I counter.

"True. Well, I'm looking forward to hanging out with him. Let's head home."

FRIDAY, JULY 24TH

Maybe it did.

Damon

WHEN I GET to the Archibald Lodge, I text Ainsley.

> **Me:** *Hey, got in earlier than expected, met up with Sammy, and dropped my bag off at the cottage. He wants to order food and have it delivered here. Is that okay with you?*

> **Champ:** *Sounds great! I can't wait to see you!*

I heart her text and then turn to Sammy. "She's cool with it."

I grab a bottle of water and go sit out on one of the front porch rockers.

Sammy comes out a few minutes later with a glass of white wine. "Got everything ordered. Tell me about your summer training. I follow football, but have never really paid attention during that time."

"Mostly, it's about getting in peak performance shape. On Mondays and Fridays, we do full-body lifting and a lot of cardio. Tuesdays and Thursdays, we work on speed skills."

"What's that?" Sammy asks.

"Different drills that help promote speed—from things like timing the forty-yard dash and trying to beat your score to agility drills, where you practice acceleration and deceleration."

"Why would you want to decelerate?"

"There's a fumble you want to go get, a defender you want to avoid. Sometimes, you have to make a quick change in the direction you are going."

"So, the fastest players win?"

"Not necessarily. It's also got to do with how you utilize your speed. Think about running backs—unless they are lucky and hit a hole in the defense and can run untouched down the field, they often have to change directions to avoid being tackled."

"And on Wednesdays?" Sammy wonders.

"Similar to Mondays with the full-body lifting, but instead of doing cardio, we play seven-on-seven football games." I grin. "So far, the team Chase and I are on is undefeated. Wednesdays are my favorite day."

"Then do you get the weekend off?"

"If we're there—since it's summer, everyone isn't there every day, but for those who are, there's a sanctioned player practice." When Sammy looks confused, I add, "It just means that it's organized by the players, not the coaching staff. They aren't mandatory, but they're a great way to build teamwork and get some additional practice in. And of course, most of us take our most challenging classes in the summer."

"I'm taking summer courses, too, so Ainsley and I can both graduate this winter."

"What are you hoping to do after graduation? Where do you want to live?"

"Kansas City area, hopefully, so I can be close to family. I think I'd like to work at a furniture store and do in-house design for their customers. I like being out with people."

Just as he finishes speaking, Ainsley pulls up in her golf cart. She's in her cute work uniform, and she looks gorgeous, as usual. I'm up on my feet and by her side before Sammy even reacts. Guess those agility and speed drills pay off in other ways too.

Her face beams with a smile, and she greets me with a kiss. A long kiss. Just the way I like.

And I suddenly wish I could make Sammy disappear, pick her up, and carry her to the bedroom.

"I'm starved," she says. "What's for lunch?"

Sammy blinks his eyes a few times, like he's just now realizing we haven't gotten our food yet as another golf cart pulls up.

I reluctantly let go of Ainsley and take a big bag from the server.

"Thanks, Greg," Ainsley says to him.

I watch as this Greg guy blushes. I think he may have a crush. *Me too, buddy. Me too.*

WE GET THE food set up in the middle of the table so that we can all share and fill up our plates.

"So, what have you guys been doing without me?" Ainsley asks.

"I was learning about summer football training," Sammy replies. "I was just about to ask Damon what classes he is taking."

"Chemistry and Calculus," I tell him.

"Oh, my two least favorites," Sammy says. "Why start with those?"

"Chemistry has lab time, and Calc has a lot of homework. Best to do them in the offseason."

"I didn't know you were taking classes," Ainsley says. "You never told me that."

"I have more fun things to talk to you about than school," I say with a smirk.

"Oh my," Sammy says with a laugh. "I don't think I want to know."

"Not to change the subject," Ainsley says, "but I managed to get you two a tee time. Two of the guys who work here, Apollo and Liam, were going out as a pair, so I was able to make it a foursome."

"What do they do?" Sammy asks.

"Both have worked here for as long as I have," Ainsley says. "Like me, Apollo started as a pool server, but now he's the spa manager. Liam is one of our most requested caddies. I've golfed with them before. You'll have fun." She takes another chicken tender and dips it in gravy.

"I didn't think you liked fried foods," I say to Ainsley.

Usually, she eats really healthy.

Sammy's eyes get huge, and he says to me, "Oh shit. You probably don't ever eat stuff like this, do you? I should have ordered you salmon and broccoli or something."

"This is a fun splurge," I say, smiling at him.

But he's right. This meal started with jalapeño poppers and pulled pork nachos, continued with the strips and gravy, cornbread-battered fish, and a trifecta of French fries—cheddar cheese and bacon, Cajun seasoned, and Parmesan truffle.

"Well, it's a good thing you are splurging today because I also got dessert!" He lifts a napkin off the top of a container he must have been hiding. "Have you had their gooey butter cake before?"

"I have!" Ainsley raises her hand. "And it's one of my favorites!"

And it quickly becomes one of my favorites, too, when she feeds me a bite.

AFTER GOLF, SAMMY heads to the bar with Apollo and Liam while I wait for Ainsley to come in at the end of her shift.

The second she pulls up, I'm at her side.

"From the little I saw when I was buzzing around, it appeared you had a good round. Or at least were having a good time. Sammy was grinning like crazy."

"Oh, that's not because of the way he played. He's got a wicked slice, and he was not putting well."

"Really?" Ainsley tilts her head in confusion. "He's usually pretty good."

"There might have been another reason. When he did poorly, Apollo was giving him tips. A few times, he even stood behind him and wrapped his arms around him, in an attempt to straighten out his swing."

"That was nice of him," Ainsley says.

"I think there was an ulterior motive. There was some serious flirting going on."

"Oh! How exciting! That's exactly what Sammy needs."

"Except he seemed oblivious. Kind of like you did when we first hung out."

"Well, he was supposed to be here with Roman. He's still in shock about all that. Did you have fun? Who won?"

"Yes, it was fun. Apollo won. I got second. At least I beat the 'scratch golfer' caddy."

"He wishes he were a scratch golfer," she says with a laugh.

"We can join them in the bar or—"

"I can't actually join them since I'm still in my uniform. Club rules. I'll have to go back and change. And I could use a quick shower."

I raise my eyebrows at her and grin. "Oh, I could use a shower too."

She fists my shirt and pulls me toward her. "You do look quite dirty. Just be prepared. The shower might take a while."

THE COOL WATER flows over me. It should be calming, but it's not, particularly when she steps inside with me. I move over, giving her more direct access to the showerhead. But she stops, our eyes meeting in a stare. We don't touch. Or speak. Like we're hoping this is real. That we're back together.

She gives me a smile, then slides under the water and immediately tosses her head back. I watch as the water trails down her beautiful body.

My hand moves of its own accord, quickly cradling her face.

She sounds slightly breathless when she whispers, "I've missed you, Damon."

"I know how you feel," I tell her as she reaches up, sliding her arms around my neck, causing our bodies to press against one another.

And when our lips come together, surprisingly, it's not rushed. It's slow, yet there's an underlying feeling of desperation.

For each other.

She leaps up, wrapping her legs around me. I put my hands under her ass to hold her up, knowing we both want more.

Need more.

The next kiss is hard. Greedy. Like she's trying to make up for our weeks apart in this one single moment.

ONCE WE'RE BOTH satisfied, she lays her head on my shoulder and says, "I could stay like this forever."

And I'm thinking the same thing. I have one hand on her back and the other tangled in her wet hair, trying to memorize the feel of her.

"We probably shouldn't show up at the bar like this," I tease, looking down at our naked bodies. "Although, at least you wouldn't be wearing your work uniform."

This causes her to laugh. "We probably should get back there. Otherwise, Sammy will come looking for us, and that might be awkward."

"I love you," I say, kissing her forehead.

She looks at me like the kiss just said everything.

And maybe it did.

Almost a year.

Ainsley

WE HEAD BACK to the bar to meet up with Sammy and Apollo. Liam must've picked up an evening shift because he's now behind the bar.

"What do you eat every day?" Sammy asks Damon the second we sit down. "I feel like I'm in pretty good shape, but I'd like to take it to the next level."

"Gotta cut out this," Apollo teases, pointing at the martinis in front of them.

"I usually eat about 4,000 calories a day," Damon tells them.

I swear, I feel like I'm eating that many calories a day myself right now, but I can't say so.

"Like, specifics," Sammy insists.

"Um, okay," Damon says, but then turns to me. "What do you want to drink?"

"I'd like a sparkling water with a lime," I tell him.

"Two of those," Damon tells Liam, then says, "I start most mornings with yogurt, eggs, and toast. Followed by lifting and then a large protein shake. Current favorite is strawberry, banana, and almond butter. Lunch is usually chicken, rice, and lots of veggies. Afternoon snack is another shake, some nuts or oatmeal, and a peanut butter and jelly sandwich with bananas. Dinner is often pasta or something similar to lunch. Bedtime snack is my favorite—a chocolate cherry shake."

"That's a lot of food. I don't know if I could eat that much. You eat like it's your job," Sammy says with a laugh.

Apollo goes, "It pretty much is, right?"

"Yeah, kinda," Damon says with a grin.

Sammy says to me, "What do you and Damon have planned for tonight? Apollo asked if we wanted to join him for some line dancing after dinner. Apparently, there's a country music band onstage tonight."

"We have live music almost every night during the summer," Apollo says.

"I think once I have dinner, I'm going to be done for the day. But I'm off tomorrow, so if you want to go dancing then, we can."

"I'm only covering here for a few hours," Liam says. "I'll get some of the other guys, and we'll all go together. Damon, you in?"

Damon shakes his head. "Nah, you guys have fun."

WE EAT DINNER, and when Apollo goes to use the restroom and Damon steps outside to take a call from his little sister, Sammy fans his face.

"Your man is hot. If only he were gay … seriously, I'm drooling. His father is no longer my obsession."

"You can't be obsessed over my boyfriend," I tease.

"I also really like him, like as a person," Sammy says, which is high praise, coming from him.

"I'm glad. So, Damon told me he thought Apollo was flirting with you today and that you were oblivious."

Sammy's eyes get huge. "Oh my goodness gracious. What the heck? How did I not realize that?" I don't get a chance to reply because he goes, "Of course, it's because I'm in the relationship-ending mourning period. Also, is Apollo gay? I did not get that vibe from him. I thought he was just being helpful because my game was horrific today."

"Damon thought you were playing bad on purpose."

"I wasn't. Roman not only took my heart and stomped on it, but he's destroyed my golf game. It's ridiculous. Seriously." He sees Apollo walking back toward us. "Tell me what you know."

"I've never spoken to him specifically about his sexuality, if that's what you're asking."

"Has he dated anyone here?"

"I don't know, to be honest."

He licks his lips. "Tonight might prove to be interesting."

"Maybe just make some new friends tonight as opposed to looking for love. I can tell you that Apollo is a good coworker, thoughtful, and funny."

"Yeah, maybe," he says noncommittally, but I'm not really paying attention because Damon is now walking my way.

SAMMY DECIDES TO stay at the bar until Liam gets off work, and Damon and I head back to the cottage, where we decide to sit out on the front porch.

"Being on the seventh green today brought back a few wonderful memories," he tells me. "I wanted to stop and pay some kind of homage to its significance."

"I still can't believe I had sex with you on the day you turned eighteen. You were barely legal," I say with a laugh.

"I was totally legal," he counters, narrowing his eyes at me. When I don't say anything, he goes, "You do realize that the age of sexual consent in our great state of Missouri is seventeen."

"What?! No, it's not! You told me you weren't legal yet when I said something about it."

"Well, technically, like other states, the age of majority is eighteen, but for sexual consent, it's seventeen. I figured you knew that. *Everyone* here knows that. How could you not know that?"

"Probably because I dated the same stupid boy who was my age all through high school and it didn't matter." I throw my hands up in the air in frustration.

"You're getting really worked up about this," he says, a smile playing on his face.

"That's because I was feeling like I shouldn't be with you!"

"You shouldn't have felt that way. I had been legal in that regard for almost a year before we ever got together."

"Hmm." I tap my fingers on the table. "I think Damon's been a bad boy."

"I've never been a bad boy, but I might be willing to make an exception for you," he says in a deep, sultry voice.

I act like I'm not impressed, even though I want nothing more than to take him up on the offer. "I think what needs to happen here is, you need to offer me some restitution for the mental trauma I went through."

He knows I'm playing around with him because a smile lights up his whole face. "What kind of payment are we talking about here?"

"I'm pretty sure it would be of a sexual nature," I reply.

He stands up and holds his hand out to take mine, then leads me into the bedroom.

Forever.

Damon

AS USUAL, I'M up early and in the kitchen, whipping up breakfast when Ainsley strolls out. Her hair is twirled up into a bun, and there are little mascara smudges under her eyes, but her face is radiant—especially when she smiles at me. She's wrapped up in a bathrobe, and that's how I feel—wrapped up in love.

She gets some orange juice and scrunches up her cute little nose at the omelet cooking on the stove.

"With fall practice starting soon, I've really got to watch what I eat. But I did make waffles and caramel sauce, just for you."

"I thought I'd smelled something sweet," she says with a grin.

"You're the something sweet," I tell her, pulling the strings of her robe toward me for a kiss.

She lets out a content sigh. "I'm so happy, Damon. What do you want to do today?"

"Well, I was thinking we could go out on our ski boat. I thought whoever stayed at the house got to use it, but Dad said they only leave the pontoon. We could take lunch, maybe fish, soak up the sun."

"Sounds perfect," she says, but then whispers in my ear, "Although I'm glad Sammy's here, I kinda wish we could be alone for that."

"I heard that," Sammy says from behind us. "And your wish is my command. Apollo invited me to the spa. He's setting everything up. Says I need to decompress to soothe my mind. Rid it of Roman."

"That's really nice of him," Ainsley says. "And I agree. It would be good for you."

"I took your advice," Sammy says to her, "and we bonded as friends last night. All three of us, really. Me, Liam, and Apollo. Liam and I get along well, but I think Apollo might be like you. One of those people who just belongs in my life."

Ainsley gives him a hug. "And sometimes, they come along at just the right time."

"That they do," he says, then turns to me and asks, "Whatcha cooking?"

I FIND A spot in a quiet cove and drop the boat's anchor.

"It's literally the perfect day," Ainsley says. "Partly sunny, not too hot. Cool breeze off the water."

"Or the perfection isn't because of the weather," I tell her, lying down next to her on the front of the boat.

"That could be true," she says, leaning in for a sweet kiss.

"It is pretty here. I've always loved vacationing in the Ozarks. I haven't talked to anyone about it yet, but I think we're going to have to continue the joint family reunion next year. That way, it's not just my family, but the whole big crew."

"That's a really good idea," she says. "I should mention it to Tripp."

"And I'll say something to my mom. She is good at making things happen."

"Like what?"

"Well, it's because of her helping Chase that he could pull off a surprise wedding."

"What do you mean, a surprise wedding?"

"Chase wanted to elope. Go to the courthouse and just get married. But Dani wanted her dream wedding. Chase's dad proposed on his and Jadyn's first date, and then he took her straight to a surprise engagement party. And I guess Chase thought it might be fun to propose, then have a surprise wedding. He took his idea to my mom. Mom pretended to want to have a reception with Van since they got married at the courthouse. But it was a ruse to get Dani to go on spring break with my mom, Jadyn, and Jennifer. She was able to look at wedding dresses and talk about her dream wedding without suspecting a thing."

"So, he proposed and then what?"

"The next morning, after she told everyone the good news, she was whisked away to meet a wedding planner, who gave her the preplanned ideas that she and Chase had come up with. I'm shocked he was able to keep it a secret from her. They tell each other everything."

"I don't know how I would feel about that," Ainsley says. "Although I suppose if the time was right and the future groom knew exactly what I wanted, it would probably be a whole lot less stressful than planning it."

"What do you want? Like, do you have a dream wedding?"

"Oh, well, I think most girls do," she says.

"And what is yours?"

"Do you have any dream wedding ideas?" she asks me.

"Yeah, I want you walking down the aisle to me."

"Any certain time of year?"

"The sooner, the better. How about now?" I say, raising my eyebrows at her.

"Like, we could get an officiant to come out here and marry us in our swimsuits on the boat?"

"Yeah, why not?"

She lets out a sigh. Like she doesn't even know what to say in response.

"I'm just teasing. I want the day to be special. I would say I'm open to any time of year, and somehow," I say, sliding my finger across her charm bracelet, "we'd have to incorporate all this stuff."

"Hmm," she says, "so we'd get married on the seventh hole of the golf course, have fireworks and a clear night sky for star viewing. We'd serve only peaches. Hire butterflies to swirl around us while we said our vows. Our getaway car would be a golf cart. The guests would be required to skinny-dip. Our theme would be butterflies and naked asses."

I grin. "That sounds awesome. I'm taking mental notes right now."

She swats at me. "Not funny."

"I don't know. I think naked asses are lots of fun. Especially when it's yours."

"Well, if you can do all that and throw in a New Year's Eve party, there you go. It's already planned."

"Dream ring?" I ask her.

She shrugs. "No idea. The one that Brad gave to Bailey was very similar to what high-school me wanted. Now, I don't know. Something simple maybe—a classic solitaire? Slightly vintage."

"And where would you live if you could live anywhere?"

"Wherever you are," she says, rolling toward me and sliding her hand down my chest. "Which you won't know until you're drafted."

"Any preference?"

"Well, of course, KC is my favorite team. But it would be fun to live somewhere warmer. Tampa? Nashville? Dallas? Do you get any say at all in where you go?"

"I'll interview with multiple teams, and I might have an idea, but you never know for sure until they call your name."

"Something you might not know about me is that I watch the draft every single year. Usually with my dad. I love the excitement of it. The red carpet. The outfits they wear. Although, I will say, those have changed with the NIL money. There was a lot of bling on the players this year." She runs her finger down the middle of my chest. "You gonna have some big iced-out necklace with your number on it?"

I chuckle. "Doubtful. I think I'd rather invest the money."

"My uncle Tripp would say you're a smart man. He's been making me give him a fourth of what I make at the resort so he can invest it for me. Someday, I'm sure I'll be richer than my wildest dreams. Or not," she says. "I just want to be happy, you know."

"And do I make you happy?"

"You do," she says, planting her lips on mine.

WE HAVE DINNER with Sammy, but he's off quickly after that to hang out with some of the guys who work at the resort.

Which is okay by me.

I take Ainsley out on the front porch, turn on some music, and sway with her in my arms—wishing we could stay like this forever.

SUNDAY, JULY 26TH

To see you again.

Damon

I WAKE UP to her running her hand down my chest.

"Morning," she says.

"Morning," I reply as her hand dips lower. I was going to talk to her about my fall schedule and try to figure out the best time for us to talk every day, but that can wait.

For as long as it takes.

"BEFORE YOU ATTACKED me, I was going to talk to you about what my life will be like once season starts."

"Which is basically this week, right, since fall practices are starting?" she asks.

"Yeah."

"I expect you will be quite busy. Learning the playbook, practices, competing for your spot."

"I think you're exactly right. Knowing you'll be coming to visit me in Lincoln will get me through it."

"I've never been to Lincoln before. You're going to have to show me around."

"I can't wait," I say, kissing her cheek. "It's hard to believe we start fall practice this Wednesday. It seems like the summer has flown by."

"Isn't that when all the media attention will really kick into gear?"

"Yeah, for sure. Like who is where on the depth charts. They're especially going to be wondering who will be the starting quarterback."

"Will that be hard for Chase to deal with?" she asks me.

"Dad's always told us not to read what reporters are saying. That they can't predict the season. That it's up to me. Us. I do expect there to be a lot of hype around Chase. So, I figure I'll try to safeguard him from it a bit until they start hounding me."

"You're Danny Diamond's son. Surely, they are going to have questions." She gives me a coy smile. "I know I have a lot of them."

"Like what?"

"When are you going to have time to call me?"

"Every night before I go to bed so I can see your gorgeous face."

She smiles. "How are your practices structured? Like, do you still work out?"

"We do. There's a flow to the practices each week. The first few days, there's no media in attendance. On certain days, they allow some players to speak to the press. And that first Saturday, we get to do an open practice for fans, which raises money for the school. Every Sunday, we are to rest and recover. Although I'm sure Chase and I will spend that time watching practice tapes and trying to up our game and gauge our competition."

"And impress your coaches, one would assume."

"That's the goal."

"Something I don't know is, how many wide receivers are actually on the roster? I mean, how many people do you have to compete against to start?"

"There are sixteen on the roster, which includes redshirted players—something I do not want to be. In each game, there will always be two receivers on the offensive side of the ball. But depending on the play called, there can be up to five."

"And what's your competition like?"

"There were two outstanding players last year. One was drafted in the sixth round, and the other was a true freshman who played in all the games last year. He's number one on the depth chart as of now. I'm probably not going to take that spot, but even being number two would mean I would start."

"Which is your big goal."

"Big goal? Nah, that's just one of my goals. The big goal is a national championship."

"Is that realistic, knowing how their year went last year?"

"I always break down my goals into smaller, more doable actions. For example, in order to reach the big goal, we have to win most every game. So, each week, that's the goal. Then that goal is broken down into smaller ones. Practicing well, being conditioned and game ready. Mental preparations. Everything."

"And what kind of mental preparations are you going to have to prepare for my visit?"

I grin. "I think, for that, I'm going to have to be in really good shape. Physically."

"Yes, you must," she says, running her hand over some of my muscles.

WE SHARE A long *can't wait to see you again* kiss when she drops me off at the airport.

"I can't believe it's going to be almost a month before I get to see you again."

I kiss the top of her head. "I'll miss you."

"I'll miss you too."

WEDNESDAY, AUGUST 12TH

Don't know if I am.

Ainsley

I'M A LITTLE nervous as I step into the doctor's office today. It's the start of my second trimester and time for an ultrasound. As the technician preps my abdomen with a cool jelly so we can see the baby on the screen, I realize it's kind of fitting since its daddy will also be making an appearance on a screen. His practice is being filmed as a stop on their conference TV tour today, and they specifically requested to speak with him.

And while Damon may not be reading what the sports journalists have to say about the team, Sammy and I have been following along obsessively. I've even been printing out articles to save.

While there has been some movement on the depth charts, the final ones won't be released until just before the start of the season—which is a little over two weeks away. Right now, they show Damon in the fifth spot. And I know he wouldn't be happy with that.

I look up at the ceiling, focusing on the ceiling tiles and the soft hum of the machine. In a few moments, I'm going to see the proof of our love. I always try to think positive thoughts, but I'm suddenly overwhelmed with a million what-ifs. *What if it's not real? What if there isn't a baby? What if something's wrong?*

The room smells faintly like antiseptic and lavender hand soap, and my heart is racing out of my chest.

The tech smiles at me and says, "Ready?"

My first thought is, *Am I?*

I nod even though I don't know if I am.

The wand glides over my abdomen, the screen flickers, and then … there.

A tiny flicker of light.

"That's your baby," the tech says softly.

My baby.

I kind of expected to see just a little blob. When the chart said the baby was the size of a peach, I thought it would look like that, with maybe a heartbeat.

"Okay, so here, you can see there is a visible gestational sac," the tech says. "As well as the heartbeat."

She points out the baby's head. Talks about the brain forming, the heart. I don't know what I expected, but I can see the spine, arms, hands, legs, and feet. And I'm overwhelmed. In awe.

Tears slip down my cheeks before I can stop them. I feel everything all at once—wonder and fear, joy and panic. I want to laugh. I want to sob. I want to bottle this exact moment and keep it forever.

I reach out toward the screen, like maybe I can touch it, hold it.

Protect it.

For the first time, this isn't just lines on a test. This is real.

MONDAY, AUGUST 24TH

This summer.

Ainsley

I GRAB A cup of coffee and take it out to the screened porch of my cottage and stare out at the lake.

Yesterday was my last day of work for the summer. But then I realize it's actually the last summer ever. I'll graduate this fall and start my career. I've made so many friends here. Some in passing, but others, like Apollo and Liam, who I think will be in my life beyond.

It's bittersweet.

But then I think about Damon. From the time we first laid eyes on each other, our families have intertwined. I glance at our special picnic spot and touch my abdomen as I think about this summer.

The summer that changed both our lives.

Even though I'm a bit melancholy about leaving, I'm excited to get my stuff packed and hit the road. To go see him. Be with him.

My phone rings in my hand. *It's him.*

"Hey," I say.

"I wasn't sure if you'd be up already," he says.

"I'm too excited to sleep in. I get to see you today!"

"I know. And I can't wait. To see you. Hold you in my arms. Kiss you."

"And show me where you live."

"My bed, specifically," he says.

"I hope I get to see more than that," I tease.

He chuckles. "We're having a party at our place tonight. You'll get to meet my friends."

"That's awesome," I say, but I'm thinking the last thing I want to do is party. I just want to spend time with him.

"When will I get to kiss you?" he says, changing the subject back to that.

"I have to pack. Goal is to leave here by ten. I'll have a late lunch with my mom, then drive to Lincoln. I'm thinking six thirty, seven."

"Perfect," he says. "Everyone is coming at seven thirty. That gives me time to cook you dinner."

"Cook me dinner? Hmm. Do I need to steal the apron from the cottage for you?" I ask, thinking back to when he cooked for me this summer, wearing nothing but.

He laughs heartily. "You'll have to find that out when you get here. So, don't dally."

"I'm calling off lunch with Mom," I say.

Very quickly, my phone buzzes, him wanting to video chat. I press the button, and his handsome face pops up. It makes me smile even more. In a few hours, I'll be back in those strong arms.

"Show me our picnic spot and the lake," he says. "Let's have one last look at it together."

I turn my phone, and then he says, "Now I want to look at

you." As soon as I switch the view again, he goes, "This summer."

"I know. I was just thinking that before you called. How this summer changed my life. How you changed my life." I start to get tears in my eyes. Because I wish I could tell him just how much.

But I can't.

He looks misty-eyed too. "Best summer of my life," he says, but then adds, "So far. Just think, someday, we'll be bringing our kids there. Our parents will be grandparents. Mimi and Papa, great-grandparents. I can't wait."

"I can't wait either," I tell him.

"All right, I have to get going," he says. "Drive careful. You've got precious cargo."

My eyes get big. "Precious cargo?" I ask, dumbfounded. *Does he somehow know I'm pregnant?*

"Yeah," he says. "You."

I PACK, GET everything loaded in my car, and then set my navigation to take me to the restaurant where Mom and I are meeting.

"Sweetie," Mom says, giving me a big hug when I arrive. "You look gorgeous. I appreciate you stopping to have lunch with me. I know you're probably excited to get to Lincoln."

"I am, but I'm glad to see you. What have you been up to?"

"Well …"

She grins big as a tall, handsome, older gentleman comes to stand next to her. And then wraps an arm around her waist.

My eyes move between them. I blink a few times. Swallow.

"I'd like you to meet Evander Hayes. Everyone calls him Hayes."

He holds out his hand to shake mine. I look down at his

hand. Feel a little sick.

"Um, excuse me," I say, rushing off to the restroom.

I gag a little, telling myself it's because I'm hungry—even though I ate road-trip snacks in the car on the way here—and not because of the fact that my mother had some random guy's arm wrapped around her.

I THINK BACK to when she told me she was sorta seeing someone. It was when I got back to the resort on Fourth of July weekend. I've talked to her numerous times since then. And she hasn't said another word about it. Or him. And now she just springs him on me with no warning?

I decide while I'm in here, I might as well use the restroom. I'm washing my hands when Mom comes in.

I just stare at her. When she gives me the eye back, like I'm in trouble, I say, "It's been almost two months since you told me you had a few dates. I've heard nothing since then, and you just invite him to our lunch and don't tell me? Do you not even care about Dad anymore? Not to mention *my* feelings?"

"What are your feelings?" she replies.

"My dad—your husband—is a gambling addict who hasn't been heard from in months. To my knowledge, you aren't divorced. Is that why you've been hiding your relationship?"

"You've never liked change," she says. "But it's inevitable in life."

"That's not an answer, Mom," I fire back.

"Your father has chosen gambling over us. Period. There is no denying that fact. I petitioned the court for a divorce as soon as your father left rehab. The court allowed a service by publication, meaning a notice was put into newspapers. He hasn't responded, so the divorce is uncontested. It will be final next month, and I'll be able to move on with my life."

"Seems like you've already moved on," I quip.

I don't know why I'm being so pissy about this. I told her that I was happy for her when she spoke of meeting someone. Of dating. But seeing her with another man … it was a shock.

"What would you like me to do, Ainsley? Sit around and wait for your father to come home?"

I sigh. "No. I want you to be happy, Mom. I do. I just—you should have told me before I walked in. You know?"

"I'm sorry. I should have, but I was excited."

"You like him?" I ask.

She smiles broadly. "I like him a lot, actually. Probably love him."

"Is he going to think I'm rude?"

"Of course not. He's out there, ordering our favorites. Shall we go join him?"

"Yeah, we should."

AFTER LUNCH, I get back in my car and immediately call Sammy. "You're never going to believe this."

"You had lunch with your mom and her new beau?" he asks.

"You know about him? How?!"

"Your mom told me. We talk."

"She hasn't really told me anything!"

"She's been trying to keep you out of all the drama. Trying to get a divorce has been a nightmare for her. But she really likes this guy. I, um, probably shouldn't tell you this, but …"

"Did you meet him before me?!" I shriek.

"Maybe," he replies sheepishly.

"Spill," I command.

"You're all happy and in love with Damon. Your mom didn't want to bring you down with the divorce stuff. And I put her in touch with my mom. Granted, it's been years since my mom went through it, but her first husband had just upped and left. Drained their bank accounts and left her with two very young children."

"I didn't know that," I say.

"To be honest, I didn't know either, but when I was telling my mom about your dad, she told me. And then they talked."

"So, what do you know about this new guy?" I ask Sammy.

"Tell me what you thought first," Sammy replies.

"He's very gracious. Handsome. Sounds like he has a good relationship with his children."

"He had to raise them when his wife passed," Sammy says. "Very sad."

"It is sad. And I want my mom to be happy. I really do."

"Why do I feel like there is a but coming?"

"There isn't. It was a statement."

"But … she shouldn't have surprised you with him?"

"That's the only but in the story. That, and the fact that I was a bit of a butt myself. I couldn't bring myself to shake his hand. I ran to the restroom instead. But in my defense, I did feel a little sick."

"Can driving make you motion sick?"

"I don't think so," I say with a laugh.

"I'm happy for your mom. She's been embraced by your dad's side of the family. Is going out and having fun. Loves where she lives—did you get to see it?"

"No. Have you?"

"I haven't. But it sounds lovely."

"I just met her at the restaurant for what was supposed to be a quick catch-up lunch on my way through town."

"Well, you got caught up quick!" Sammy hoots.

"And on that note, I think I should focus on driving. I'll text you when I get there," I tell him.

"No need. I'm tracking you," he says in a way that sounds a little devious.

Be loved.

Ainsley

I CALL DAMON when I arrive in Lincoln, and he comes outside and shows me where to park. I'm barely out of the car when he leans me against it and gives me a wonderfully steamy kiss, making me to want to start shedding my clothes right here.

"I love you," he says, caressing my cheek as I stare into his gorgeous eyes, taking in the soft scruff on his cheeks and his brilliant smile.

I swear, he looks older than he did the last time I saw him in person.

"I love you too," I tell him. "And I'm excited to see where you live."

"You're just trying to get me into the bedroom, aren't you?" he says with a smirk.

"I maybe hoped for that. Sorry I'm late. There was an accident on the interstate that had traffic at a complete stop. Are your friends already here?"

Damon glances at his watch. "A few, but we're going to go upstairs the back way and have dinner in my condo before we join them."

"Sneaking me in so your parents don't know I'm in your room?" I tease.

He smiles, grabs my bag, slings it over his shoulder, then takes my hand and leads me to a freight elevator. When the doors part, I don't know what I expected, but it wasn't this.

Shirts are folded and lined up in neat rows on industrial shelving. A bank of tables and shipping supplies are on the other side of the wall, which are painted dark gray. And there's a huge sign with angel wings that says One Eleven Sports.

"You have a lot of inventory," I say, surprised, sort of thinking this was just a fun little side hustle.

"Gearing up for the season. Chase's mom is glad to have her garage back. She and Haley brought it all here this summer. Decorated. Organized. It turned out nice, I think," Damon says, then leads me to a wide hallway lined with doors.

There's lots of exposed brick, and the floors look like they are original to the building.

I can hear voices toward the end of the hall, but Damon stops and says, "Home sweet home," then opens the door.

And his condo is so cool.

"Do they all look like this?" I ask him.

"Most of them are two-bedroom condos, but there are two with three bedrooms. They were decorated with our parents and our little siblings in mind. The rest have slightly different styles and color palettes, but the floor plans are the same."

I take in the high ceilings, exposed brick wall in the living room, the deep green kitchen cabinets, wood floors, and comfortable furnishings.

"Want to know why I chose this one?" he asks me, pulling me back into his arms.

"Why?"

"Because the kitchen matches the color of your eyes," he says.

"Really?"

Because he can't be serious. It's a condo. They probably all have green cabinets. But he did say they have different colors, and Jadyn's designs are always amazing.

"Really," he says, sealing it with a kiss, then taking my hand and leading me into his bedroom.

There's a cognac leather padded headboard behind a king-size bed. The walls are painted a shade lighter than the cabinets. Floor-to-ceiling windows offer views outside.

"This is really nice," I say, which is a total understatement, but it's hard to think about pesky things like words when Damon starts kissing my neck.

I slide my hands under his shirt, wanting to take it off him.

"I promised you dinner first," he murmurs.

"I want you first," I tell him. "Even if it's quick."

AND IT IS. But we have three days together before he leaves for his football game and I go to school. Lots of time to take it slow. Plus, I could smell the red sauce the second I walked in. And I'm starving.

Since our clothes were never fully off, it's easy to get ourselves put back together, then go into the kitchen, where he pulls out a chair for me to sit in.

I notice things I didn't see before, like the fact that he already has the table set. That he included cloth napkins and candles on the table.

"Would you like wine with dinner?" he asks me.

"I thought you didn't drink during the season."

"I don't, but I wanted to offer you some," he says.

"Nah, I'm okay. Thank you. I'll just have whatever you're having."

He grabs a big bottle of sparkling water out of the fridge, fills our glasses, then adds a lemon to each.

A few moments later, he adds a big bowl filled with salad, a pan of lasagna, and cheesy bread to our table.

"This looks and smells wonderful, Damon. Did you cook all this?"

"Well, I bought the bread and added the cheese, but everything else, yeah."

"You're amazing." I smile at him as he dishes up our plates, and we start eating.

"I read a quote recently about how the only happiness in life is to love and be loved," Damon says. "While I agree with the sentiment, I feel like there's so much more to it. Because it's not just your love that makes me happy every day. It's hearing your voice, seeing your face, making you laugh, touching your skin. Whether we are together or apart. Happy or sad."

"Possibly because you are in love with me?"

He rolls his eyes. "So, you're saying all that goes back to the quote? That I'm happy because I'm loving and being loved?"

"I guess it depends if you feel that way when you hear everyone's voice."

He leans across the table and gives me a kiss. "I most certainly do not."

"I also don't think the poet was just referring to romantic

love," I tell him.

"That's true. Although it's different, the love I feel for my family, my friends, my dog also makes me happy."

"I think the physical side of our relationship adds another dimension to it."

"Speaking of that, we need to stop talking and eat so I can get you back in my bedroom," he says, his eyes turning dark with desire.

I point down the hall, where I can hear voices. "Does that mean no game night?"

He sighs. "I want to wrap you up in my arms, hold you close, and keep you to myself, but I also want you to meet everyone."

"Is that your answer then?"

"Yes," he says in a begrudging tone.

"Can I talk to you about something else?" I take a bite of food, waiting for him to reply.

"Of course," he says.

"When I went to lunch with my mom, she introduced me to a guy. Who she's dating. I am struggling with that, to be honest."

"We talked about divorce in the Ozarks. Floating around the lazy river. Remember that?"

"I do, and I appreciated it then. It's just … no one has heard from my dad. My uncles have tons of money. You'd think they could find him."

"Ainsley," Damon says, "your dad is an adult. If he wanted contact with his family right now, he'd call. It sucks that he hasn't, but there really isn't much you can do about it."

"And what about the fact that my mom is dating when they aren't divorced yet?"

"You can't control your parents' lives," he says with a shrug.

And I know he's right.

AFTER DINNER, HE leads me out to a big gathering area.

"This is like a sports bar. Couches. Televisions. Tables."

"Yeah, it's awesome. Fun to have our friends here, and the space functions well during game weekends."

"I bet. I can't wait to see you play," I tell him sincerely.

"Speaking of games," Damon says.

"Where did your friends go?" I ask him.

"I'll show you." He takes my hand, leading me to a set of French doors, then up some stairs to a rooftop deck.

I don't know what I was expecting when he said they were having friends over. But it wasn't this. There are several people sitting at a big teak table, playing cards. Soft music in the background. No beer in sight.

"Stupid question," Damon says to me. "But do you like games? Cards, stuff like that?"

"I love them. And I should warn you, my competitiveness doesn't end with golf."

"Oh boy. Should I mentally prepare for defeat?"

"No, only winning for you—just maybe not when you play cards with me."

He puts his arm around me, and we walk to the table.

"It's about time the lovebirds joined us," Dani says with a smile, quickly getting up and giving me a hug. Then she says, "Everyone, this is the famous Ainsley. The Ainsley my brother won't stop talking about."

"His future wifey," a guy says. He's tall and buff, and he looks like he plays football.

"That's right," Damon says. "Ainsley, this is Treyvon. He was

Chase's roommate last semester and plays wide receiver."

I reach out to shake his hand, but he pulls me into a hug.

"Oh, girl, I feel like I already know you. Most everyone else here is all booed up, but I'm very, very single."

"Me too," another guy says. "Hey, I'm Eddie. Frat boy and Dani's ex-love."

My eyes go wide while Chase and Dani laugh.

"Why do I feel like there's a story here?" I ask.

"Oh, because there is," Eddie says. "Dani and I became friends. She asked me to go home with her for Thanksgiving last year."

"And I was extremely jealous," Chase says. "Wanted to hate Eddie, but he's impossible to hate."

"It was a disaster, to be honest," Dani confesses, "but it all worked out in the end."

" *'Cause we're married!*" Eddie and Treyvon say in girlie voices while holding up their empty ring fingers.

Everyone laughs, including me.

"And we're Amber and Garrett," Garrett says while Amber shows off a sparkling diamond. "Recently engaged."

"Congratulations," I tell them. "It's nice to meet you."

"And last but not least, me," a pretty girl says. "I'm Lauren. Single. Got my eye on Eddie, but he's clueless."

Eddie goes, "You do?"

"What are you playing?" Damon asks them.

"Spoons," Chase says. "Killing time until you finished dinner."

"But now that you're here, we have a card game we want to try. It's supposed to be sort of like a fast version of Monopoly, where you gain properties to up your net worth, but the fun part is, others can steal them from you."

"That sounds fun," Damon says as we take seats around the table.

AND IT IS fun. Mostly because I win the first round. But by the middle of the second, I can't hide my yawns anymore even though it's only nine o'clock.

When the round is over, Damon says, "We're out. Ainsley was up early and drove here all the way from the Ozarks."

"And is yawning like crazy," Eddie says.

"Sorry," I reply. "You are all so welcoming, and I'm having fun."

"You also won the last two games. We're cool if you go to bed. Give one of us a chance," Amber teases.

Gave some energy.

Ainsley

I WAKE UP to the sound of Damon getting out of bed. "What time is it?"

"Five thirty."

"That's early."

"It's what time I've gotten up every day since fall practice started. I make a shake here before I leave, go do some cardio, eat breakfast, then lift. I have a pretty strict routine."

"I'm not very routined," I tell him.

"I have to be if I want to get everything done. Especially during the season."

"So, when will I see you today?"

"Hopefully, I can get back here by eight. Although, most days, I'm at the facility until closer to nine."

"What do you do there all day?"

He glances at his watch, and I can already tell I'm messing with the routine.

"That's okay," I say. "I'll find something to do. Wander around Lincoln. Check it out."

"Dani told me she was hoping you two could hang out today. She gets up around seven."

"Perfect," I say, snuggling back in my pillow.

Damon leaves the room, and I hear the sound of a blender. Then he comes back into the room, dressed in workout clothes, holding a cup and drinking from it.

He sits on the bed, smiles at me, and runs his hand across my cheek. "You fell asleep so fast last night."

"It was a long day. Although probably not as long as yours." I squeeze his biceps. "But then again, you're in better shape than me."

He leans down and gives me a strawberry-flavored kiss.

"You taste good," I tell him.

"Do you want some? I made extra for you."

"Yeah," I start to say, but he's up and back in a flash with a cup for me.

"Enjoy," he says, kissing the top of my head. "I'll see you tonight. Save some energy for me."

I drink the smoothie and go back to sleep.

I WAKE UP an hour later, throw one of Damon's sweatshirts over a pair of my shorts, patter into the kitchen, and open the fridge, thinking I can have some leftover lasagna. There's bottled water, Gatorade, milk, and fruits. No pasta to be found.

The pantry is also sparse, but it does hold a loaf of bread, a jar of peanut butter, an assortment of nuts and seeds, and a bunch of protein powder. Basically, it's a smoothie shop.

Does he eat out for his meals?

But then I remember the big kitchen in the gathering space and wonder if they keep their food there instead of in their individual condos.

The second I open the door, I smell bacon cooking, along with something sweet.

I find Dani manning a waffle iron, three pans of bacon on top of the stove behind her.

"Morning," she says cheerfully. "Get any sleep?"

She raises her eyebrow, and I think she's insinuating that we must have been up all night, having sex. And honestly, we should have been.

"I had a long day," I tell her. "Fell asleep pretty much the minute I got into bed. And now I feel bad about it."

"You shouldn't."

"Except we haven't been together in a month."

"You hungry?" she asks, changing the subject.

"Kinda. Damon gave me some of his shake before he left. I drank it and went back to sleep."

She takes a waffle off the cooker and adds it to the pile she already has.

"That's a lot of waffles! You expecting guests?"

"No, just food prepping. Chase's mom always does stuff like this. And it's smart. Instead of making them every day, she'll make a big batch and freeze them. Then, when you're rushing around in the mornings, you can just pop one in the toaster."

"That is really smart."

"I'm going to fry up a bunch of hamburger next and do the same. Then we can pull it out and quickly whip up tacos or a meat sauce for pasta."

She starts cooking another waffle.

"Can I help?" I ask.

"Yeah. The bacon should be cool now. Break it in half and

put it in those containers," she says, pointing. "I'm almost out of batter. The last two are for us." She grins. "Then I thought I could show you around Lincoln. We could have lunch. It's kind of boring around here right now. My friends are busy with Rush Week, and the boys are at the facility all day."

"What do they do there all day? I mean, work out, practice. What else is there? Or is it that they just like to hang out there?"

"I was hoping to get a facility tour set up to show you. They have gorgeous brand-new facilities, but things are closed this week for game prep. Not even the media gets to see what's going on. Lucky for you, as part of my job with the conference network, I got to do a behind-the-scenes tour, where we highlighted everything. We can watch it while we eat if you want?"

"That sounds great!"

I help her package up the waffles and am thinking about how Sammy and I should do this sort of thing.

Once that's done, she makes our waffles, covers them with butter and warm syrup, and throws on a few pieces of bacon.

Then we sit down at the bar, and she presses play on her computer.

Her pretty face comes on the screen, and she speaks about the new facility—how it is state of the art, one of the best in the country, and why players will want to come there.

I notice that the video is just over thirty minutes. So, it must be a pretty extensive tour.

It starts with her introducing the strength and conditioning coach in the weight room. First of all, the space is beautiful. Open, airy, while at the same time, you can tell it's serious business. He talks about how they have enough for half the team to do workouts at the same time. There's a cardio studio and lifting stations. And all sorts of other things to become an elite athlete.

"This part is really cool," Dani says as on-the-screen Dani says something similar. Which makes me laugh.

"A refueling station," I say. "Although it makes me think of a gas station, not a café, where they get healthy snacks."

Dani pauses the video and says, "Each snack they eat isn't just like you or me grabbing an apple or something because we're hungry. Each athlete has a plan created in coordination with sports nutritionists and strength and conditioning coaches. You hear guys say they want to bulk up, which usually means they're adding more fat to their bodies. Chase and Damon are both working to add lean muscle mass."

"They both seem like they're already in great shape."

"They are when you just look at them, but we want their bodies to be more durable."

"What do you mean by that?" I ask. "While I've always enjoyed the game, I just sort of assumed when they weren't playing, they just … I don't know … lifted some weights, ate a lot, and practiced."

"It's a lot more scientific than that. Football is physically demanding, and bulk allows them to absorb a hit. It helps to reduce injuries. For Chase, any strength he adds to his core and legs allows him to put more force in his throws—meaning a tighter spiral and the ability to throw the ball farther. It will also give him a stronger presence in the pocket. Although you might think of Damon's job as just catching passes, on running plays, he becomes a blocker against bigger defenders. And when the play *is* a pass, it allows him to be more explosive—faster and more agile. When he goes up to make a catch, the majority of the time, he's fighting for position against a defender."

"When Damon was visiting me at the Lodge, we hung out with my roommate, Sammy, and a couple of guys I worked with. Damon was telling them what he eats in a day, and I remember Sammy saying that Damon eats like it's his job. I kind of laughed, but it pretty much is, isn't it?"

"It definitely is. And so is sleeping."

"Sleeping?"

"Yeah, it's crucial for repairing and growing muscles."

I nod in understanding. "And so, when they left early this morning, they went to work out?"

"Yeah, each collegiate team is limited to twenty hours of practice a week with one day off and a max of four hours a day."

Which brings me back to my original question. "Then why are they there so much?"

"Well, there are rules relating to what they call CARA, or Countable Athletically Related Activities—which means any athletic-related meeting or activity supervised by the coaching staff that has an athletic purpose."

"That's a mouthful," I tease.

"I had to say it in an interview recently. It was the one thing I thought I would screw up, and I practiced it incessantly," she says with a laugh.

"So, you had your internship, which is over, but you're still working?" I wonder.

"Yeah, I'll be on the sidelines for a few conference games. Interviewing celebrities, big donors, and former players. I'll be talking to them—which, at first, I didn't really want to do because I thought it might be tabloid-ish. But Chase told me to keep the talk about what we were there for—the game. So, I'll ask them to make scoring predictions, talk about their favorite players, favorite football memories. That sort of thing. And now, I'm excited about it."

"That's going to be a great experience," I tell her.

She nods, then says, "Okay, back to their day. So, after working out and refueling, they need to recover."

She clicks on the video, which now shows a calm, soothing, almost-spa-like area with even better amenities. Sure, they have the usual hot tubs, saunas, cold plunges, but also things like hydro, compression, sensory deprivation, and red-light therapies. There are sleep pods, massaging recliners, and zero gravity chairs. There, they can also do yoga, work with a chiropractor, or get a massage. Recovery is touted in the video as a hugely important part of their process, as is getting enough sleep. They even have areas for napping.

The video goes on to highlight the trainer space. This is where they do research on faster recovery and injury healing. Where they try to protect against future injuries and rehabilitate when they happen.

"I will admit," I tell her, "I'm shocked by all of this."

"You haven't even seen half of it yet," she says with a laugh. "Are you bored, or do you want to keep watching?"

"I want to keep watching. It's fascinating, and I love being able to visualize where he is all day. Where he's calling me from. What he's been doing."

"Next up is the locker room. Look, you can see Chase's name and picture"—she pauses it—"right here, along with his game-day outfit. The other side of his locker has room for him to keep his backpack, jackets, whatever he wants. And just outside of this is another area with all his practice gear."

We watch a little more, and she goes, "And this shows their

indoor and outdoor practice facilities."

"They don't practice in the stadium?" I ask. I don't know why, but I assumed they did.

"Not usually. They try to keep the turf game ready."

I take a moment to polish off the rest of my breakfast. "Thanks for a wonderful meal," I say graciously.

"You're welcome," she says as she presses play again. "This is the players' lounge. It's where they get a little downtime, interact with their teammates between classes and practice. They can watch movies, play video games, play pool, and even get their hair cut."

"For one of my design classes, we got to see plans for a new corporate campus, and in a way, it reminds me of that. They had so many perks for their employees—from a gym to a pharmacy, on-site physicians, restaurants, and even a Starbucks. The idea was that if they didn't have to leave for coffee, lunch, appointments, and meetings, they would save time and therefore make the company more efficient."

"Exactly, like this," Dani says happily. "Of course, once you see their training table, you'll wonder why I even bother cooking for them."

She shows me where the team eats their meals. "Food buffets are split into nutritional categories," she says, "to help them choose what their bodies need, with sections that focus on things like protein and immunity. The boys say the brisket at school is incredible and one of their favorite things. Beyond that is the Life Skills and Learning Center. We're talking study rooms, tutors, tech, and staff. Then my favorite part—the coaching area. Someday, maybe I can talk Coach into letting me sit in on meetings. I just find the coaching and motivational part of football so interesting."

"Would you ever want to coach?" I ask her.

"I don't think so, but as I go through the process of learning more and more about the game that I always thought I knew everything about, I keep calling my dad and asking him questions."

"I bet he loves that," I say with a smile.

"He does. It's also why he's such a good announcer. He understands the game so deeply. And I'm trying to soak up as much of that as possible so I'll be a good announcer someday."

"Like call the game? Be on *Monday Night Football*?"

"I'd take any night, but yes," she says.

"You have big dreams."

"We all do. What about you, Ainsley? What's your big dream?"

"Ideally, I want to own a company similar to the one my uncle Tripp bought from Chase's mom. I adored my internship, working on the hotel renovation, and learned so much. I'm hoping I'll find a job on that side of the business."

"It's good to have goals and dreams." She glances at a ring on her finger. It has little diamonds set in gold that spell out *dreams*. She notices me looking. "Chase gave this to me before we were dating. Even back then, he wanted to play pro ball, and I wanted to be on the sidelines. Now, it's an everyday reminder, or confirmation maybe, that we're living it. Working toward those dreams."

"You and Chase know each other so well. I haven't even scratched the surface with Damon."

"While you might think it's a downside, I don't. We're all always learning and growing and facing new challenges, and it's good to go through those things together." She lowers her voice even though we are the only ones here. "I had a pregnancy scare recently."

"Really?" I say, my mind all over the place.

"I want kids. We both do. But we want to wait, ideally, until we achieve some of our career goals. And I was—well, I had mixed emotions. I was relieved, but there was a little part of me that was disappointed. Although I literally can't imagine me or Chase having that on our minds right now. He needs to focus on football."

"Yeah, I'm sure that was a lot of emotions to deal with," I say, feeling sick.

I find myself wanting to curl in a ball while also kind of wanting to confide in her. Based on what she just said, I believe she'd keep it a secret. I haven't told anyone that this is happening. And she, probably more than anyone, would understand why I'm not going to tell Damon until the end of the season. And I'm very grateful she confided in me because it solidifies the fact that I'm doing the right thing for Damon.

She looks at me and says, "It was! And now I want a mimosa. Want one?"

"I'll take some orange juice," I tell her.

She gets up, opens a single serving bottle of champagne, grabs OJ and two flutes, then pours us our drinks.

She looks at me and toasts, "To the boys we love."

I clink her glass, then take a drink of the cold juice.

"All right," she says, closing her laptop, "let's get ready, and I'll show you around Lincoln."

SINCE IT'S WARM out, I grab a pair of jean shorts and a tank top. When I put the shorts on, I realize they are a little tight in the waist. I pull them back down and look at my belly in the mirror. My stomach feels harder than it used to, but there's not a bump yet. I may look a smidgen bloated, like I do when I have my period—which then makes me laugh. This is why I didn't get my period.

We meet back up and take the elevator down to the garage and get in Dani's car.

"I love your car," I tell her.

I don't know why I'm surprised that she would have an expensive car, considering who her parents are, but I am.

"I've had a hate-love relationship with it. I had a Mercedes coupe in high school that I loved. But when I came to college, Dad was worried about me being up here by myself, and he traded it in for this G-Wagon. I told him I looked more suburban mom than hip college student," she says with a laugh. "Although, I will admit, when I had to drive in the snow, I was thankful. Now that I've gotten used to driving this beast, I love it and am not sure I'd want to go back." She pulls out of the garage space, and we take off down the street.

"I have a sedan, but it is all-wheel drive, and with all the snow we get at school, I, too, am thankful I have that."

"I can't wait for it to snow," Dani says dreamily. "There's just something so magical about it. Did you notice that there's a hot tub up on the rooftop deck?"

"I didn't see it. I was too busy kicking butt at cards," I tease.

"There's nothing better than sitting in it when it's snowing out. One of my favorite things in life." She pauses for a moment, then says, "So, I'm sure you know that Lincoln is the capital of Nebraska. It was named after, duh, Abraham Lincoln. We're going to drive by the State Capitol Building."

She stops when we get to the building, whipping into an open parking spot.

"It's a cool building," I say. "Architecturally."

She laughs. "That's the same thing Auntie Jay says. I know you like design. Do you like architecture too?"

"Yeah, I love all of it. I did a semester abroad in Italy and was immersed in it."

"Well, let's see if I can remember some facts."

"Let me guess," I say. "It looks like they combined styles. Like, I see old Roman temple vibes, mixed with a Byzantine church and hints of Art Deco."

"Ha." She laughs. "That's more than I know. I was going to say something about Rome. I do know that the huge bronze figure at the top of the dome is called The Sower, obviously having to do with the state's agriculture. And probably why our team is named after a crop worker."

We drive through town. It reminds me of many other Midwestern towns. Then she pulls into a drive where there is a sign that says, *Sunken Gardens.*

"My mom always likes visiting this garden when she's in town for football games. Each year, they have a different theme. One of my all-time favorites was when it was decorated based off the book, *Alice in Wonderland.* This year's theme is Enchanted Ocean. The cool thing is, it changes with each season. I was here this spring, but it will look different today."

On a sign it says, *Guests are invited to trade the prairie horizon for a dive into wonder, where magic shimmers beneath the waves. Soft washes of white, lavender, and blue ripple like the sea's hidden depths while playful splashes of yellow, orange, and pink dance across the scene like seashells scattered on sun-kissed shores.*

"This is all so pretty," we say at the same time, then laugh.

WE ENJOY A long, leisurely stroll through the gardens, pointing out flowers and floral displays, then get back in the car.

It surprises me when she drives back to the condo building and parks.

She sees the quizzical look on my face and goes, "Just parking the car. We can walk everywhere else. Next stop on your tour for today is the campus."

"Oh, I'm excited for that."

We go out of the garage and onto a sidewalk.

"You can see the stadium and campus from here. We're lucky that we can walk to class."

"That is nice. I'm able to do that at K-State too."

She checks her watch and says, "Let's go over to sorority row. Rush is this week. It's hard to believe just last year, I was going through it." She smiles. "And now I'm married!"

"And seem very happy about your decision," I tell her.

"Oh, I am."

As we get to the center of campus, I take in the wide green lawns, dotted with old trees. The brick buildings.

And a whole lot of girls running around in matching shirts. It's fun to see their outfits though. How they personalize them with skirts and fun shoes and jewelry.

"It's day two," Dani says. "Did you go through rush?"

"Notre Dame doesn't have sororities, so no. And I wasn't really interested when I switched schools."

"It's funny. My mom and Auntie Jay met because they were sorority sisters. I was bound and determined not to follow in their footsteps. Tried so hard not to like their sorority. But in the end, it was my first choice."

"I loved the serenading that was done during your wedding weekend."

"Yeah, it was special. But at the same time, I'm glad I'm walking around campus with you right now instead of doing all the rush planning and stuff. Amber and Lauren have been working nonstop. In fact, I was shocked they were able to come hang out last night."

She shows me her old sorority house and Eddie's frat house. When we head back toward the stadium, she glances at her watch again.

"I really appreciate you showing me that video. I feel like I can picture exactly where Damon is."

She sends a quick text, grabs my elbow, and practically skips down the sidewalk, then comes to stand in front of a building.

She giggles. "While the girls are rushing, the boys are *rushing* in a different way."

"Like rushing for yards?" I wonder aloud.

"Yep," she says as Chase comes out the door, quickly giving her a hug and a kiss.

A few moments later, Damon strides out—and holy shit. I've seen him sweaty after workouts, dressed in tuxedo perfection at the wedding, even naked.

He's always sinfully good-looking.

But right now? He's in full-on athlete mode. Compression top clinging to every muscle and shorts hanging low on his hips. Even though both boys are wearing the same style shirt—Chase's in white and Damon's in red—somehow, Damon makes his look better.

My gaze catches on his hair. It's shorter than it was this morning, like he trimmed it just to drive me crazy. So I would want to run my fingers through it instantly.

But then my eyes trail lower, taking in his tall frame. Those broad shoulders. The way his biceps strain against his sleeves.

Maybe it's because he's been lifting this morning, causing the testosterone to ooze from his every pore, but he looks manly, almost primal. Like a lion ready to pounce.

Heat rushes through me so fast that I instantly wish he could skip practice and drag me back to his lair.

"Hey, Champ," he murmurs, pulling me in for a kiss that leaves me lightheaded.

But honestly? He's the one who looks like the true champion—like he could've been carved out of marble, timeless and godlike, straight out of Olympus.

Only in red.

I said that already, didn't I?

After the kiss, he says, "We should finish early today, so hopefully, I'll see you before seven. That work?"

"I have no plans," I tease. "Of course it will work."

"Well, you should have plans," he practically purrs. "And if you don't, you should be making them."

"I'm confused," I reply.

"Plans is code for all the things you want to do with me tonight. In bed—or wherever."

I let out a breath. Nod. "I can do that."

WHEN WE GET back to the condo, we find a bouquet of flowers sitting outside the door.

Dani picks them up and hands them to me. "These have your

name on them."

A wide grin breaks out on my face. Because these flowers are adorable. And very patriotic—no, wait, not patriotic. They are collegiate maybe?

No, more like school spirit.

Anywho, there are a whole bunch of red roses, mixed with white carnations. On some of the carnations are little red N's. Others have footballs. There are picks with other decorations on them in between the flowers—a jersey with Damon's number on it, a corn cob, a team pennant, team mascot. It's a crazy, fun, and romantic gesture.

I love it.

I think about how Sammy put it out into the universe that I would meet someone in the Ozarks. And I'm hoping it will also help me find a job here, so Damon and I—and our baby—can be together every day.

I take the flowers upstairs and put them on the kitchen counter in Damon's condo. Then Dani takes me to a nearby restaurant for lunch, followed by some shopping.

A matching set.

Damon

WHILE I'VE BEEN fully engaged in my workouts, practice, and meetings today, I have been looking very forward to getting home to my girl.

I open the door to my condo and am greeted with two things.

The wonderful aroma of sizzling meat and Ainsley, clad in nothing but the apron that I wore for her in the Ozarks. When I left the facility, I was feeling a little tired, but that's all gone now.

"You're home!" she says cheerfully, turning to face me.

"What happened?" I say, my eyes wide when I see that she has a bruise under her eye.

"Oh yeah," she says. "I've been trying to forget. Remember how I told you that I'm athletic, but I can be a bit of a klutz sometimes?"

I move toward her, pull her into my arms, letting my hands glide down to cup her naked backside, and nod.

"When we were shopping today, I maybe sorta had a run-in with a clothing rack."

I grin at her and kiss her lips. "Am I going to have to go kick its ass, like I did that bush in the Ozarks?"

Laughter rings out. And it's joy to my ears.

She rolls her eyes. "Maybe."

I stop smiling and gently touch her face. "Does it hurt?"

"No, and don't think you're getting out of what I have planned for you tonight because of this. It's barely swollen."

"And what exactly do you have planned for me tonight, Miss Archibald?"

She smiles and pulls my shirt up over my head. "Nakedness."

"And what are you cooking?"

"Fajitas. They are cooked and waiting in the warming drawer. The question is, which are you hungry for first? Them or me?"

I sweep her off her feet and carry her straight to my bed in reply, undo the apron strings, then slowly explore her body like it's the first time.

And in a way, it feels like it.

Until she got here yesterday, it had been a month since I'd seen her. And I want to make up for all those moments. Rejoice in the way she giggles every time I kiss a certain part of her. The purring in her voice when she whispers what she likes in my ear. The boldness of her hand when she's ready to stop being teased and wants more. The sweetness of her lips and the forcefulness of her tongue. Her athleticism and gracefulness as she flips herself—

"Ouch," I mutter out, backing away as her elbow connects with my face.

Make that the bridge of my nose. I quickly close my eye and cover it with my hand.

"Oh my gosh!" she says. "I'm so sorry! I told you I'm such a klutz!"

"I'm fine," I say, blinking a few times and laughing while pinning her down on the bed.

She reaches up and caresses my face. "I love you."

"I love you too," I reply, then proceed to show her just how much.

A GLANCE AT the clock tells me that I've gotten another hour of *working out* in for the day, and my stomach is letting me know it.

Just when I'm thinking about mentioning it, she goes, "I'm starving. How about you?"

"For more of me or food?" I tease.

"Right now, food."

"Me too," I say, kissing her forehead. "But before we do, I want to know what you think of Lincoln."

"It's very nice," she tells me. "I just want to be wherever you are."

I get up and out of bed, smile at her, then hold out my hand, pulling her up.

SHE GETS ALL the food she made out of the warming drawer and sets it on the table. I notice the flowers I'd sent her arrived and are on the kitchen counter. They are just as fun as I hoped they would look.

Years ago, when my dad and Jennifer were dating, my dad sent her a crazy Halloween bouquet, featuring a ton of orange roses but filled with all sorts of other glittering floral arrangement things. Jennifer loved them so much that she planned her wedding around that bouquet, so I was pretty specific in my request for these flowers. Okay, so I maybe had to call Jennifer and ask her what everything was called so I could order them, but still.

Ainsley follows my gaze. "I forgot to thank you for the flowers when you got home! I love them. I've never seen a bouquet like that, and they are just so festive!"

I grab her around the waist and say huskily, desire growing again, "That's because you weren't wearing much when I got home."

She swats me away. "Oh, no. No more of that sexiness until after we eat dinner."

I let her go. "Fine. What all do we have here?"

"Steak and chicken fajitas with mushrooms, peppers, and onions. Homemade tortillas I bought this afternoon. And all the fixings."

We don't chat a whole lot during dinner. We're both just chowing down, but then she stops and looks at me.

"Your eye, um … shit. We're going to be a matching set."

I feel the top of my cheek and realize it's a little swollen. I get up and look in the mirror by the front door and laugh. "We are."

WEDNESDAY, AUGUST 26TH

Damon

WHEN CHASE AND I get home tonight, Dani and Ainsley are nowhere to be found.

"I wonder where they went," Chase says after double-checking both his condo and the One Eleven office space.

"Did you let Dani know we were headed this way?" I ask him.

"No. Thought I would surprise her with being home early."

"Looks like it's us who got surprised," I say with a sardonic chuckle, feeling a little let down as I grab my phone out of my backpack and text her.

Me: *Hey, where are you?*

Champ: *That all depends. Where are you?*

And I don't know why exactly—probably because I can hear her flirty voice saying it—but her text instantly turns me on.

Me: *At home.*

Champ: *Oh!!! You're so early! Yay! We're up on the roof!!*

"They're upstairs," I tell Chase, who is digging through his backpack, still looking for his phone. "And it's in your jacket pocket."

"Thanks," he says, finding it.

I head up to the rooftop deck. The girls are sitting there, drinking out of champagne glasses. Ainsley stands up and rushes toward me, lips first.

After a long kiss, I ask her, "Day drinking?"

"Well, technically, it would be evening drinking. It is after six. Either way, I love seeing your face so much earlier than yesterday."

"Since we head to Cincinnati tomorrow, practice was a little shorter."

"That makes sense," she says.

"We're sitting up here because it's unseasonably cool," Dani adds. "We have some dinner options, but does anything sound good?"

"Since it's nice, why don't I grill everything up here?" Chase offers. "Maybe some chicken and veggies. We could throw some rice in the cooker?"

"That sounds perfect," Dani says while Ainsley nods in agreement. But then Dani looks at me and goes, "What did you do to your eye?"

Chase starts laughing. I punch him in the arm.

Ainsley raises her hand like she's in a classroom and says, "Um, I might have caused that. I accidentally elbowed him."

"In bed!" Chase hoots. He thinks it's hilarious and has been giving me shit about it all day.

Dani is still laughing. "The best part is, you match!"

"Yeah, we know," I say.

"Must have been some night," Chase teases.

"It actually was," Ainsley says boldly. And seriously. Quickly shutting him down.

"Wanna go play a round of pool before dinner?" I ask Ainsley.

"I'd be careful," Dani says. "Those sticks can be dangerous."

As we're walking down the stairs, Ainsley says softly, "I think *your* stick is the dangerous one."

I slap her butt. "Wanna find out now?"

She stops and seems to consider it. "Do you?"

"I can wait until later if you can."

"Actually, I can't. It's our last night, and you're home early," she says, pulling my shirt off and leaving the pool table in the dust.

WE BARELY MAKE it in the door before she has my back pinned against it, kissing me hard.

And it's really hot.

Of course, I was turned on from the moment I read her text.

I pick her up, walk us over to the nearest chair, and sit down. She's straddling me, wearing a flirty little dress. When I reach my hand underneath to strip off her underwear, I find none.

"Were you really sitting up there with no drawers on? How much day drinking were you doing?" I murmur into her neck as I kiss up it.

"I was waiting for you to get home so we could do this easily. And our day drinking was sparkling water."

I don't get a chance to reply because she pulls down my shorts, freeing what she wants, then glides on top of me.

"I WISH I could come home to this every day," I tell her, kissing her gently.

"We just have to get through this semester," she says.

And the way she says it, there's something in her voice, something different from the fact that she'll miss me.

"Do you not think we can make it?" I ask, a lump forming in my throat.

She runs her hand through my hair. "I wasn't sure before, to be honest. Which has nothing to do with what I want. I want more than anything for us to be together, always."

"Always, like daily?" I ask, feeling vulnerable, almost afraid to know what she was thinking before. "Or like longer?"

"Damon …" she says.

Her eyes, which feel like they hold the answers to my universe, gaze into mine.

"What?"

"I love you. I want us to be together forever. But I was nervous about getting through the semester."

"But you're not now?"

"No. Dani showing me the facilities and explaining what you do each day really helped me. My mind won't be thinking up things you could be doing because I know what's really happening. Now, I know things can happen—you know, after practice—but she told me about how important sleep is and your routines. And I feel like I'm a part of it now, somehow."

I let out a sigh of relief. "I want to be yours forever."

She gives me a kiss. "I want that too." But then she gives me a smirk. "Although you might change your mind once I kick your ass at pool."

"I'm pretty good," I tell her. "Been playing since I was a kid."

"Well then," she says with a sly grin, "I wish you luck."

WE STRAIGHTEN OUR clothes and go back out to the common

area and play a game of pool.

She wins.

Not once.

Not twice.

But three times.

And Chase thinks this is hilarious. "Getting beat up by your girlfriend in more ways than one. Whatever will this do to your ego?" He chuckles. "I'm a little scared it might mess with your game."

When he says that, Ainsley's eyes get huge. "Will it?" Her eyes are now moving frantically between me and Chase. Then she turns straight to me and says, "I just got lucky."

I smirk at her and go, "Oh, I know."

Which causes her sexy little mouth to drop open. And I know she's thinking about sex earlier and not the game.

"I know your winning was just a fluke," I reiterate.

She rolls her eyes and punches me in the shoulder. And she uses a little bit more force than a playful one.

And I like it.

I love that she's competitive. That she's not the kind of girl to just let me win because she doesn't want to bruise my ego.

She's going to be a great mom, I suddenly think. Then I shake my head, wondering where that thought just came from.

I don't think my dad ever purposely let me win. He wanted me to push harder. Try harder. And in between, he taught me the skills to excel.

But as I look at Ainsley, I realize he taught me a lot more than about sports. He taught me how to treat a woman with respect. His and Jennifer's relationship just oozes love. It can be serious one minute and playful the next. The funny thing is that when I first saw Ainsley, I couldn't imagine any of that. I didn't know what it would be like. I was just drawn to her.

"You're never going to mess with my game," I say seriously to her.

"True," Chase finally admits. "He does think pretty highly of himself."

"I'm confident," I tell him. "And you damn well know the difference."

He just smiles and nods.

"You two seem more like brothers sometimes than friends," Ainsley says with a laugh.

"We are brothers now," I say, rolling my eyes.

Chase and Dani hold up their ring fingers and say in unison, " 'Cause we're married!"

AFTER DINNER, AINSLEY and I go back to the coziness of my bed. I know I'll get to see her next weekend, but I was bound and determined to make sure she wouldn't be even remotely tempted by another man.

And now, I'm quite tired.

She's snuggled up in my arms, and I'm ready to go to sleep when she jumps up and goes, "I almost forgot!"

I sit up in bed while she runs into the closet and comes back out, holding up a shopping bag.

She hands it to me, slides back into bed, and sits cross-legged in front of me.

Did I mention that she's naked? And that I'm not so tired anymore?

"I got you something today. It's a little *corny* though," she says with a goofy smile.

I reach into the bag and pull out a pair of yellow socks that look like a cob of corn.

"They are sort of for good luck. At your game, you know."

I laugh. "They certainly *are* corny."

FRIDAY, AUGUST 28TH

My last time.

Ainsley

YESTERDAY, I GOT up early with Damon and had a teary goodbye because I wasn't ready to leave him. Normally, that isn't something I would cry over, but just looking at his handsome face and thinking about the fact that I was carrying his baby really hit me. At a slightly inopportune time.

And I feel bad because it made him a little teary too.

It's then that he told me that it was okay that I wasn't going to be at his game because he wasn't named a starter. I could tell it pained him. But he put a smile on his face and told me that he hoped he'd get some playing time so he could prove himself.

I wished him luck. And he pulled up his sweatpants leg and showed me he was wearing the socks.

Since I was up anyway, I ate one of Dani's waffles and some bacon and hit the road.

Sammy wasn't here when I arrived home three and a half hours later, so I unpacked, went shopping, got organized, and went to bed early.

SAMMY ISN'T HERE when I get up either, but I do see a text from last night, saying that he wouldn't be. I have a leisurely morning, then get ready and go to the campus bookstore to buy my books and new school supplies.

Buying new school supplies is something I've always loved, and as I put them in my backpack when I get home, it hits me that it's my last time doing this.

I put my hand across my abdomen and realize the next time I do it will be when our baby starts school.

Which makes me cry. Imagining how I will feel. I've spent a lot of time with my nieces and nephews. Babysat a lot when I was a teen and then again while working at the resort. I've always loved kids.

But this is Damon's baby. *Our baby.* And someday, they will go to school.

I'm sort of bawling when Sammy bursts through the door.

"What's wrong?" he immediately says.

I wipe my tears. "Nothing. I'm just … packing my backpack with school supplies for the first day of school for the very last time."

He sits down on the seat next to me with a thud. "Wow. You're right. I always loved going to buy new pencils and paper. I was a big doodler. No surprise. And I'd go through paper so fast. In fact, that's how I studied. I took notes. Then rewrote them to prep for exams."

"You are a very visual person," I tell him.

"And you should see who I feasted my eyes—and other body parts—on last night," he says. "New guy. Hot. Not as hot as Apollo, of course, but very fine."

"I figured you were out whoring around when you didn't

come home last night."

"I texted you last night. You know exactly why I didn't come home," he counters.

"I went to bed early."

"You went to bed at eight?" He gets a wide grin. "I take it, Damon wore you out. Oh, tell me about your time there. I need all the details."

I laugh. "You're not getting all the details, but I'm going to text you a link to a video. I watched it with his sister, and she explained what Damon does all day at the football facilities, which are so well designed. And I feel like I have such a better understanding. Like, when he says he's up at five thirty and home at nine and goes to bed shortly after, he's not joking. And I see why he's tired. Why sleep is so important. I know all the things!"

"That's really good, Ains. And I'll watch it. Just like I'm going to watch the game with you tonight. I've been feeling like I'm in a rut with my game-day snacks, so I've been collecting recipes … well, since I met Damon. I've been inspired."

"To eat junk food?" I tease.

"No, everything I want to make is super high in protein. And starting today, I'm cutting out alcohol. I went to the gym this morning with the new guy."

"What's his name?"

Sammy waves his hand through the air. "It doesn't really matter."

"Not seeing him again?"

He shrugs. "Who knows? Plus, you and I are going to work out together, right? Get in great shape?"

"That's the plan," I tell him.

Which is almost comical. While I am going to continue to

work out during my pregnancy, I know that while Sammy slims down, I'll be getting … well, I'll be growing a baby.

"I can't believe it's already opening weekend for football. Did you watch any of K-State's home opener last night?"

"Uh, no. Totally forgot about it."

"But we're still going to games together this season?" he asks. "Like when you're home."

"Yes, we are. In fact, maybe you should come to a game in Lincoln with me."

"I thought you'd never ask! Of course, I was going to invite myself at some point."

I chuckle. "Okay, so while you cook, I'm going to take a nap. Otherwise, I'll never be able to stay awake for the whole game. I wish it didn't start so late."

"It starts at eight," Sammy says, studying me curiously.

"Fine, I had a lot of fun with Damon this weekend and need to catch up on my sleep. Is that what you want to hear?"

"For goodness' sake, yes. Thank you! Have a good nap. I'll wake you up at seven so we can watch the pregame. Which should be fun. The game is at a pro stadium, not at the school's stadium. In theory, a neutral location, but not really. And some big celebrities will be there. You know who I'm talking about."

"I do," I say, then head to my bedroom and lie down.

Just as I do, I get a text.

Damon: *At the stadium. Just wanted to say hi.*

Me: *Hi. Are you doing okay? Part of me wants to say I'm sorry you're not starting, but no. Just like meeting me, this is part of your life journey.*

Damon: *My dad says I'm supposed to learn a lesson from* *this, but didn't tell me what lesson. And I have no clue.*

Me: *I'm not going to say work harder because I know you give your all in everything you do. Maybe you're supposed to learn patience. Good-things-come-to-those-who-wait sort of thing.*

Damon: *I already learned that lesson. I waited three years for you.*

Me: *And what a moment that was. It went from nothing to greatness in just a few weeks. You will too.*

Damon: *You think?*

Me: *Yeah, I do.*

Damon: *You watching the game?*

Me: *Sammy is making us snacks, and we both are. Wouldn't miss it for the world. Speaking of that, I know your families always come for games and stuff, but is there any chance Sammy could come up one weekend, see a game, watch you play?*

Damon: *I'd love that. Actually, Daine's concert in Lincoln is September 17th. Why don't we plan for that weekend?*

Me: *That would be really fun.*

Damon: *Okay. Love you.*

Me: *Love you too.*

I close my eyes, feeling happy.

SAMMY WAKES ME up. I put on a Nebraska shirt that I stole from Damon for good luck and go sit in front of the TV.

"On tonight's menu is jalapeño poppers; buffalo wing chicken tenders, coated in Parmesan cheese; homemade potato chips, fried in beef tallow; homemade ranch dip; and for dessert, a chocolate mousse, made healthy with avocado," Sammy says with a flourish.

"It all looks amazing. And not healthy."

"It's all about the protein and lack of carbs and sugar, girl."

"I love it. I'll go grab some water real quick."

"Oh, I almost forgot!" he says, rushing to the fridge and bringing back a new thermal pitcher with a football on it and two martini glasses. "I made us mocktails! A mocktail mule, to be exact."

He pours us each a glass, and then he holds his up. "To victory and Damon having a good game."

"I don't think he's going to play tonight. He is, like, fifth on the depth chart. So, unless they're up by a bunch—"

"But he's a five-star recruit!"

"I know. I don't understand it. He doesn't either. It should be an interesting game."

IT IS.

And not in a good way.

The offense struggles.

It's not that Chase is playing poorly—more that the offensive line is. The defenders keep getting through, and Chase is constantly under pressure—either running for his life or getting sacked.

And when he has managed to throw the ball, the receivers are … just off. Like it just hits their hands. There is a lot of punting on both sides. Three-and-outs.

With just thirty seconds left in the game, we're up six to three. The other team gets another first down, putting the ball at the sixteen-yard line with enough time for them to score. On their first down, they run the ball, but fortunately, the defense holds them to just two yards. On the second play, they give the quarterback just enough time to throw the ball toward the end zone for a game-winning touchdown.

And it's a beautifully thrown ball, headed straight for their open receiver, who's literally standing in the end zone, waiting for it.

"We're going to lose," Sammy says, but then suddenly, one of our players flies across the field and grabs the ball out of the air.

"Interception!" Sammy yells, standing up. "We win!"

I jump up with him, and we hold hands and do a little happy dance.

"It wasn't pretty," I say.

"A win is a win," Sammy counters.

I can't help but think the win would have been bigger if they'd let Damon play. I wonder why they wouldn't put their five-star recruit out there, but then I realize that a famous quarterback's son who was highly touted has been sitting on the bench for two years, coming into games only occasionally, waiting for his time.

And I can't imagine Damon being willing to wait that long.

HE TEXTS ME just as I'm getting into bed.

Damon: *What are you wearing?*

Me: *Honestly, a workout shirt that I might have stolen from you.*

Damon: *That makes me smile.*

Me: *Rough game. But a win is a win, right?*

Damon: *It was hard to watch and not be able to do any-thing about it.*

Me: *I bet it was.*

Damon: *To be honest, it pisses me off. I've never had to deal with this. With not being the best.*

Me: *Not even your freshman year of high school?*

Damon: *When you get on ESPN as an eighth grader who almost won a high-school state championship playoff game, you start the next year.*

Me: *True. I love you. And I know you will play. Soon. Just keep working hard.*

Damon: *Love you too, Champ. And I guess if I'm going to be with someone named Champ, I'd better become one myself too.*

Me: *Exactly!*

SATURDAY, AUGUST 29TH

Even better.

Ainsley

I WAKE UP with a start, worried I'm going to be late for class. It's my last semester, and the school wonderfully scheduled a senior-level course to start on Monday mornings at eight. *Yes, I'm being sarcastic.*

I grab my phone and check the time, seeing that I have an hour before class and a text from Damon.

Except … wait.

I look at my phone again. It's Saturday. I don't know what I was thinking. Actually, it is what I was dreaming. I was dreaming I was late for class.

And possibly walked in naked.

Damon: *We flew home right after the game. Got home late. People met us at the airport. Fans. Cheering for us. Cheered for the crappy way we'd played.*

Me: *I think they were cheering for a victory. For an exciting finish. The last few years, it didn't go our team's way.*

Damon: *Our team?*

Me: *Yes, our team.*

Damon: *You and me?*

Me: *That too.*

Damon: *What if I'm not as good as I think? What if I don't go pro?*

Me: *Where's that champion mindset right now?*

Damon: *It's in fifth place.*

Me: *You have a backup plan.*

Damon: *Yeah, you're right. Their showing up meant a lot though. And I've been thinking a lot this morning. And I might have come up with a plan to play.*

Me: *What's that?*

Damon: *Well, the starting receivers weren't exactly lighting the field on fire last night.*

Me: *So, you're going to light it up in practice this week?*

Damon: *I need to, yes. See, my girl is going to be at the next game. And I need to show off for her. So, I have to make it happen.*

Me: *I can't wait! And I think even if you don't start but you get to play, we celebrate the way we promised.*

Damon: *Fried chicken and champagne.*

Me: *Exactly.*

Damon: *Naked.*

Me: *Even better.*

Leave them no choice.

Ainsley

I'VE JUST ARRIVED in Lincoln and gotten inside the condo building when Dani rushes over and says, "Oh my gosh, you're never going to believe it."

"Believe what?" I ask her.

"One of the starting receivers got suspended for tomorrow's game. The papers are all over it. It's a huge scandal. First, the police were called to the apartment he shared with his girlfriend yesterday afternoon because they had been fighting. I guess a neighbor had called, but the police didn't see any evidence of abuse, and the couple told the police it was just an argument. And they were sorry if they were loud. But then, last night, he got pulled over for reckless driving."

"Oh, that's not good."

"It's not. But it should be good for Damon. He will definitely be playing in the game. And you know what that means?"

"He'll be happy?" I ask.

"He and Chase will connect. Like they always do. You're in for a good show."

"That's exciting. He really wants to be a starter. It's killing him not to be."

"I know. I hear about it a lot. But he'll get there. Maybe sooner than we thought."

"Do you think it will affect the team morale or anything?"

"Of course, stuff like this is always a distraction. Something coaches hate. Everyone is just finding out the news. Chase called me about fifteen minutes ago. Damon a few minutes later. I'd barely hung up when both my parents called and wanted to know what I'd heard. Auntie Jay called and asked how Chase was handling it. So, you know it's going around like wildfire. And you know our opponent is looking for ways to turn it into an opportunity on the field."

"When Damon first got here, he told me that their coach said they had to be really careful. That he didn't want any trouble before the season started. No scandals, arrests, or headlines."

"Probably would have been better if this had happened before the season started, but here we are."

"It's really too bad he went off on his own like that. That he didn't call a teammate if he was upset."

"He should have. Even one of his coaches."

"Will he get kicked off the team?"

"Right now, it's a one-game suspension. I assume they need to get more information before they make any further decisions." She pauses, then goes, "Oh, and Chase and Damon should be coming home between practice and when they have to report to the hotel." She rolls her eyes. "Although I suppose that might change. Let's hang out here and have a movie night, if that sounds good to you. I'm in the mood for popcorn and junk food. I try not to eat it around the boys since they're so strict with their diet, but since they won't be here," she says with a smile on her face, "we can be bad."

"That sounds fun. It's been a long week. How was your first week of school? Do you like your classes?"

"I think they'll be fine. Mostly, I love my schedule. All my classes are on Tuesday and Thursday. And without sorority, I have so much free time compared to last year. I'm loving it. How are yours?"

"They're good. It helps that Sammy and I have our classes together. And I love that I don't have class on Fridays. But the first day, they told us about all the projects we'd be doing, and it's going to be a lot of work. Fun because I enjoy it. But graded, you know."

"If only we could just learn and not have to get grades, college would be so much more fun," she says with a laugh.

"Will your family not be here tonight?" I ask.

"No, they'll all fly up together first thing in the morning. Chase's little brother Ryder made varsity football and has a game tonight. That's why we're having a quiet night because tomorrow will be chaos. And it will be even more than usual with Chase's birthday celebration."

"When is his birthday?" I ask her.

"On Monday, the seventh, but the family won't be here for that, thankfully." She holds up her hands. "That sounded bad. I just mean that it will be nice for Chase to have a quiet birthday."

THE BOYS DO get to stop by before they have to go to the hotel. And I'm pretty sure it's not to get their stuff, but because they are looking for a quick roll in the hay. Chase leads Dani into their condo the second he arrives, and Damon kisses me intensely before leading me back to his.

"I don't have a lot of time," he says.

"We never have enough time," I tease. "But we can probably make do."

Clothes are removed, bodies pressed together, and our love is consummated.

I'm kissing up the side of his neck, feeling happy and fulfilled. In love.

"Did Dani tell you the news?"

"That I'm going to get to see you play?" I ask in between kisses.

"Yeah. I'm glad you're here."

"Me too. Sounds like everyone else will be here," I tease.

"Oh, tomorrow, before and after the game, this place will be hopping. They usually fly in and out for morning games, but I know they are planning a party for Chase's birthday, and I don't know if they will spend the night or not. If they do, the following morning will be a little crazy too."

"Either way, I'm sure it will be fun. Also, I think we'll be celebrating something besides a birthday."

"Like what?" he says, glancing at his watch.

"Hmm. Time to go?" I ask him.

"Yeah, unfortunately."

"It's okay. I'm just glad we got to spend a little time together."

He kisses me, then gets out of bed.

I get up and get dressed too.

When we walk to the door, I block it and pull him close. "What we'll be celebrating is your phenomenal game. The kind that will leave them no choice but to make you a starter."

He gets a big grin. "I like that."

"Do it for me?" I flirt.

He gives me a salute. "Yes, ma'am, Champ, ma'am."

"You're silly," I tell him.

"And *you* are perfect."

SATURDAY, SEPTEMBER 5TH

Very wrong.

Ainsley

"SO, HOW ARE the boys doing? The team doing?" Chase's mom asks Dani the second she steps through the door. "Do you think the suspension will distract them?"

"He said the coaches and captains have spoken to the team. I think since it's just a one-game suspension, at least right now, it'll be okay. Chase has been trying to keep the offense focused on the game. And the bonus for us is, it means Damon should play today."

I get a big hug from my uncles as well as Damon's mom, Jennifer, and Damon's dad. It's kind of cool that his parents seem genuinely happy to see me.

"Did you see this? Did Damon?" Damon's dad asks, handing me a newspaper.

I look at the circled article. It's talking about how five-star recruit Damon—the son of a Super Bowl–winning quarterback and Nebraska legend—wasn't good enough to play in the first game. They speculate on why.

That he doesn't have the mindset. *Wrong.*

That he's used to things being given to him because of his name. *Wrong.*

That he doesn't work that hard. *Wrong.*

That he doesn't have that good of hands. I smile. *Very wrong.*

In the end, they wonder if he'll be asked to redshirt, sit out this season and wait until he's ready. Which, to them, seems stupid, seeing as he got a lot of NIL money to come here. They basically imply that he was a bad investment.

"It's not very nice," I say with a frown. "But he says he's going to light the stadium up today. That there's no need for fireworks."

"Really?" Damon's dad says.

"Yeah. He says he's getting his chance to show them."

Damon's dad looks a little worried. "I hope he does."

Big corn energy.

Damon

WE WERE ABLE to get a few pregame on-field passes. Dani has a press badge that allows her access to every game, and while I wait for everyone else to get down, I notice Chase sneaking up on Dani, then flipping the hem of her skirt just a little. When she turns around, he winks at her.

"Look at us," Chase says. "We're both exactly where we promised we would be."

"We are," she says, moving close to him and putting her hand on his chest, pressing on the pads underneath.

And I know what she's thinking because she's told me before—that the pads are there to protect his ribs and heart. That he used to need that kind of protection from her, but not anymore.

"I should tell you to have a good game. To wish you fortune and glory, but I have something else to say."

Chase's eyes sparkle, and I wonder what she's going to tell him.

"I've decided dating an underclassman would be totally cool," she says.

"What are you saying?" he asks, looking bewildered.

"I'm asking you to be my boyfriend, Chase."

He laughs, then says, "That's kind of scandalous, isn't it? Since you're already married?" But then he picks her up, kisses her, and swings her around.

I think about that summer. The promises they made. Then broke.

When Haley, Ryder, and Ainsley join them, I realize that so much has changed—that we're all starting to live out our dreams.

And today, I plan to showcase mine. For the girl who is walking toward me. Who's wearing a shirt that features a mascot made of corn and says, *Big Corn Energy.*

I think about the socks she gave me and can't help but laugh.

"Big Corn Energy?" I ask, taking her hand.

"You should see the one I got for you," she says in a flirty tone. "If you do good today, I'll give it to you tonight."

My smile is wide when I say, "I'm going to do better than good. I'm going to light this place up. Just wait, fans will be cheering my name."

"You know I will be," she says sweetly.

Shock and awe.

Ainsley

I CAN TELL you that once you've watched a football game in a suite, you'll never want to go back to sitting in the stands. It's hot out, and just walking down to the field made me all sweaty.

Now I'm being treated to sweet, cool air-conditioning.

There's a buffet filled with food, a fridge full of cold drinks, a well-stocked bar, and our own private bathroom.

There are bar-top tables to sit at, multiple TV screens so that you won't miss a play, and padded seats lined up in rows with views of the fifty-yard line. We're up high enough to have a good view, but not too high.

The mood is festive, but I'm feeling nervous. I want Damon to play. To do well. To show everyone that he's not overrated.

Dani grabs my hand and leads me down to the seats right by the window. "Best spot in the house," she says.

"Are you working during this game?"

"No, I just get to watch. But beware, I talk during the whole game."

"I think that will be good for me. I'm trying to learn the intricacies of the game."

"Then you've come to the right spot," Haley says, sitting on the other side of Dani and rolling her eyes.

"Oh, come on. You love it," Dani says to her.

"Yeah, I do. To be honest, I was always too busy cheering to really pay much attention to the *intricacies* of the game. I just knew to yell when they did something good."

PRETTY SOON, THE team takes the field for the first offensive play, but Damon isn't lined up.

"I don't see him," I say softly.

"He said he wasn't starting, but expected to get playing time," Dani says. "We don't know what that exactly means. Like, how much or when."

"Okay," I say.

BY THE END of the first quarter, the score is tied three–three.

And the game is, well, for lack of a better word, dragging on a bit.

"I didn't expect this to be a defensive battle," Dani says. "And I don't understand. The offensive line is holding, and Chase has time to throw, but no one is open. I know the other team's defense is playing man-to-man, but *someone* should be able to break away. Do a pick or something!"

The teams switch sides of the field and play starts again—us with the ball.

"There's Damon!" Haley calls out. "He's in the huddle!"

I watch as Chase says something to the guys, and when they break to take their places, Chase gives Damon a fist bump.

"What was that for?" I ask.

"Shock and awe," Dani says. "I hope."

"What's shock and awe?" I ask. "I mean, in regard to football. Wait, Damon mentioned that at your wedding. In his best-man toast. He said they called him and Chase the shock-and-awe package. I meant to ask what that was, but then he made me cry with the rest of the speech, and I forgot."

"You'll see," Dani says cryptically as Chase gets hiked the ball and Damon takes off running.

And he's fast.

Like, really fast.

Or maybe it's that his defender isn't, but he runs right past him, flying down the field. Chase throws the ball—launches it into the air really. And a few moments later, Damon catches it mid-stride and runs another twenty yards into the end zone.

The suite erupts with cheers.

I stay seated, tears filling my eyes, so proud of him. His mom is sitting behind me, and she places her hand on my shoulder. I turn around and look at her and realize she's teary too.

"This is just the start," she says to me. "He just needed to get on the field."

I nod in agreement.

NEEDLESS TO SAY, the rest of the game is quite thrilling.

Both Treyvon and Damon make multiple receptions and score a couple of touchdowns apiece.

And because of the team's success in the throwing game, Dani says it helps to open up the run game. Meaning all the offense seems to be clicking.

Chase hands the ball off to a running back, who runs for a first down.

On the next play, after Damon catches another pass and scores, the commentators announce that Damon has tied the school record for most touchdown receptions in a game—with only two others sharing that spot. They speculate that since it's only the beginning of the fourth quarter, it's possible we could see a new record.

The stadium feels electric. We're winning by twenty-one points, but no one is sitting down. Even in the suite, with its comfy chairs and amazing view, we're all standing.

And when our team takes the field on offense again, the announcer's voice booms through the air, "Mackenzie back to pass. He's looking right—no, he's going deep, down the sideline …"

And there Damon is, breaking free from his defender. The ball arcs through the air and goes toward him like it's a magnet and he's metal, zooming to connect. Damon stretches out, his arms up high, and snags it. Then he uses those ballet skills he told me about, dragging two feet across the turf and into the end zone.

"Touchdown!" the announcer yells.

And the place erupts. I thought they were cheering loudly before, but this is crazy. Almost deafening. The student section seems to be losing their minds.

As is pretty much everyone in the suite.

Damon's teammates swarm around him, smacking his shoulder, his helmet, giving high fives.

After a quick replay to verify the play, the announcer says, "The record is broken. Damon Diamond, son of Nebraska legend Danny Diamond, has done it. Four touchdown receptions. I think we'll be seeing more of this young man in the future."

"Yeah, on Sundays," the other announcer says.

When Chase and Damon run together to the sideline before the extra point is kicked, I can see the grins on their faces from clear up here.

WE GO BACK to the condo after the game, everyone incredibly happy. Both Damon and Chase broke school records today. Chase for throwing the most touchdown passes in a single game and setting a record for most passing yards for a freshman in a single game. As well as Damon's four touchdown receptions.

When we get inside, the condo gathering room has been transformed into a party space. Food, drinks, and a big red cake are lined up on the island, and there are balloons wishing Chase a happy birthday.

Damon's dad quickly switches on the television and listens to a sportscaster talk about the game, about Chase and Damon's friendship and how they chose to go to the same college, despite experts telling them they should do otherwise.

And I learn the story of how the boys became known as the shock-and-awe package. How the nickname started when a skeptical local reporter, who thought the boys were only getting hype because of Damon's last name, came to see one of their games when the boys were only in high school. He wrote later that he was *shocked* at Chase's throwing technique and accuracy and *awed* by Damon's agility and ability to catch pretty much anything thrown his way.

And now we can all see, the man was right.

EVERYONE IS IN a festive mood, and the party has most definitely started already even though the boys won't be back from the stadium for a while.

I go into Damon's condo and send him a quick congratulatory text.

I'm surprised when he texts me right back and tells me that he was asked to do a postgame interview with the press, that I can watch it online, and that he will be here in about an hour.

Even though there's lots of food, I place an order to be delivered in a couple of hours.

THE FIRST THING Damon does when he and Chase arrive is grab my hand and pull me into his condo.

"You were literally amazing," I tell him. "And I learned what shock-and-awe meant. Like, both the origin and, well, seeing it in person."

"You inspire me," he says, pulling me into a tight hug.

And I don't know what happens to my brain when he hugs me, but I want to blurt out that I'm pregnant. That we have a lot to celebrate.

I take a deep breath and know that I can't. He needs to keep this going. Have his perfect season.

"Coach told us that we should remember how this game felt. To savor it. And to know that every game we play this season is going to end with us victorious."

"The coaches were pretty pumped up when you set the record. Hell, the fans in the stands—something like eighty-five thousand—were too. You should have seen your parents. Your mom was teary-eyed, like I was, after your first touchdown. When you set the record, your dad was … overcome with emotion. Your parents really love you."

"I know they do. I should probably get out there. Celebrate."

"Yes, you should." I glance at my watch. "For about an hour, and then we have to take care of our own celebration."

WHEN I GET a notification that our food is almost here, I tell Damon I'm going to get it and to meet me in his condo in ten minutes.

Which gives me time to go downstairs to retrieve the order and get it all set up on his dining room table.

When he comes and looks at the food, he smiles. "Oh, I have

a better idea."

He grabs a big wooden tray, puts all the food on it, carries it into the bedroom, and sets it in the middle of the bed.

"Hey, can you grab the bottle of bubbly in the fridge and a couple of flutes? Then get your pretty ass back in here."

I do as told, relieved to see that the bubbly is a nonalcoholic version.

HE OPENS THE bottle, pours us each a glass, and clinks his glass against mine. "To big corn energy and my lucky charm."

"Speaking of that, I have something to give you." I run and grab a wrapped package from my suitcase.

When he opens it and reads what it says on the shirt, he eyes me. "*Big COB energy*, huh?"

"Well, corn energy is for the game. The *cob* energy is for me," I say in my sultriest voice.

SUNDAY, SEPTEMBER 6TH

Wherever.

Ainsley

I WAKE UP to the sounds of banging noises and cheers.

"Oh shit. I should have set my alarm," Damon says, jumping up.

"What's going on?" I ask, jumping up, too, and getting dressed, afraid they might be going door to door or something.

Damon throws on a pair of shorts and leads me out the door. I see the whole group from yesterday is still here, and they are lined up outside of Chase and Dani's condo.

The singing of a loud and rowdy rendition of "Happy Birthday" commences. And when Chase opens the door, they start throwing stuff at him. Confetti, little trinkets. His little brothers are throwing things hard. Almost pelting him.

What is even happening?

Even Dani is tossing little crocheted cupcakes at him.

"Mackenzie family tradition. The birthday confetti toss. Otherwise known as the birthday throwdown," Damon says, wrapping his arms around me and leaning down to rest his chin on my shoulder.

"It's more than confetti," I reply.

"It is," he says, pointing at the floor. "Looks like this year, like most years, it's football and Nebraska-themed. Plus, the ones and nines since he's nineteen. And the candy. The candy was always my favorite part."

"I helped you throw stuff at them for their wedding exit. It makes sense now why it wasn't just confetti."

AFTER A BIG home-cooked breakfast with more birthday cake, the families head to the airport, and Chase and Damon get sprawled out on the big sectional.

"This morning, you get to see what dating a football player is like," Dani says with a chuckle.

"They lie around on the couch on Sundays?" I ask.

"For a bit. They'll study game film, then go do a light workout and any recovery therapy they might need. Chase has a big bruise on his forearm from when he got sacked. How was Damon's body last night?"

It was damn fine, is what I think, but what I say is, "I didn't notice any bruises, and he didn't complain about anything hurting."

"They will today. But overall, it looks like they fared well."

I go sit next to Damon. He snuggles me into his arms, and I fall back asleep while he watches himself play football.

DAMON CARRIES MY suitcase and puts it in the trunk of my car. Even though tomorrow is Labor Day and we don't have school, Damon has to put in a normal football day, so I'm going to head home now, missing the holiday traffic, and do some homework.

"I had an amazing weekend," I tell him.

He gives me a smirk. "Which parts were the most amazing?"

"Hmm, it could have been that you set a new record."

"On or off the field?" Literally, he's beaming. "I think you know what I'm referring to," he says, pulling me close and planting a big kiss on my lips.

"Your reception record. *In bed?*" I raise an eyebrow at him.

"Exactly."

"Didn't we have a conversation about your athletic prowess the night of Chase and Dani's wedding?"

"Oh, yeah, we did. I know you acted like you were talking about football, but you were totally thinking about me in bed."

"You're right. I was."

He looks genuinely surprised. "Really?"

"Yeah. I wanted to sleep with you. Have a fun little summer fling. You told me that prowess was like prowling. That I was on the prowl for you, but that I thought I couldn't have you. And that I was making up excuses in that pretty little head of mine."

"Just a fling?" he says, fake clutching his chest. "And here I thought it was love."

I laugh out loud. "Of course. Thus why you told me I could discover your prowess in the bedroom—*or wherever.*"

"I guess I'd better get you in this car and let you go before you disillusion me more." He slaps my butt and then opens the car door for me.

I slide inside, put the key in the ignition, and turn the key. But it won't start.

Damon gives me some instructions on different ways to start it or when to press on the gas and when to let off. But the result is still the same.

The battery is dead.

Twenty minutes later, my car has been jump-started, is running, and I'm getting told where to watch the bar for the battery's charge and to try not to shut the car off until I'm home.

WHEN I GET home, I race past Sammy to use the bathroom. I've had to pee for the last twenty minutes but was afraid to shut off the car.

"You not able to stop and use the bathroom on the road suddenly?" he asks with a laugh when I come back out.

"Actually, no. My battery was dead, and we got it jump-started, but Damon told me not to turn it off until I got home."

"Oh," he says. "Come on. Let's go check it out and get your stuff unloaded."

Thankfully, when I turn the key over this time, the car starts right up.

"What a game!" Sammy says, then proceeds to give me the play-by-play like I wasn't in attendance.

THURSDAY, SEPTEMBER 17TH

Do it up right.

Ainsley

NEBRASKA WON THEIR game in Michigan last week. It was a high-scoring game, full of offense. The reporters are now predicting Damon will shatter all reception records as a true freshman.

And I hope he does.

The game, however, was STRESSFUL!

A nail-biter, coming down to a Hail Mary throw and catch in the end zone by Treyvon as time expired.

Sammy and I skipped class today so we could get to Lincoln well before Daine Kirkwood's concert tonight. One thing I like about Sammy is that while he could talk for the entire journey, never once running out of something to say, he prefers to listen to music and eat snacks during road trips. But since he's working out hard and being careful about what he eats, our snacks aren't the usual chips and candy, but rather dark chocolate-covered date balls. Which I am obsessed with, by the way. And surprised at how healthy they are for something so sweet.

Our trip is going well when, all of a sudden, there's a loud bang, and my car immediately lurches to the right. Which is not a good thing because there is a big truck coming up alongside me. It's extremely hard to steer the car, and there's a really bad vibration, making the whole car feel like it's shuddering over whatever just happened.

My heart beats wildly.

"Whoa!" Sammy yells out, bracing his hand on the dash.

"I think it's my tire!" I yell back, struggling to maintain control of the car.

Although I've never had something like this happen before, I somehow instinctively know that I shouldn't hit the brakes or make any sudden movements.

"I think so too! Slowly take your foot off the gas," Sammy instructs.

I do, which makes it a little less bumpy, and grip the steering wheel firmly while trying to breathe.

But that's difficult because my body is on high alert, adrenaline coursing through me.

The car rattles and thuds as I fight to get it onto the shoulder.

When we finally roll to a stop, I let out a sigh of relief.

Sammy turns around. "I can see a bunch of shredded rubber behind us. Definitely a blowout. Although, at first, I thought the car's whole transmission just fell out."

He reaches over and turns on my hazard lights.

"What are we going to do?" I ask. Even though it's a stupid question.

Sammy runs his hand down my arm. "It's okay. We're safe. You did a great job maintaining control of the car. We're lucky it happened when we were in a fifty-five speed zone instead of seventy-five," he says. "The car could have flipped."

I swallow hard. My mind immediately goes to the baby in my belly. The thought that we both could've been hurt brings tears to my eyes. And I start crying.

Sammy says, "Do you have a spare?"

"Yeah, I do."

"Then it's not the end of the world," he says flippantly, which makes me sob.

He pulls me into a hug. "Seriously, Ains, we're all right. Everything is all right. We'll change the tire and be back on the road. And if you want, I'll drive."

"Okay," I say shakily.

"Come on. Let's go check out the damage and find the spare. Worst case, we call a tow truck or something. We won't miss tomorrow's game. I'll rent a car if need be, and we'll keep going."

"That's true," I say even though I wasn't even thinking about getting to the game.

I'm thinking about the fact that I could have just died. And they would've told Damon I was pregnant. He would have found out from someone else.

I run my hand across my belly and take another deep breath.

Because I'm okay.

We're okay.

I follow Sammy out of the car, just as there's a clap of thunder and rain starts pouring down.

I look up at the sky, wondering what I did to deserve this.

Sammy shrugs his shoulders. Like, *what can we do?*

I guess at least there isn't any lightning in the vicinity.

Thankfully, a state trooper pulls over behind us and helps Sammy change my tire. The good news is that my dad insisted that there be an actual tire in my trunk and not one of those little doughnut spares that you can only drive fifty miles on. And that means we can get to Lincoln without a problem.

SAMMY TAKES THE wheel, and after a few minutes, we've left the rain behind us, and the sun is shining brightly.

"I want to stop at the next gas station. I think we deserve more than date balls after all that. I must have burned a few thousand calories in seconds."

"What do you want?" I ask him.

"Hmm. If I'm going to cheat, I might as well do it up right. King-size Reese's Peanut Butter Cups, Cheetos, and a full-sugar Coke. What about you?"

"Peanut butter M&M's, a Heath bar, sour cream and onion potato chips, and a water."

"I want to check the pressure on all your tires. Have you done that recently?"

"Um, no," I say. "But I always look at my tires before I drive a long distance to make sure they aren't looking low."

"Maybe you hit something in the road that punctured it," he says, pulling into the gas station.

He checks the pressure while I use the restroom and buy the snacks.

When I get back in the car, Sammy says, "You really need new tires."

"I know the tread is getting low, but I just can't afford them right now. Not with all the school books and stuff I just bought."

"Then I'll buy them for you," he says sweetly.

"I'll figure something out," I tell him, happy to be back in the car.

"I can't believe how hot it is," Sammy says, sliding behind the wheel. "A few miles back, it's pouring, and here, it's"—he turns the car and checks the dash—"ninety-two. I hope it's not that hot for the game tomorrow."

"We'll be in a suite," I say with a grin as he pulls out of the station and gets back on the road.

"We will be?"

"Yeah, with his whole family, Chase's family, and probably Uncle Tripp."

"Very cool," he says. "Open my snacks for me. I'm ready!"

We're happily munching away and only about an hour from Lincoln when he goes, "Shit."

"What's wrong?"

"Your car is overheating. The *Check Engine* light just came on."

"Can we make it to the next gas station?" I ask just as we pass a sign telling us of an exit just a mile ahead.

"Yeah. Hell, if the trip keeps up this way, I may need you to drive so I can sit in the passenger side and drink."

"You do realize, I've driven this before, by myself, and never had a lick of trouble."

"Are you saying this is my fault?" he asks, pretending to be aghast.

"Just stating facts." I smile at him. "I'm not sure if I should be glad you're here to help me or if it wouldn't have happened if you hadn't been."

"Oh hush," he says.

AFTER ADDING MORE fluid to the radiator, we continue on our trip, and we're both thrilled when we finally arrive.

I push in a code to get access to the building, and we ride the elevator up.

Haley is the first one to greet us. Letting out a happy screech when the doors open.

"It's about time you got here!" she says, wrapping us both in hugs.

"I'm Haley," she says, hugging Sammy again. "Damon's told me so much about you. I feel like I already know you. So, hugs are a given. Plus, now you're like family."

"It's nice to meet you, Haley," Sammy says. "And I'm excited to meet your beau tonight."

"Oh, he's not my beau," she says. "I mean, like, we're not a couple. We're friends. Good friends. Really good friends. But that's it. For now. Maybe forever. Who knows what the future holds? But we are just—"

"Good friends?" Sammy asks.

"Yes, exactly." She turns to me and points to her leg. "No more restrictions. I can dance the night away."

Dani comes out of her condo and greets us, gets introduced to Sammy, and then she turns to Haley and says, "There are *some* restrictions."

"Fine," Haley says. "So, I'm not supposed to jump yet, go skydiving, anything like that."

"And what did you decide about volleyball?" I ask her.

"I'm on an unofficial college recruiting visit this week. That's how I got a Get Out of Jail Free card—I mean, an excused school absence for the trip. And I don't know if you've heard, but I decided not to play with my team this year. I'm doing the private coach thing. And I think it's going to be great. Certainly no drama. And there's plenty of that going on at school, but I digress."

I laugh. Haley is funny. And I remember what it was like to be sixteen.

CHASE AND DAMON are home in time to change for the concert, and while we're walking there, Sammy is telling everyone about our trip. About how we almost died. And on and on. About how many miles my car has. I finally get tired of him shit-talking my car.

"She's been a great car. I've had her since I was sixteen. She wasn't new, but she was new to me. It was just a fluke. Sammy thinks I hit something on the road, and that punctured the tire. I am very glad Sammy was with me though. I had been taught how to change a tire, but haven't had to do one since."

THE CONCERT IS fun. Haley stays backstage most of the time because Daine wants her to see what goes on behind the scenes, but the rest of us, which is a pretty big group, are in a cordoned-off VIP section. It's basically everyone from the game night—Amber and Garrett, who talk a lot about wedding planning; Eddie and Lauren, who have finally decided to date and are quite lovey-dovey at the moment; as well as Treyvon and a bunch of other guys from the team. I was introduced to them all, but I can't remember their names. Sammy will though. He's excitedly chatting about their upcoming game, and he doesn't seem to be suffering any aftereffects from our scare today.

I'm exhausted, if I'm being honest. The music is great and all that, and Daine is quite talented. It's super cute when he plays a new song, one dedicated to *a special girl who happens to be here tonight.* I can see Haley just on the edge of the stage, her arms crossed, hands held against her chest. The song is a sweet ballad about the power of friendship. But yet there's a lot of love in there. And I think it's pretty clear what page Daine is on regarding Haley even though she still insists they are just friends. And they should probably be. He's older and traveling. She's still in high school. I remember at the Ozarks this summer, he told her she had been the constant in his life.

Once the song is over, Daine says, "All right, Lincoln, it's time to kick it up a notch. Get this party started. Rumor has it, you've got a pretty good football team this year!"

Of course, the crowd goes crazy over that.

"And I heard a few of those boys in red are in the house tonight! Chase, Damon, Treyvon, give us a wave!"

The guys do as the band starts a rowdy song about Friday night lights in the country.

Everyone is dancing, but I'm sort of just standing motionless. I swear, I think I could fall asleep, standing here.

Damon pulls me into his arms. "You doing okay?" he says into my ear.

"I'm quite tired. Today was … a lot."

"Sammy said you were pretty shook up."

"It was scary," I say, looking into the eyes of the boy I love and feeling happy that I'm here to do so. "The car, like, lurched, and I felt like I didn't have control. And it just happened so suddenly. Like there was an explosion sort of sound, and then—boom—the steering wheel didn't want to cooperate."

"I'm very glad you are okay," he tells me, then gives me a kiss.

"Me, too, because I'm here with you."

"I know the concert isn't over yet, but let's go home. Get you to bed."

And all I really remember after getting in bed is him giving me a kiss.

not just any girl.

Damon

I KISS AINSLEY'S neck, waking her up. There's something I want to talk to her about before I head to campus.

"Morning," she says, looking up at me with sleepy eyes.

I roll onto my side and lean up on my elbow, my head cradled in my palm. "Morning."

"Last night was fun," she says. "Daine is really good. Thanks for bringing me home early, and I'm sorry if I fell asleep on you."

"We were mid-kiss," I say to her, smiling while absent-mindedly twirling a piece of her hair. "But that's not what I wanted to talk to you about. I'm kinda worried about your car."

"Yeah, me, too, but not much I can do about it right now. It's paid for, and until I get a job, I can't really afford a new one."

"Look, you're driving up here for me all the time. And I want—no, I *need*—for you to be safe while doing so. Would you allow me to buy you one?"

"No, I wouldn't, Damon," she says, but then softens. "You'd do that for me?"

"Of course."

"I just couldn't accept a gift like that."

"It would really be for me and would ease my conscience. I wish that we could rotate. That I could come see you every other weekend, but I can't during football season."

She purses her lips.

"After you fell asleep, I started online shopping and found one that I was going to surprise you with. But when I texted Dani to ask if she would go with you to pick it up today, she said you should get to help pick it out."

"I'll think about it," she says, and I can tell she's just saying that when she has no intention of doing so.

"Think about this," I say, pulling her in tight and kissing her sweet lips.

Things heat up quickly from there.

A LITTLE LATER, I'm kissing her neck, and my fingers are tangled in her hair. I'm awash in that content feeling that comes after sex with her. Like everything is perfect in the world and nothing else matters.

If only that were true. I'm worried about her car and the fact that I'm still not starting. Which is crazy, considering I've been setting school records.

"What if I have Dani take you to the dealership and show you the car that I was going to get you? You can take it for a test drive, choose your favorite color, and if you like it, you can drive it home on Sunday."

She crinkles up her nose in response.

"I'm going to buy it either way. And if you care about me and my mental well-being, you will drive it."

"What if we break up?" she asks.

"The thought never crossed my mind because we are never breaking up."

"You can't just go around, buying cars for any girl you date. That's not exactly fiscally responsible," she chastises.

I pull her hips into mine. We're still naked, snuggled under the covers.

"You're not just any girl, and you know it. What if I buy it and let you drive it? Then you don't have to worry."

"Unless we break up," she mutters.

I tickle up her sides. "You are quite stubborn—do you know that?"

"I'm practical, Damon. Realistic."

"And I'm in love with you, and I care about your safety. I agree to let you drive it until the end of the semester, whether we break up or not. And once you get a job, you can either buy it from me or give it back. How's that?"

"It *would* be nice not to have to worry," she says tentatively.

I smile at her and kiss her forehead. "I agree. And car shopping is fun. Enjoy it."

"I've never been car shopping before," she says.

"You've never been shopping with my sister before either," I say with a chuckle. "You're in for a treat."

"Actually, we did shop a little the first time I visited you. She made me buy team apparel, and that's where I found those corn socks."

"I love the corn socks. Did you know that I've been wearing them to every game?"

"I didn't know that," she says with a grin.

"And we haven't lost. So, that's on you."

"It's because of the corn socks that the team is winning?"

"Pretty sure."

She kisses me deeply, then says, "You're silly."

"I won't see you until tomorrow. We'll go straight from practice to the team hotel."

"I know the routine now," she says, giving me a really good kiss. The kind that will linger on my lips until tomorrow. "Although, last time, you did manage to make your way back."

Absolutely.

Ainsley

"I HEAR WE'RE going car shopping!" Haley says when I go out to the common area.

"I'm still not sure I'm comfortable with this," I tell her.

Dani stops stirring what I think is sausage gravy and says, "I get it. You want to be an independent woman. Buy your own car, right?"

"Yeah, and I know my car had some issues on this trip, but it has been a good car and just has to get through the semester."

"And it would," Dani says, "if it wasn't for the fact that you're putting so many miles on it, driving here and back for him. He just wants you to be safe. The car he picked out is pretty. I think you'll like it. I like it."

"That means it's expensive," Sammy says with a hoot.

Dani rolls her eyes but smiles and shrugs.

"So, besides that, what do you guys have planned today?" I ask.

"We have a ton of orders that need to be shipped out. The shirts all arrived earlier this week, and we want a quick turnaround. If you guys want, you could help us," Haley says.

I turn toward Sammy, wondering what he thinks.

"I'm cool with that," Sammy agrees.

Dani says, "I thought we'd eat, go to the dealership, pick out the car, and come back here and work. Then we need to take Daine around town and out to lunch. I thought we'd do dinner here up on the roof." She turns to Sammy. "I hear you're a good cook. Would you want to grill?"

"Of course I can!" he says, sounding shocked anyone would think otherwise. "I grew up in Kansas City and come from a big family. I'm practically an expert at grilling."

"Perfect," she says to him. "I've got some big steaks, potatoes, and veggies waiting for us."

"And I'll whip up some brownies," Haley says. "Speaking of Daine, do you think I should go wake him?"

"I'd let him sleep," Sammy says.

I love how he's so easily become part of the group.

"Everyone up but me?" Daine asks a few minutes later.

He moves toward Haley and whispers something in her ear that makes her blush. They're cute together.

"The concert last night was amazing," Sammy says. "And the new song? Love it!"

"People seem to like it," he says humbly. "What's the plan for today?"

Haley fills him in, and we all eat breakfast.

WE WENT TO the car dealership and brought home the car Damon had picked out—which, I will admit, I love. It's a luxury brand, and it's probably going to ruin me for future cars. It's also an SUV, which means once I have the baby, it will be so much easier to deal with a car seat than in my current car.

It's practical, I keep telling myself. Even though I still don't know how I feel about it all.

Damon calls me when we're working on One Eleven orders.

"Hey, Champ," he says.

I step out of the room and walk down the hall so we can speak in private.

"What do you think of the car, really?" he asks.

"It's amazing. Way more than I was expecting. Are you sure about this?"

"Absolutely," he says.

I smile. "Do you remember another time you said *absolutely* to me?"

"Not exactly," he says.

"Then I'm going to remind you. Remember when you gave me the charms and you showed me how you had the number seven engraved on the golf flag?"

"Of course," he says.

"You told me that night on the golf course, where you broke the drought, was literally the best night of your life so far," I tell him. And I can't help but think about how it was also the night I got pregnant. "When I asked if you really meant it, you said—"

"Absolutely," he says, finishing my sentence. "I also practically started crying when I showed you the most important one."

I look down at my bracelet, touch the butterfly charm. "The butterfly."

"Yes, because you're my butterfly. My soulmate. And you always will be. That's why I wanted you in a safe car, really."

Tears fill my eyes just like they did that day.

"Remember, this is just a blip in the timeline of our life to-gether," he says.

SATURDAY, SEPTEMBER 19TH

This moment.

Ainsley

SINCE SAMMY GRILLED up a bunch of steaks last night, we start the day with steak, eggs, and fried potatoes. It's darn good. And since the game doesn't start until two-thirty today, we have some time to kill.

And we do so by sitting up on the rooftop deck, watching all the people who are already tailgating. It's awesome up here because I feel like I'm part of the festivities while being out of the crowd.

Daine and the band join us, as they'll be in the suite with us today. As do Amber and Garrett.

We listen to the sounds below and play cards. It's a fun way to kill some time. Garrett and Sammy hit it off at the concert and are now best friends.

And seem to be teaming up on me, trying to steal my stacks of money in the game. Thankfully, it doesn't work, and while I don't win any of the games, neither do they. Haley seems to have the hot hand today.

ABOUT THREE HOURS before the game, the group from Kansas City arrives—Chase's dad, Damon's mom and Uncle Van, Uncle Tripp, and Damon's dad. Apparently, Jennifer left yesterday to fly to Milan for some Fashion Week events. It's crazy to think the young girl I idolized in a movie married a football player from Kansas City and lives a very normal life—like when she's not jetting off to Milan. And I guess Chase's mom didn't get to come today because of a big soccer tournament that Madden is playing in. And I heard something about the grandparents taking care of the little girls.

ONCE THEY'VE ALL gotten cocktails, Damon's dad says to Dani, "Come on. It's homecoming! We've got to go see all the decor, don't we?"

Dani shrugs. "I suppose. Eddie told us to stop by his frat house. I guess their decor is cool. They re-created a cornfield or something. I don't know."

"And I'm an alum, so we have to stop by my house," Chase's dad says. "Well, technically, it's not where I lived. They knocked that place down years ago and built a new one. But still. Some of my frat brothers said in a group text that they'd be here. It'd be good to see them."

"Why don't you boys go explore?" Dani's mom offers. "We'll meet you at the game."

I can tell the idea of wandering around on campus doesn't thrill her. Of course, I wouldn't want to walk anywhere in the high heels she's wearing.

I'M SITTING IN my usual spot next to Dani when in the beginning of the third quarter, Damon scores his first touchdown of the game. I'm not sure why, but the game has been kind of slow. Like they've have been playing just hard enough not to lose, rather than to win.

And when I stand up to cheer and everyone in the box is calling out Damon's name, I feel it. A flutter in my belly. *A kick?*

I touch my belly as I look around at all the people in the suite and the boy down on the field and wish I could share this moment with them.

With him.

MONDAY, OCTOBER 12TH

Ainsley

I'M SITTING AT the doctor's office, waiting to get called in for an ultrasound. The last few weeks—well, almost a month—have been the longest of my life.

I've been sick. Exhausted.

The week after I was in Nebraska for homecoming, Damon had a bye week and was finally going to visit me. See where I live. But we couldn't risk him getting sick.

The next week, their game was in Maryland, and it was K-State's homecoming. My mom was supposed to attend the game with me, Sammy, and Sammy's parents, but I told her not to come.

This past Saturday was a huge game. So big that a major network chose to broadcast from Lincoln because the matchup featured us against last year's national champions. Two undefeated teams. Conference rivals. Everyone was excited even though some critics predicted a big win for the other team.

I was so looking forward to being there, but what I thought was just a cold turned into a bad case of bronchitis, and Damon insisted that I watch from home and get some rest.

I was really proud of how our team played. It was another high-scoring game, both teams offensive powerhouses, but in the end, we lost by a field goal. Sammy was excited though when he saw that we had moved up to a higher rank despite the loss.

And after a round of antibiotics, I'm finally feeling more like myself.

I get called in and am excited to see the baby again. Hear the heartbeat. See how it's grown. Get scan photos.

When she's about finished up, the tech asks if I'd like to know the sex of the baby. It should be a simple yes or no question. But I immediately think about Damon. I can't find out without him.

"Um, is there any chance you could maybe put the results in an envelope for now? I'd like to find out later," I say.

I don't tell her that the father doesn't know I'm pregnant. That I have been keeping everything to do with the baby—from the positive test to all the doctor notes and information to the ultrasound photos—in a pretty box to share with him after his football season.

"Oh, fun," she says.

When she comes back, she gives me photos of the baby from today as well as a white envelope with the words *BOY OR GIRL?* written in pink and blue marker across the front.

"Just open it when you're ready. Are you doing a gender reveal party?"

"Uh, yeah," I lie. "Thank you."

I go home and add the photo and the envelope to the box, along with the photo of the flowers he sent me when I was sick.

I'm just getting in my car when my mom calls.

"Hey, Mom," I say.

"How are you feeling?"

"Much, much better. Thank you."

"Guess what," Mom says.

"What?"

"I accepted a job with Tripp's foundation."

"That's amazing, Mom. Congratulations. I hope you love it."

"I'll certainly love the hours. More free time. My last day at work is tomorrow. Then I'm taking a couple of weeks off. Going on a vacation." She pauses. "With Hayes."

"Oh, wow. Really? Um, that's nice."

"Do you really feel that way?" she asks.

"We haven't talked as much as we usually do," I say in response. "I feel sort of left out of the story. Did the divorce get finalized?"

"It did."

"I'm assuming Dad never showed up?"

"He didn't."

"Do you worry about him?" I ask her.

"I did, but it just caused me stress. For my own personal mental health, I had to let go. I cannot be expected to be responsible for him anymore. And I won't be. You should let go too," she tells me.

"It's not like I have a choice," I say. "Tell me about Hayes. About what's going on."

"I haven't been keeping it from you on purpose. I just ... you haven't been telling me about what's going on in your life much either."

And she's right about that. I was afraid she would guess that I'm pregnant. Or that I would slip and tell her. I want to tell her. I wish I could tell her. But I can't. Damon has to be the first to know.

"I was planning to tell you when I came for homecoming that we were getting more serious, but then you were sick. And I was worried if the divorce would go through or not. It's been stressful. I'm sorry."

"Thanks, Mom. And I'm happy you're happy."

"Thank you. I'm very lucky to have found him so soon. But at the same time, it feels like a long time coming. On one of our very first dates, we talked about places we wanted to visit. Our dream trips. Funny enough, we wanted to go to the same place. Switzerland. A few days after the divorce was final, he suggested we go."

"That's really sweet," I say.

"And how are things going with Damon? I hear from Van you are a regular in the suite."

"I am. Damon's great, Mom. I really love him. He says we're going to be together for a long time, and I very much hope that he's right."

"I hope so too," she says.

The inside scoop.

Ainsley

"I'VE GOT THE snacks ready," Sammy yells to me as he's spreading food out on the coffee table.

Not sure why he's yelling this when I'm sitting at the kitchen counter, doing homework while he's been cooking.

"So, Minnesota is up today. Should be an easy win," he says when there's a knock at the door.

Sammy rushes to answer it. He leaves the door open and turns to me and says, "It's for you."

I get up and am completely shocked and relieved to see my father.

"Dad!" I say, rushing toward his open arms to get a big hug. "How are you? Where have you been? Why haven't you called?"

"Do you think maybe I could come in before you start in on the twenty questions?" he asks.

"Oh, sure. Sorry. We were just sitting down to watch a football game."

"Yeah, the one your boyfriend is playing in," Dad says.

"How would you know that?"

Dad shrugs. "I don't know. Someone told me."

"Oh, well, I would've loved to tell you myself. Seriously, where have you been? I've been worried about you."

"I'm fine. Just getting my life together."

"And does that life not include me anymore?"

Sammy slowly sits down on the couch. The volume on the TV is turned up, and I notice he doesn't mute it.

"I went to the hospital to see your mom. They said she doesn't work there anymore, and they wouldn't tell me where she lives."

"Why did you go to see her?"

"Do you think I could sit down maybe?" Dad asks.

I mean, we are standing in the open doorway, and it's kind of chilly out.

"Sure," I say with a wave of my hand toward the kitchen table. "Have a seat. Would you like a soda or something?"

"Whatever you have," Dad replies.

While I'm pouring him a Coke over ice, I take a moment to study him. He looks different. Hair cut shorter and in an actual style. He's wearing a bomber jacket with the words Versace on it. And I wonder if it's real. I sort of assume it is because he certainly doesn't look like he's been living on the streets.

"How did you get here?" I ask him as I set the drink on the table in front of him.

"Drove. Got a new car. It's hot."

"What kind is it?" Sammy interrupts.

"Maserati. Want to come see it?"

A Maserati?

"Can we wait until halftime?" Sammy asks. "Our game is about to start."

Dad nods toward the couch. "Mind if I watch it with you?"

Sammy shrugs, but I say, "Yes, I mind!"

Dad rolls his eyes. "Fine. I left rehab because I didn't need it. I don't have a problem. I just made a couple of bad … we'll call them business decisions. It's all cool now. I'm golden. Back on top. Loving life."

"So, let me get this right. You're still gambling, and you've made enough to show up here in a Maserati, wearing Versace, but you didn't ever have the time to call your daughter and tell her you were still alive? Or to give back some of the money that you lost?"

"Yes. That's correct," Dad says, shutting me down.

I stand in stunned silence.

But then Dad goes, "So, give me the inside scoop. I heard that Damon was questionable for today's game."

Sammy shakes his head. "He bruised his thumb at the end of the last game. He's fine. I think, sometimes, they extend injuries so the other team doesn't know what to expect."

"So, he's playing?" Dad's eyes get big, and he grabs his phone. "That makes a difference."

He presses a few buttons, and I suddenly realize what just happened. He placed a bet. He only came here to get the scoop on Damon.

"Why did you go to the hospital to see Mom?" I ask him.

"She changed her phone number, and I don't know where she lives now, so I—"

"I didn't change *my* number. Neither did your brothers. Also, did you know that you are now legally divorced?"

Dad looks quite surprised, but then a smile spreads across his face. "Sweet. That's what I wanted to talk to her about. I've met someone new."

"Awesome," I mutter as he moves to the couch.

HE STAYS FOR the whole game, constantly checking his phone and constantly asking me and Sammy for information.

I shake my head imperceptibly at Sammy, so he usually just shrugs.

When the game is almost over, Dad hops up and says, "Well, it's been real." He pulls out a card and hands it to me. It's like a business card—white with gold embossed letters that spell out his name and phone number. "Keep in touch. I'd love to hear more about Damon's season."

The second he breezes out our door, I turn to Sammy, who looks at me with wide eyes and says, "What the hell was that?"

"He was making and checking bets the whole time. Do you think the only reason he came here was because I'm dating Damon?"

"Yeah, that's exactly what I'm thinking. I'm glad we didn't tell him anything. Not that we know much, but still. It would be like a big deal if someone related to Damon was betting on his games. Like, it would be serious. He could get kicked off the team."

"But we're not related," I argue as I look it up on the phone.

But then I read what all it says about it.

I set my phone down with a sob. "I'm never going to be able to marry Damon."

"After the game, tell him what happened. Maybe he can tell his coach. Put it on record so they can never come after him for it."

AND I DO, spilling my guts to Damon the second he video-calls me after the game.

"We didn't tell him anything. Well, that's not true. He asked about your thumb injury. Heard you were questionable for the game. Sammy was like, *Oh, no, he's fine.* And then I know Dad placed a bet. That's all he did during the game—press buttons on his phone. Scroll through statistics. And you know what that means, right?" I ask him, tears filling my eyes. "This could jeopardize your career."

Damon looks shocked, then concerned. "First of all, are you okay? I can't believe your dad just showed up like that, unannounced."

"If he shows up again, I will not be inviting him in. Mom's right. We don't deserve the stress, and he doesn't deserve my love. At least not right now. Not when he's like this. I don't even know who that person was."

"Let me talk to my dad about all this, okay?"

"Okay," I tell him.

LATER THAT NIGHT, when he calls me before bed, he tells me that he spoke to his coach.

"I explained the situation," he says. "Told him what happened. That you don't plan to have further contact with your father, but that you might have shared something others didn't know before the game started. We reported the violation, explaining the circumstances and what we expect to happen, going forward. You really can't talk to him about me or anything football related again."

"I won't. I'm so sorry, Damon."

"It's not your fault, Champ."

"Thanks. I love you. Good night."

"Sweet dreams," he says.

Rethink that.

Ainsley

"YOU LOOK A little puffy. Are you retaining water?" Sammy asks me this morning. "You're supposed to drop pounds when you eat healthy, don't drink alcohol, and work out. Not look like you've been bingeing. Do you think you need to go to the doctor?"

"I'm fine."

"Maybe it's food allergies. Have you thought of cutting out— I don't know—like sugar, or dairy, or gluten?"

"I'm having a hard time with sugar. I've been craving it, probably because I stopped drinking wine."

"Yeah, I've heard that could happen," he says. "And are you still driving up to Lincoln today?"

"Yeah, I was planning to leave in a couple of hours," I tell him.

"Hmm, you may want to rethink that. They are maybe supposed to get an ice storm. The news called it a two-faced storm. Like a bad best friend," he hoots. "Apparently, depending on its track, people on one side of the storm will get ice and snow, and the other side will get severe thunderstorms with hail and possible tornados. Lincoln is right on the line."

"It seems awfully early for that," I tell him.

To be honest, I've been nervous about going up there this weekend. I'm twenty-four weeks now and most definitely showing. I can hide it under baggy sweatshirts—and although Sammy just hinted about my weight gain, he hasn't even once wondered if I could be pregnant. But my relationship with Damon is much different, and he would notice. In fact, even though it's not the end of his season yet, I've resigned myself to the fact that I'm going to have to tell him earlier than I thought. It's crazy, really, how my body has changed. How growing a baby does that. It's both beautifully amazing while equally terrifying.

But if there's a storm … it would give him a little more time.

"I should probably call Damon," I tell Sammy. "See what the weather up there is saying."

"You definitely should. Did you know that one time, when I was a little kid, my parents were driving down I-70 between Lawrence and Kansas City and they could see not one, but two tornados in their rearview mirror? They were twins! Twin tornados."

"What happened?!" I ask, my eyes wide. Because I can't imagine having my child in the car and seeing something like that.

"My mom looked up the radar and saw they were supposed to go north, and she made my dad turn south, even though that's not where they were heading to. It was a good call because those tornados ended up doing some damage in northern KC."

"You were lucky." I nod.

"And I'd like *you* to be lucky by staying home with me this weekend. I'll be a nervous wreck if you try to drive through that. And you might go all the way up there, only for them to cancel the game. And maybe even Halloween! I'm calling Damon," he says, quickly picking up his phone and hitting a few buttons. "I need to hear this firsthand."

I can't help but laugh.

"Damon," he says into his phone, then puts it on speaker so I can hear. "I'm glad I caught you. Tell me about this storm. I'm worried Ainsley is going to be stubborn and try to drive through that mess."

"I was actually just going to call Ainsley about it," Damon says.

"You're on speaker," Sammy tells him. "Say hi, Ainsley."

"Hi, Ainsley," I tease.

"Champ," Damon says, making my heart melt with just one word. "I agree with Sammy. I don't want you driving up. There's even talk of postponing or rescheduling the game, depending which side of the storm we end up on. If we get some snow, it wouldn't be that bad, but thunderstorms can cause issues. We certainly can't play during severe weather."

"They are saying that fall and winter weather will be separated by just a few miles," Sammy says, playing into the hype. He gives me a pointed look.

"Fine," I say. "I'll spend Halloween with Sammy. Oh, the joy," I say sarcastically.

"More like an Almond Joy," Sammy says. "I'm going to buy all the candy."

"Will you have trick-or-treaters at your apartment?" Damon asks.

"Well, if I have to lure a hot guy or two here," Sammy replies, "candy might work."

"And I think, on that note, I need to be getting back to my

workout," Damon says.

"Bye! Call me tonight!" I tell him before Sammy hangs up.

"Looks like you're stuck with me," Sammy says. "Maybe we should stop the ban on alcohol and drink tonight. I'll even splurge for wine in a bottle."

"I probably won't, but I will pour for you. And I'll even take care of dinner."

"Hmm." He seems to seriously think about this because he thinks he's a better cook than I am. But I might purposely let him think that. "What would dinner consist of exactly? I'm not being critical, just need to pair the wine properly."

"I think you know if I'm taking care of dinner on a night like tonight, when my plans have gotten all messed up, it means pizza will be involved," I say with a laugh.

"A red wine it is then."

SATURDAY, OCTOBER 31ST

Most delicious.

Ainsley

SAMMY AND I turn on the Nebraska game. They are playing USC, and it's supposed to be very close, if you follow the betting lines.

For obvious reasons, I do not, but even though Sammy doesn't bet on games, he says he likes to know what the experts expect the game to be like.

Lincoln ended up on the thunderstorm side of things, but it moved through the area quickly, meaning their mid-afternoon kickoff time was not affected. Nearby Omaha has two inches of snow.

It's funny. I remember Halloween as a kid. How Mom would make sure my costume was big enough that I could wear my coat under it if need be. I think about my own baby, taking it trick-or-treating someday.

"This game is too close," Sammy says, opening another Toot-sie Roll.

He's been nervously chewing on them most of this quarter. He was serious when he said he was buying a bunch of candy. And he got his favorite peanut butter cups and Snickers bars for me.

To be honest, as a kid, trick-or-treating freaked me out. First, I'm told not to talk to strangers and especially to never take candy from them, and then I'm told to walk up to their front door and ask for just that.

And Sammy is right. The game is too close. We're down by a field goal, and there's only a few minutes left in the game.

"I thought you were supposed to find a, um, partner to share your candy with," I tease as the opposing team takes a time-out.

"Yeah, well, I had options, trust me, but I'm still really not over Roman."

"Tell that to the random men you've been seeing."

"Fine, I'm rebounding." He rolls his eyes. "In the most delicious of ways, but eventually, that gets old, and you just want someone to love."

"Are you still talking to Apollo?" I inquire about the guy who works at the Archibald Lodge.

"We keep in touch. He was telling me though that rumor has it that your uncle is considering a new project in Kansas City next, and if it turns out to be true, he'd love to transfer there. Which means we'd be in the same place. And he said if we were, he'd be interested in exploring our relationship further."

"And how do you feel about that?" I ask, not wanting to interject my feelings into it.

"I think he could be my penguin, honestly."

"Your penguin?" I ask.

"Or my wolf, or my bald eagle, my goose, or my beaver."

I break out in laughter. "I don't think you have one of those."

"Oh, hush, you. I'm just naming animals that mate for life."

"Ahh, that's sweet. You think it could be something?"

"In my dreams, yes. Do I think, in reality, a guy like him

would want me?" He shrugs as the game comes back on and our team lines up.

"Oh, come on. You are very good-looking, Sammy. And if you weren't gay …"

He rolls his eyes at me. "Keep the compliments coming. I love them—oh, go! Go! Goooooooooo!" he yells, standing up and pretending to run along with Damon.

Chase throws a beautiful, long spiral, and Damon is running down the sideline into the end zone when he looks over his shoulder and adjusts his speed, the ball landing in his outstretched hands.

"Touchdown!" Sammy yells. "We win! We win!"

AFTER THE GAME, Damon calls me.

"That was quite the catch to seal your victory," I tell him.

"It's crazy, isn't it? That we've only lost one game this year? I mean, that was our goal, of course—to go undefeated—but at the same time, the team didn't even go to a bowl game last year."

"I think it's amazing how two best friends, who are talented and confident, can have an effect on a whole team. I'm so happy for you."

"I'm happy you're happy. Kind of weird though, not having you or the family here to celebrate after the game. It's just me, Dani, and Chase tonight. Although Treyvon is here too. Dani made us tacos with all the fixings. Can't wait to dig in."

"I'll let you go do that. Again, congrats. You're amazing."

"In bed?" he teases. It's become our running joke.

"One hundred percent," I say with a grin as we end our conversation. "And happy Halloween, Damon!"

TUESDAY, NOVEMBER 3RD

I'm not telling you.

Ainsley

"I CAN'T STOP thinking about you," Damon says to me during one of our nightly phone calls. "I miss you so much."

I'm sitting on the couch, smiling, when Sammy walks in the door.

"I miss you too," I tell Damon, then say, "Hey, Sammy just got home and we have to work on our project, so I should probably go."

"That's okay. I have homework too. Love you, Champ," he says as I end the call.

Sammy comes to stand in front of me, looking perplexed. But then he crosses his arms across his chest and starts tapping his foot.

"What's up?" I ask, wondering what his latest drama is.

"Are you pregnant?" he asks me.

My eyes get big. "Do I look pregnant?" I ask, trying to look offended and not guilty.

"You did just now. We talked the other day about how you look puffy. I haven't wanted to just come out and say it, but you've most definitely gained weight this semester. And although I was trying to be careful about broaching such a delicate subject, I've been worried about you. Looking up weight gain causes, like thyroid issues, food allergies, even cancer! But now it's so obvious to me. You're sleeping more, eating more, so incredibly picky about food."

"I'm tired, hungry, and trying to eat healthier," I reply.

"When you were on the phone, you were rubbing your belly. And it just hit me. You're having his baby. Aren't you? But the real question is, why haven't you told me?"

I let out a sigh. "Because I haven't told anyone. And I'm not telling you now."

"Not even the father?" he asks, looking stunned.

"That's correct."

"But why? It's not like you can really hide it anymore."

"No one has noticed at school. You didn't notice until just now. If I'm pregnant, trust me, Damon will be the first one I tell. But he needs to get through this season first."

"This season?! That's bullshit. If you don't tell him, I will!"

"I would deny it," I say seriously.

Sammy sighs. "You really love him, huh?" he says softly, sitting down next to me.

"Yes, I do. And you know that."

"You two talk all the time. You're still together. It wasn't just some summer fling. So, what I don't understand is, why? Why haven't you told him? Or told me? I feel very emotional about this. You and I tell each other everything. And now I'm distraught!"

"I told you, Sammy. No one knows until he knows. Period. I have my reasons. Important reasons. And that should be good enough for you."

"Well, it's not! I could've been there for you. This whole time. You shouldn't have kept it a secret. And he's a great guy. You can't do this to him. Seriously, if you don't give me a good reason this second, I'm going to call him."

I judge his serious expression. And know he's not fibbing about that.

"For one, it will cause a huge scandal if anyone other than Damon finds out. And that would take his focus off his game, his season, his career. *His dream.* I can't do that to him. He deserves this time to focus."

"So, you're going to hide the baby until he gets drafted?"

"Just until Thanksgiving."

"That's only a few weeks away."

I nod.

"How far along are you?"

"I'm not telling!"

He marches off in a fury. "You are so stubborn sometimes!"

BUT THEN HE comes back a few moments later, sits next to me, and just pulls me into a hug. "You've been going through this all on your own."

"Yes," I exhale, the weight of his statement hitting me. "I'm doing it for him."

Sammy sighs. "It's kind of romantic," he says to me.

"I think so."

"Do you really think this is smart though?"

"You've seen how they're doing. What they are capable of this season with focus. He's going to find out soon anyway."

"And then we will really find out if he can handle the pressure."

"You're right. And it's given me time. To adjust to the news. To feel the baby grow. To make sure Damon is not only going to be a good dad, but a good partner."

"I love you, Ainsley. You know I'm here for you—always. No matter what. And for your baby."

A tear falls down my cheek as I rub a circle across my stomach.

It's then that I feel another kick.

SATURDAY, NOVEMBER 7TH

Turbulence.

Ainsley

"ANOTHER SATURDAY, ANOTHER win," I say to Damon when he video-chats with me after his game. This week, they played in California. "Sammy went back home for the weekend, so I made myself some hot wing dip and watched it by myself. I might have yelled at the TV a time or two."

It was the first game I hadn't either been at or watched with Sammy. And I might have been doing my own play-by-play, talking through the game and telling our baby exactly how their daddy was doing—which, for part of the game, was not that great. The team really struggled.

"It was a rough one," Damon says. He's freshly showered, his hair still wet. And looking different from when I watched him speak at the postgame press conference a little bit ago. "We had bad turbulence on the plane going there, and it seems like it was indicative of the game we played."

"It *was* turbulent. Chase threw two interceptions. Got sacked multiple times. The reporters, of course, were going for the kill. Saying that your weaknesses were being exposed."

"They were, honestly. Our offensive line was being manhandled, and I don't know how many sacks they ended up with, but it was way too many. The defense was lethargic. We were a mess."

"But you stuck with it. I'm always amazed how one play can change the momentum in a game."

"Yeah, the defense's pick six was huge and put us back within two touchdowns."

"The comeback of the century, according to those same reporters, who were suddenly singing your praises. They thought you were going to go the safe route, kick the field goal, tie the game, go to overtime, and hash it out there."

"But we had other plans," he says with a smile.

"As usual, I watched your postgame interview. You did really well, Damon. But you always do. You're good at public speaking. I think I would get up there and freeze."

"I just try to talk to them like I would a friend," he says with a shrug. "That makes it easy."

"Except they were pretty brutal with some of their questions. Especially the one about if you are overrated."

He rolls his eyes, causing me to laugh.

"That's exactly the expression you had when he asked. You rolled your eyes."

He chuckles. "I try not to do that. To let them get to me, but …"

"You stood up for your team. Mostly Chase. Is he feeling okay? Some of those hits were pretty brutal."

"I'd say he's going to be sore tomorrow, but right now, he's flying pretty high. We all are."

"And did you happen to see who lost today?" I say, referring to the team that served up their one and only loss of the season so far.

"We sure did. If things keep going as planned, we'll be playing in the conference championship."

A lusty blur.

Ainsley

"HEY, CHAMP," DAMON says when I answer his request to video chat.

I let out a dreamy sigh the second I see his handsome face. Because how did I get so lucky to have such an adorable boy fall in love with me? He's so sweet and confident. Family and friendships are incredibly important to him. And he's so driven to perfect the game that he loves.

"You look sexy," I tell him, doing a little whistle at his shirtless torso, mussed hair, and the little blond scruff on his face. *And that smile?* I swear it lights up my world.

The baby has been quiet, but the second it hears Damon's voice, it perks up. Like the baby has some innate pull toward the amazing man who helped create it.

"It would be sexier if you were here with me."

"That I know," I say with a grin. "But me finding a job is pretty important. And I'm starting to get nervous I'm not going to find one. I've submitted over a hundred résumés over the last month, and it's like they all just went into some kind of vortex and disappeared from the face of the earth. Seriously, only about ten percent have even acknowledged the fact that I applied. I have excellent references and grades. What is even more incredible is that after I flunked a semester during my freshman year, I'll be graduating with honors."

"Don't stress," he says. "You do have a fallback plan."

"No, I don't," I say, looking confused.

"Yeah, you do. I can support you. Actually, I'd prefer that was *the* plan, not the backup."

I laugh. "Because we know that Damon Diamond doesn't do backup."

"Damn straight," he says with a grin. "But seriously, we have a free place to stay and could live very comfortably on my NIL money until I get drafted. Like Chase and Dani."

"Dani has career dreams of her own. Big ones. Like I do. I also worked hard to get my degree, and I want to be able to support myself." *And my baby—well, our baby.*

"And I appreciate that," he says. "So, how did the fair go?"

"I had three prescheduled interviews and gave résumés to five other places, so hopefully, someone will want to talk with me further."

"I'm sure they will," he says. "Are any of the jobs anywhere near Lincoln?"

"A couple are work from home."

"And if you got one of those, would you come here?"

"Hmm, you might have to talk me into it," I tease.

"Oh, well, in that case, Miss Archibald, I should mention that a job in Lincoln would offer some very special perks." He raises his eyebrows and grins.

"And what kind of perks are we talking about?" I know exactly what he's thinking, but I want to hear him say it.

He stands up, revealing the rest of himself.

"Damon! Have you been sitting there naked this whole time?" I screech-laugh.

"Just got out of the shower. Making sure I'm thoroughly dry before putting on my suit for the walk to the stadium."

"Now I really wish I were there," I say. "You're so beautiful."

"Are you referring to me or him?" he says, pointing downward.

I put my hand up to cover my eyes. "I wasn't prepared to see that. But I like it. And I'd say both."

"Excellent," he says. "Now for the most important question of the day. Are you going to be reading while you're watching my game?"

To this, I laugh. "I can't believe I even told you that," I say, remembering our time in the Ozarks. "You told me it was unacceptable."

"I definitely remember. And if I recall, I told you that you could read, but that I'd be trying my best to get you to look up."

"Well, whatever you're doing is working. You've been winning a lot of games."

"Does that mean you're going to be cheering my name?" he teases.

"Pretty sure I already have. *In more ways than one.*"

"You have a naughty mind," he tells me.

"Because you're naked!"

"So, enough about me," he says.

"No, wait. Are you going to win? Like, do you think you will?"

"We're playing a worthy opponent."

"Sammy says that Vegas predicts it's going to be a close game, but you are expected to lose."

"Whatever. We're going to blow them away. By at least two touchdowns."

"That would move you up in the rankings significantly, wouldn't it?"

"It would put us into the top eight, which is what we need to make the playoffs—that or a conference championship. It's been six years since we won one, so I think we're about due. Of course, that was before they had me and Chase."

"Here comes the cocky boy I know and love."

"You love me?" he whispers.

"I do," I tell him.

"Then I will do my best to make you look up."

"I've been doing that all season, Damon. Actually, that isn't true. I haven't even thought about reading. It's possible that you might have turned me into a diehard fan."

"Good," he says. "Because although I like having lots of fans, you're the only one I need."

"Then win for me today," I tell him.

"That I can do."

WHEN HE CALLS me after the game, he says, "Looks like I'm going to have to promise to win every game for you from now on."

"You definitely shocked the announcers, but they quickly got on the bandwagon. And you, Damon, played spectacularly. That reception where you went up over the defender and caught it with one hand—actually, not even your hand. It was like your fingertips. They showed the replay of it four times!"

"Remember in the Ozarks, when we were working out?" he asks.

"I think watching you work out is kind of a lusty blur." He laughs, but then I say, "I actually do remember. You told me you were lifting those colorful little dumbbells with just your fingertips for finger strength. That Chase needed it for throwing, you for catching. At the time, I thought it looked silly, but I'm sure glad you've been working out. Congrats on a great game."

Which news?

Ainsley

"It's about time you got home!" Sammy says the second I walk through the door.

"Was I supposed to meet you or something?"

"I've just been dying to tell you. I accepted a job offer this morning!"

I give him a hug. "That's amazing. Which job?"

"In-house designer at that high-end furniture store. I think it will be so much fun. The customers will come to me, and I can become an expert at what the store has to offer. Plus, this extrovert will love the daily interaction with all the people who come to shop. It's a combination of salary and commission, and I'm pumped. And my store location is in Country Club Plaza, and you know I love that area of Kansas City. I'll only be about an hour from my family."

"Congratulations, Sammy," I say sincerely as tears I can't seem to control roll down my cheeks. "I'm so happy for you."

He gives me a hug. "You'll find something."

"Damon wants me to move to Lincoln. Says he can support

me.”

"And why are you not doing that?"

"Because I didn't go to college for four and a half years to be—"

"A full-time mother?"

"Would you suggest I go live with Damon if I wasn't pregnant?"

"Heck yeah, I would. To be honest, when Roman and I were dating this summer, the thought crossed my mind. He mentioned that with his schedule and income, I wouldn't need to work. I could live a life of leisure."

"Would you have done that?" I wonder.

"Obviously, in retrospect, that wouldn't have worked long-term, so I'm glad I have a job of my own—ah, I love saying that. I have a job of my own. It's totally empowering."

"And see, that's how I feel. I need to be able to support this child on my own."

"Don't give up hope. You had some good interviews."

"I did, and with Thanksgiving this week, I'm sure I won't hear until after the holiday weekend. In the meantime, I need to get something to eat and then focus on my design project."

"Just wondering, if you don't get a job in Lincoln, maybe you could find something in KC and live with me. We could save money that way, and we get along so well. I can't imagine having another roommate, and I'm not sure I'm ready to live alone."

"Even with a baby?" I ask, surprised.

"Yes, Ainsley, even with a baby."

"You're so wonderful, Sammy. I'm so lucky I met you."

"I feel the same," he says.

WE'RE JUST SITTING down for a lunch of pasta with red sauce and spinach when my phone vibrates.

I answer, feeling excited when I see the name of one of the companies I interviewed with yesterday.

When I get off the phone, Sammy grins and says, "So?"

"That was the online design company. They want me."

"I heard that," he says, "but why didn't you accept right away?"

"Because they told me to take the weekend and let them know on Monday." I no more than get the words out of my mouth when my phone rings again.

"It must be both our lucky days," I tell Sammy after I end my call.

"Two job offers in one day?!" he says excitedly. "I'll drink to that. In fact, I think I will." He gets up, grabs two glasses, and fills them with sparkling water, then sits back down. "First, a toast. To us. May we make millions doing what we love."

"Hear, hear," I say, clinking my glass against his.

"So, which job are you going to take?" he asks.

"I don't know. I'm going to think about it this weekend."

"And how is Thanksgiving with the family going to work exactly? Seeing Damon? It's pretty obvious that you're pregnant right now."

"I have a plan."

"And what is that?"

"It's just my mom and me for Thanksgiving this year. Everyone else is either vacationing or going up to the football game. Even though I want Damon to be the first to know, I don't know if I will be able to hide it from my mom. Either way, I'll drive to Iowa for the game on Friday and tell Damon."

"How do you think he'll take it?" Sammy asks. "Because I think he's going to be pissed."

"There's not much I can do about it now. I'll explain why I waited. It was for him, remember?"

"Yeah, I remember. Totally disagreed, just for the record. But I know your heart is in the right place, and I understand. It's pretty clear you're crazy about him."

"It is, but I was thinking about my parents. How my dad didn't lie to my mom at the beginning of their relationship, but rather omitted a big, important truth. And I know I'm doing that now. I keep thinking about my dad. I didn't tell you, but he texted me and asked me about a game. I blocked his number."

"I'm sorry."

"I just don't want this to erode my relationship with Damon. Because you're right. I can't wait any longer. And I miss him and want to see him. Funny thing is though, no one at school has said anything."

"You're carrying the baby well. But in general, people are afraid to, in case you just gained weight or something."

"I suppose that's true," I say, checking the clock. "But back to the jobs. I know which one I will accept. In fact, I'm going to do a video call with Damon and tell him the news."

"*Which* news?" he asks with a smirk.

I wave my hand through the air and grab my phone. Damon answers right away.

"Hey," I say, practically bursting with excitement.

"You sound happy."

"That's because I just got offered two jobs."

"That's amazing. Congrats. What would you be doing and where?"

"Well, the one I am going to accept will allow me to live anywhere I want."

My comment hangs there for a second before his face breaks out in a wide smile.

"Does that mean we get to be together?"

"If you still want me," I tell him.

"Oh, I most definitely want you," he says. "I'm so excited you're coming to my game against Iowa this weekend. Sucks that it's away, so we won't get to hang out much. But I'll have some free time on Friday. And a lot of family will be there."

"I can't wait!"

He tells me that he's got to run to his team meeting, which is starting shortly, so we end the call.

And I just sit and think dreamily about finally telling him. And pray that he takes it well.

WEDNESDAY, NOVEMBER 25TH

Ainsley

"IT'S REALLY GOTTEN cold out," Sammy says, tightening his coat against his neck as we walk home from a dinner with some friends from class.

"As Pooh Bear would say, *It's a blustery day*," I tell him, but then again, I love fall.

"The wind is cold. And look at the sky. It almost looks like it could snow," he says.

"No way. It's too early for that. Plus, it can't snow. I have places to go this weekend. And so do you."

"I'm just sayin'," he says.

When we get home, I go to my room, take off my shoes, and put on my warm slippers.

"I'm turning the heat up," he says, just as my phone buzzes with a weather alert.

"Wow, you were right. Our area—really, a lot of Kansas and Nebraska are in a winter storm watch."

He grabs the remote and flips on the TV to the local news. And what it's showing is not good.

"Sleet starting tonight, wintery mix on Thanksgiving, and snow on Friday and into Saturday," he says. "Well, shoot. That's going to mess up both our plans."

"And we purposely let ourselves get low on groceries since we were going to be gone."

His eyes get big. "Give me your keys. I'm going to the store."

"To get what?" I ask him.

"I don't know! Everything! Before it's all sold out!"

ABOUT THIRTY MINUTES later, Damon calls. "Have you seen the weather forecast?"

"Sammy and I were out to dinner with some friends from class, so we saw it when we got home."

"I don't want you driving in that. They are saying that your area could get two to three inches of ice tonight with snow tomorrow."

"I think my mother just heard you," I say as a text pops up from her. "She doesn't want me driving either. Will they cancel your game?"

"The weather isn't supposed to be bad in Lincoln until Friday afternoon, but they moved up our timeline so that we'll leave before the ice hits. The good news is, if the storm follows the predicted track, it will miss Iowa City."

I let out a sigh. I was eager to see him.

Eager to tell him.

To get it off my chest. To stop keeping this secret.

And just to see his face.

I pray every night before I go to sleep that he will be happy. That he will still love me. That he won't hate me.

And that it won't negatively impact him. His game. His team.

Us.

"That was a big sigh," he says. "I'm disappointed too. I haven't held you in my arms in way too long."

"I know. It sucks."

"And it's going to be crazy busy between now and Christmas. If we win this game, we'll go to the conference championship."

"Where will it be held?"

"Indianapolis. You think you can come? I'm sure my dad will get a box. It's next Saturday."

"Gosh, I don't think I can. I have to finish my final design projects. I don't know how I'm going to get it all done. One is on lighting, and it's very technical. I can pick out light fixtures, place lamps, and choose the perfect light bulbs, but the mechanics of getting it all on the architectural design is literally my least favorite thing. For my internship, we didn't have to deal with it. The hotel lighting plans were done, as they should have been, by an electrical engineer. But they want us to understand it all. I have most everything chosen for my other interior project, but it's still a lot to put together. Then Sammy and I graduate on the twelfth. But I'll try."

"That's before finals week, isn't it?"

"Yeah, I guess when they used to hold it after finals, a lot of people didn't attend the ceremony. I mean, everyone is always ready to leave as soon as their tests are over."

"I want to come to your graduation, but if we win the conference championship, I'll have practice that Saturday. If we don't, I'll be there, for sure."

"While I'd love for you to be there, I would much prefer you keep winning," I tell him. "Do you know yet when you will get to go home for the holidays?"

"Coach already said that if we end up in the playoffs, we should plan on only getting two days off—Christmas Eve and Christmas."

"Hmm, so our Christmastime plan may not work out either?"

"No. I'll be home for the holiday. Actually, I'll be wherever you are. Where will you be?"

"In Kansas City, at my mom's place."

"Perfect. That means you can come to Lincoln with me the day after Christmas, and we'll get you all moved in. It may not be a long Christmas holiday together, but at least we'll be living together after that."

"Sounds like a dream. It feels like this semester has flown by, but at the same time, it seems like it's been so slow because I've been counting down the days until we can live in the same place."

"I'm really glad you chose the job you did," he says.

"Neither job was a dream job, so I chose the one that would allow me to live with you. Do you think it will work?"

"Us?" he asks.

"Yeah. Like, us living together. On a daily basis. Every-single-day kind of thing."

"When Dani and Chase moved in, they each had their own condo. My sister felt like it gave them both space, and she says it allowed them to date. To keep some of the mystery before they decided if they were going to be together forever. You could do that too. We don't have to live together completely."

"I want to live with you, Damon. Do you want space like that?"

"I do not. At all. I want you as close to me as you can get. And most definitely in my bed. Every. Single. Night."

And the way he says it makes it sound like a threat.

Of the most delicious kind.

"All right," he says, "I've got to go. I'll text you before bed. Love you, Champ."

"Love you too," I say dreamily.

I'm still sitting here in a sexy daydream when the front door bursts open and slams against the wall.

"You have no idea!" Sammy says. "The bread was nearly gone. Everyone was buying up all the water and toilet paper. We're talking three, maybe four days of slick streets. It's not the apocalypse, people."

I get up and hold the door open for him. "Did you manage to get anything?" I ask, but I can see that he did because he's loaded down with a bunch of bags.

"Of course I did. I'm a forager. I bought a turkey and all the fixings. We'll have our own Thanksgiving dinner. I created a list of planned meals, game-day snacks galore, and lots of ice cream and chocolate. I even got a few bottles of wine for myself. I figure we'll be either watching football, movie marathoning, or card game playing."

"Or maybe working on our projects?"

"Can't really do that. The school is closed for the holiday. All our stuff is there. And besides, how often do we get snow days? We're going to bask in the glory of it. We're going to reflect on our time together and celebrate our futures." He gets misty. "Our futures apart. I can't believe I'm not going to get to live with you anymore. I'm going to be so lonely. Maybe I'll get a fish."

"That should be a suitable replacement for me," I tease.

"Oh my stars! I did *not* mean it that way."

I grin at him and start putting food away. "I know you didn't. And I agree. We'll have fun."

"I was thinking about something on the way home. This is sort of a freak storm. We usually don't get ice this early. Maybe you really *aren't* supposed to tell Damon until his season is over."

"The regular season will be over this weekend, but if they win, they will go to the conference championship, and if they make the playoffs, they could play up to four additional games."

"Which go until mid-January," he says.

"Right."

"So then, whenever you see him next, however those stars align, that's when you'll tell him."

"Yes, I will."

You're fire.

Ainsley

"AINSLEY," MY UNCLE Tripp says when I answer his call.

I'm sitting on the couch, reading, while a Kansas City game is playing in the background.

"Hey, how are you?"

"Good. Wish you could have come to the game on Saturday. We ended up being able to fly up for it, and we've already secured a suite for the conference championship. You want to hitch a ride?"

"Is it possible to let you know at the last minute? All my final projects are due that Monday. I'm pushing to get them done before. And if they make the playoffs, I will definitely take you up on it."

"Of course. I'll hold you a seat and a ticket. Damon's a really gifted player."

"I know, and I actually started watching the whole game instead of reading through them," I say with a chuckle.

"Now that the small talk is over," he says. "Your mother told me that you were offered a job. Have you accepted it yet?"

"I actually got two offers. I'm supposed to call and let them know tomorrow."

"Are you excited about them?"

"Well, one is with a commercial firm based out of Des Moines. They specialize in workspaces for offices, so I'd mostly be doing CAD designs of cubicles. It won't be nearly as fun as working with you, Jadyn, and the team. And I'm not thrilled about the location. So, I'm planning to take the other one. It's residential design, which isn't my preference, but I can work from anywhere, and it pays decent, so it makes sense."

"You don't sound all that excited."

"I am excited that I could work from anywhere."

"Anywhere, like Lincoln?" he asks.

"Exactly," I reply.

"Well, I'm about to throw a monkey wrench into your plan because *I* want to offer you a job. The only problem is, it's also not exactly what you're looking for, and you'd be based in Kansas City. At least for the first two years."

"Is it for your hotels? Or something else?"

"It would be for the hotels. As you heard me tell my investors on the yacht, we're going to build a hotel near the stadium, but the plan has grown significantly since then. We've been buying up land all around it, and we finally got the area rezoned for retail development."

"Oh, wow. Can I just accept it now?" I say with a laugh.

"You can't do that. Don't ever do that," he chastises. "You need to know everything about the role—where it would be located, the working conditions, as well as the compensation package—before you make a decision."

"I was kind of joking. But I would love to hear about it."

"You would office out of our corporate building in The Plaza. I think you are aware that when Jadyn sold me her company, we agreed she would consult and not get involved in the everyday decision-making. But she's as passionate as I am about what we're doing and is working more than she should. Your job would be a hybrid role. Part of the time, you would serve as Jadyn's executive assistant."

"Oh," I say, trying to not sound disappointed. I mean, I'd love to work with her, but I want to design spaces.

"Before you say anything," Tripp says, "the other part of your role would be making design choices and project management. It would give you a chance to learn every aspect of what she does."

"I like the design part," I say tentatively.

"Ainsley, you are quite organized, incredibly talented, and I can't think of anyone better for the role. And the reason why I'm hoping you are interested is because it would be on-the-job training. You would learn everything you can from Jadyn. After six months, you'd start taking over tasks. In eighteen months to two years, you'd take over completely, and she would only consult a few hours a week."

"Are you serious?" I gasp. *Talk about the dream job.*

"I am. Aside from your talent, I need someone in this position who I can trust. And so far, even with some of the designers we've outsourced to, we haven't found the right person. I'm hoping that person can be you."

"I would love that."

"Excellent. And now to the terms."

He runs through the full compensation package. How I would need to spend a couple of days a week in the office, but could choose to work from home or wherever on others.

Once he's done, he says, "So, it's up to you. And there are additional perks," he tells me, a smile in his voice. "You're going to need an SUV to haul around materials and such, so a new company car could be in your future. And of course, a country club membership. We do a lot of business on the golf course, so you'll need to keep up on your game."

"What? Are you serious? It's an amazing offer, Uncle Tripp. Can I have a few hours to think about it?" I need to call Damon.

"Just call me tomorrow with your answer."

I could eventually run the design team?

I glance down at my belly.

In a few weeks, I'll tell Damon he's going to be a dad.

He wanted me to move in with him without knowing I was pregnant. With a baby in the mix, he definitely will want me to.

But how do I pass up an opportunity like this?

Before I chicken out, I call him so we can video chat.

"Hey, beautiful," he says.

"Hey to you," I say, noting his sleeveless T-shirt and how every time I see him, his biceps look bigger. I want to just sit and stare at them. "Um, I have something to tell you. I got another job offer. An incredible offer, and I just don't know how I could turn it down."

"Well, congratulations then," he says.

"There's a catch. It's based in Kansas City."

"Oh," he says, looking disappointed, which breaks my heart. "I thought we were going to move in together."

"I did too. But this job wasn't on the table until just now."

"Tell me about it," he says sweetly.

"I'd be working with Jadyn, half executive assistant, half designer, but more importantly, I would be learning everything she does so that, eventually, I could take over her job, and she would just consult. I'm talking a corporate car, country club membership, and a nice compensation package."

"That's awesome, Ainsley, seriously. I know you were excited to move in with me, but you loved your internship. Every time you talk about it, you just light up."

"Like you do with football. It's my passion."

"So, you won't be coming to Lincoln. It's too good of an opportunity to pass up," he says. "I'm excited for you. It just makes me sad, I guess. Because I thought after this semester, we'd finally be together."

"I know. So did I."

"I keep coming back to the fact that I have enough money for both of us. That you don't need to work."

"Damon, we already had this conversation, and you know that I want to work. I want a career. And you know what happened with my parents. How my mom is so grateful she never quit her career even though my dad had tried to get her to numerous times. And I just feel like it's not really fair of you to ask me to give all that up. You're still in college. You have at least two more years before you go pro. And as much as I want to be with you—I mean, you are happy and fulfilled, playing football, which is essentially your job. Shouldn't I get to feel that way too?"

"I get what you're saying. I do. And I agree. It's just … you know I miss being with you. I think I tell you that every time we talk."

"I know you do, and I miss you too. But at least this spring, you won't have games, and we can spend more time together. And I only have to be in the office a couple of days a week. The rest of the time, I can work remotely. So, I can come up there, and you'll be able to come down here."

"What if you meet someone else?" His voice cracks slightly.

"Well," I say with a wide smile, "I'm sure I will meet a lot of new people, but no one that I will like more than you."

"You're supposed to say love," he says, his cocky grin coming back after a brief moment of vulnerability.

And it gets to me.

"It's what I meant, Damon. In fact, I love you so much that I—" I stop speaking, realizing that I was about to tell him I'm pregnant. The words want to slip out just like they did the day I told him I loved him.

But I can't tell him right now. Not over the phone. Not at this point.

"That you what?" he asks, studying me.

"That I've become, uh … a diehard football fan," I tease.

He arches an eyebrow at me.

"Fine, I'm just a big fan of you."

He grins, but then turns serious again. "I'm a big fan of you. I'm sorry for what I said earlier about you just moving in with me. Both Jennifer and my sister would be disappointed in me. I'm excited for you. It's your dream job. And we'll make it work. Do you know where you will live?"

"I literally just got off the phone with Tripp and had to call you. But since Sammy's job is also in KC, I'm hoping maybe we could still be roommates. Both my office and the store where Sammy will work is on The Plaza."

"It's going to be hard," Damon says.

The baby gives me a swift kick to the ribs, taking my breath away. I let out a gasp.

"Are you okay?"

"Yeah, sorry. I don't want to upset you, Damon."

"I know it's a couple of years off, but we've both expressed wanting to be together in the future. How would that work once I get drafted? I can do distance for a while, but I don't want to do it forever. I want to have kids. A house. A dog. You as my wife."

"I want that too. And although it will suck, not being together every day, it will allow me to get going in my career while you're in school, so that by the time you get drafted, I'll be able to work from wherever I want. Which will be wherever you go."

"I'm going to hold you to that."

"You'd better," I say with a grin. "I love you."

"I love you too," Damon says, blowing me a kiss before ending the call.

"What the hell?" Sammy says, plopping down on my bed. "You got another job offer and didn't tell me?"

"It literally just happened."

"Yeah, right. Like they called on a Sunday."

"They do when they're your uncle," I fire back. "He wants me to work with Jadyn to learn the ropes so that, eventually, I can take over her role, and she can just consult."

"Holy smokes! Girl! You're fire!" Sammy says.

"Want to share an apartment with me?"

"You mean, with you and the baby," he states, giving me the eye.

"Don't look at me like that. You know I'm telling him as soon as he's back home for the holidays. Then scandal be damned."

"In that case, I'd love to still be roommates and besties."

He pulls a bag from behind his back. I try to look surprised over the fact that he got my favorite takeout even though I smelled it the second he walked in.

He gets everything set up while I think about the logistics.

"Our lease is up in less than a month. We're going to have to find a place to live fast. It helps that we'll both be working in the same area. We'll find an amazing apartment. I can't wait."

"Are you sure you're okay with having a baby around? We might not get much sleep."

"You mean, *you* might not. I will be wearing earplugs. You know I need my beauty rest. I'll grab my computer so we can look at options while we eat. I just don't think I'm going to be able to go with you though. Why I decided to take so many hours so I could graduate with you is beyond me right now. I have three projects, an essay, and two finals between me and being done with college forever."

"That is a lot. I'm feeling a bit overwhelmed, but I only have two projects and one final. So, why don't we pick them out together, and I'll go look at them, um"—I glance at my phone—"the day before graduation? I should have my final projects close to being done and only have one final to study for. Plus, I need to tell my mom. Alone. So I can explain the situation. I don't want her showing up at graduation and just seeing this belly."

"How do you think she'll take the news?"

"I'm sure she will be surprised—both that I didn't tell her and that I am. But I think once she gets over the shock, she'll be very supportive. She and my dad got pregnant with me very early in their relationship. But that doesn't mean I'm not nervous."

FRIDAY, DECEMBER 11TH

A lot happened.

Ainsley

IT'S BEEN A busy couple of weeks. Nebraska won the conference championship last week in spectacular fashion.

The whole day was pretty spectacular, really.

Sammy and I watched the game at home. We had hot wings and fries at kickoff, which was something I had been craving like crazy. I could literally eat them every day.

When Sammy went to Lincoln with me for the game this fall, Chase's dad was talking about how he and his friends used to do shots of cinnamon schnapps when their team scored. How it could get a little crazy during high-scoring games. And even went on to talk and laugh about some bowl game that was scoreless for so long that they started doing shots for first downs instead. Sounded like there were some drunk people that night.

Since then, Sammy had been obsessed with the idea, but had yet to try it due to his moratorium on alcohol.

But as soon as our team scored their first touchdown, Sammy filled up a shot glass with Fireball whiskey, yelled out a cheer, then downed it.

The team scored a lot. Damon had three touchdown receptions himself, and Sammy had a fair bit to drink and kept ordering more delivery food—starting with curry and followed by pizza.

And then he threw up.

Which made me throw up.

Which was kind of funny.

He was hungover on Sunday when we watched the playoffs selection show and found out that Nebraska would be playing in Dallas on New Year's Eve.

I finally got my projects done, which is a huge relief. I wasn't all that thrilled with the electrical design one, but hopefully, the aesthetic choices that went with it will impress the professor enough.

Now, I'm driving to Kansas City to look at apartments.

I think back to this summer. How I drove on this same road on my way to pick up my parents. How we were going to the Ozarks for the Archibald family reunion and grand reopening of my uncle's resort.

A lot happened there.

It was the place I learned of my father's gambling addiction and the real reason why he didn't get along with his family.

The place where my mom told me that they were getting a divorce.

And the place where I flirted with an adorable guy.

One who I didn't take too seriously.

Until he sort of rescued me from a run-in with a bush.

And then kissed it to make it better.

I was already falling for him, but when he kissed me for the first time, I knew that I wanted to be with him forever.

A few days later, when we were on a romantic picnic, he told me, *I'll never forget the way you look, what you say, how you kiss me, and how you make me feel. I know we've been flirting and kissing, but today feels like one of those moments. The start of something we'll never forget.*

And he was right.

I glance down at my belly. I've gained what the doctor says is a healthy amount of weight, and I definitely had to buy maternity jeans, but with a baggy sweatshirt over my bump, people still don't really notice.

I mean, they would if I wore a tight top, which is very stylish. And while I tell myself that I'm not trying to hide my pregnancy, I kind of am.

But it's like I can't really admit it until I tell Damon.

And it's been so hard.

So many times, I've wanted to tell him about the miraculous things that I've experienced—from hearing the baby's heartbeat, to seeing it on the ultrasound, to the first kick and everything in between.

My goal was to let him get through the season before I told him. And he has. But I kind of forgot about post-season play, where the stakes are even higher.

I just can't wait any longer.

Graduation is tomorrow.

And afterward, I'm going to drive to Lincoln and tell him.

But first, I need to try to find a place to live.

BY LATE AFTERNOON, I'm exhausted and depressed, so I call Sammy.

"Did you find us the perfect place to live?" he practically sings.

"No, I did not. Our budget isn't going very far. Most of the places that were within our budget were either old and tired or they were over by the college and that area was busy. Parking's a nightmare. I know it's the end of the semester, but there were parties going on in the middle of the afternoon!"

"You sound like an old woman," Sammy says with a laugh. "What about the one that was expensive but doable? Probably. The one with all the amenities?"

"It was nice, but they have different amenity packages that you pay extra a month for. Which would put us into the less doable range. There were a few people working in the clubhouse. They looked very hip."

"You have a problem with that? I'm hip. I think. I'd fit in perfectly," he says. "But here's a question. Does the baby really need its own bedroom? Maybe if we took it down to two bedrooms instead of three—"

When he says that, I start sobbing.

"It's okay, Ainsley," Sammy says. "Don't cry. I'll get through my finals, and then we'll look together. Keep in mind, you might even get some money from the baby daddy."

"He's not a baby daddy! He's the father. And I love him. He wasn't just some summer fling!" I yell through my tears. "I got a good job and can take care of my baby without any help. And honestly, once I tell him the truth, he's probably going to hate me. I haven't told you, but I've been dreaming over and over about his reaction. And it's not pretty."

"In your warped mind, you did it for him."

"I know. But I realized that taking my dream job instead of moving in with Damon means that I also have to be able to do this all by myself. I'm sure once he gets over being mad, he'll want to be involved. But he'll be at school in Lincoln. And I'll be in

Kansas City. And I just was sitting here, feeling sorry for myself, and so I scrolled through his social media because I wanted to see his happy face. And there was a girl who tagged him in a post from a birthday party. Her name is Annabelle, and he kissed her in the picture."

"What?" Sammy asks.

"I know. I didn't expect to see that. And now I'm a wreck. I think he's in love with her. And if he's in love with her, how can he be in love with me? How can I trust him?" I sob. "And his sister even commented on the post about how it was true love. TRUE LOVE! *I'm* supposed to be his true love. His fucking butterfly."

"Butterfly?" Sammy questions.

"Yes, his butterfly, slut-terfly, shut-the-fuck-up-fly soulmate."

"Oh, girl, you need to calm down. Just take a deep breath. It will all be okay. You have a lot of—"

"I swear to God almighty, if you utter the word hormone, I will reach through the phone and strangle you. You won't be able to breathe. Ever again."

"Um, wow," Sammy says.

And I start boo-hooing all over again. "How could I ever say something like that to anyone? I am going to be a horrible mother, aren't I? I had a dream that I dropped the baby. In a pool. And an alligator jumped up out of the pool and had my baby in its jaws. And I woke up just as it was about to clamp down."

"Um, Ainsley, sweetheart. I just looked at the photo he was tagged in. It's from the girl's fifth birthday party. They were just little kids. Are you really jealous of a five-year-old? I mean, obviously, she's probably grown up since then."

"Oh, *she has*. And she's gorgeous. And skinny. And I'm just … not."

"Why don't you stop looking for places today?"

"I have to. There are no more on the list."

"We'll make a new list. Let's get through graduation and finals, and then we'll look together. We'll find something perfect, I promise."

"Are you sure?"

"Yes, sweetie, I'm sure."

"Okay," I say with a relieved sigh.

"Maybe you should go to your mom's and spend the night instead of driving back," Sammy says.

"I suppose I could do that, but I might have to drive through somewhere on the way. I need chocolate. No, hot wings. Ice cream? I don't even know what to eat, Sammy. What's wrong with me?"

"You're growing another human. That's what. And that takes a lot of energy. I bet your mom has chocolate."

"You're right. And strawberry ice cream. That's her favorite. You're a lifesaver, Sammy. Bye."

But as I'm driving, I realize I can't just walk into my mom's house pregnant.

So, I call her.

"Hey, Mom," I say when she answers. "I'm in Kansas City. I drove up to look at apartments today, and I'm tired. Do you think I could spend the night with you? Drive back tomorrow morning?"

"Of course. How did it go? Did you find anything?" she asks, causing me to burst into tears again.

"It was horrible. Everything we can afford has something wrong with it. And I'm sorry, Mom. I'm horrible. I'm on my way there, but I have to tell you something first."

"What, honey?"

"I'm pregnant."

"You are?"

"Yes. Anyway, I'm a mess. I've been crying. And I pray you have a magic wand to help me find a place and some ice cream."

"I'll be waiting with both," she tells me.

SHE GREETS ME in the driveway of a beautiful home.

"I can't believe you haven't seen the house yet," she says, giving me a hug. But when she does, my bump crashes into her. "Oh my. You aren't just pregnant. You're like—how far along are you?"

"Thirty weeks. I'm due February twenty-second."

She gets tears in her eyes. "I can't believe my baby is going to have a baby. Do you remember when we were in the Ozarks and I told you that my role as your mother is to help you through rough times? Not judge you. I won't ever judge you. And I mean it. And remember, I got pregnant very quickly with you. Sometimes, love does that. Now, obviously, you've known about being pregnant for a while. Why didn't you tell me?"

"Because I haven't told the father yet."

"Oh," she says, but then she nods like she understands. "Come inside and sit down."

We enter the home, and normally, I would be looking at the architecture. The design choices. But instead, I plop down on a sofa and let out a pathetic sigh.

Mom says, "Stay there. I'll be right back."

A few moments later, she comes back with a pint of strawberry ice cream and a spoon for each of us.

She holds her spoon up toward mine and says, "Cheers," so I

clink mine against hers.

Eating the ice cream helps calm me down.

"Do you want to talk about it?" she says.

"I got pregnant in the Ozarks. At our family reunion. Who does that?"

"Someone who falls in love with a very handsome man who is *not* a blood relative," she counters.

"I was going to tell him. The second the test turned positive. I was shocked, but at the same time, I was happy. Really happy. And I know that Damon wants kids. I know he'll be a great dad."

"So, what stopped you?" she asks.

"We hadn't spoken on the phone for a bit. He was moving to school and then started practice, and I was working long hours to get the project plans all done. And he was just so excited to tell me everything. He was going on about football—the facilities, the coaches, his teammates—and how great everything was. I was so happy for him. He seemed in his element and loving every minute of it.

"I was ready to just blurt it out, but then he mentioned a party a lot of the guys were going to that night. And how the coach said he didn't want anyone getting into any trouble before the season even started. I still remember exactly what he told me his coach said. *No arrests or scandals and absolutely no headlines until we open fall practices to the press.*

"And all I could see were the headlines. Five-star recruit gets his twenty-two-year-old girlfriend pregnant. Danny Diamond's son, five-star recruit Damon, who just turned eighteen, is expecting a baby with his older girlfriend. And I just couldn't do that to him."

"I assume Sammy knows?" Mom asks.

"He does. But I didn't tell him either. He just—well, it started to become obvious."

"And you've gone through pregnancy all on your own? Have you been feeling well?"

"I have. Mentally, in some ways, I've been sort of pretending that I'm not pregnant."

Mom narrows her eyes at me.

"That didn't come out right. I've been doing everything I should be. Seeing the doctor, eating right, taking my vitamins, exercising, talking to the baby, listening to classical music. But if it wasn't for the fact that I didn't want you to be surprised at graduation tomorrow, I wouldn't have told you. Same for Sammy. I want Damon to be the first to know, you know? And I needed to wait until he got through his first season. Proved himself. They've done so well. They made the playoffs and could have three more games, but I decided to drive up there tomorrow after graduation and tell him."

"His mom told me that he asked you to move in with him."

"He—well, we both wanted that. I got offered a job where I could work from anywhere and told him that I'd be moving in with him. We were really excited. But then a few days later, I got offered the dream job."

"The dream job? What will you be doing?"

"Learning from Jadyn Mackenzie how to run the business she sold to Tripp. I'll sort of be a combination of executive assistant and design manager. The goal is that in two years, I will completely take over, and she will consult."

"That's amazing, honey. Congratulations."

"Thank you. The only downside is that my office is in Kansas City. And I had to tell Damon. And he wasn't happy. Told me that I didn't need to work. But I have to! But he finally agreed we could continue to do the distance thing. But really, I think it will be okay. He has two more years before he can get drafted. I'll have two years of learning. And after that, I can work from anywhere."

"That sounds like a good plan. Except for the part that you're having his baby."

"I know. It's complicated. And I'm sorry I lied to you and told you that I was looking for a place for Sammy. We'll be staying roommates for a little longer, if we can find somewhere to live."

"There are lots of lovely apartments in this town."

"I know, but we'll both be working down here, in The Plaza. We were hoping to live nearby. Sammy and I will try again after finals week."

"Come in the kitchen," Mom says, getting up. "I need to make a quick work call. Then we can talk more."

And this time, I do take in my surroundings. The house is gorgeous. Because Damon's mom lived here, I would have expected it to be heavily decorated, but it's actually really soft and pretty. There is a ton of light coming in big transom windows that overlook the backyard, which features a sparkling pool.

Mom opens a well-stocked pantry and says, "Grab anything that looks good. I'll be right back."

WHEN SHE COMES back a few minutes later, I'm happily dipping pretzels in peanut butter and drinking a bottle of sparkling water.

"Who did you have to call? Are you loving your new job?"

"I'm enjoying it a lot actually. And I called Lori Archibald."

"Damon's mom! Ohmigawd! You didn't tell her, did you? *Did you?*" My heart is racing with panic, and I start to feel faint.

"No, I didn't. I wouldn't do that. I simply asked her a question," Mom says. "And based off her answer, I have something to show you. Come with me."

I get off the kitchen barstool and follow her out the French doors to the backyard.

"It's really pretty back here," I tell her. "I bet you are just loving living here. So posh and pretty. Amazing location."

"I am loving it." She doesn't say anything further, just leads me past the pool and down a path.

And set back in the trees is a little cottage.

"Do you have a she shed too?" I ask, but then on further inspection, I realize what it is. "Oh, wait. Is that the original carriage house?"

"It is," Mom says, giving me another short answer.

"That's cool. Did you get a new car or something that you want to show me?"

"No." When we get to the door, she opens it and says, "Go on in."

"Oh, Mom, this place is adorable! Do you spend any time out here?"

"I agree, but, no, I don't. The house is too big for me as it is. This cottage has two bedrooms downstairs and a loft bedroom upstairs."

"Cool. So, once they sell the house, are you going to live back here? Like rent the place?" I wonder.

"I'm actually going to be staying in the house for a while. Van said that real estate is a sound investment, and I am welcome to stay for as long as I want. I know you need your own space, and I don't know how this compares to the apartments you have been looking at—"

"Are you saying Sammy and I could live here?! With you?"

"Well, on the same property, yes, but you'd have this space to yourself."

I throw my arms around my mom and break down in tears. "That would be incredible. Thank you so much."

"Come sit down. We should talk."

"Why do I feel like I'm in trouble all of a sudden?"

"You aren't, honey. While we were in the Ozarks, Sammy called me because he couldn't reach you. You know how he is."

"He can't keep his mouth shut about anything," I say with a laugh.

"And he might have mentioned the drought." I cover my face with my hands and shake my head. "And it's my understanding that the rain finally arrived."

"Oh my goodness. He has such a big mouth. But that is when I got pregnant. Are you terribly mad at me for not telling you?"

"I do wish you would have told me earlier, but that's water under the bridge now. What I wanted to talk about is your support system. If you're going to live in Kansas City while Damon's at school, I want you to have help. Support. From all our families. And when Damon does visit, I think you should have a space for just your family. For you, Damon, and the baby."

"But what about Sammy?"

"I have an idea for Sammy. We'll talk about that later. Do you think you should call him? Like, before you go see him? Like you did me maybe?"

"Remember the night I told you I was feeling a little under the weather when I was in Fort Worth? I took a pregnancy test that night. It was, obviously, positive. And I can tell by the look on your face that you think it was … kinda wrong of me not to have already told him. And trust me, I've wanted to so many times."

Tears start to fall down my cheeks.

"Ainsley," Mom says, giving my hand a squeeze.

"But I just couldn't do it. He has so much he wants to do in life, and I don't want to distract him from it. And I don't want a scandal for him."

"Having a baby is hardly a scandal," Mom argues.

"I don't want to be just some baby mama either."

"Well, you already are, so—"

"And I don't want him to transfer schools. He's meant to be there. He's meant to live out his dream."

"And that's why you haven't come home?" she asks me.

"Yeah."

"You're not being fair to the father or his family. And to be honest, you're not being fair to your baby."

"What do you mean?" I ask with a gasp.

"I mean that there is a whole wonderful, loving family that your baby is going to miss out on if you lie to them. Not to mention the missed bond of the baby's father."

"You're acting like I'm never going to tell him. I just haven't told him *yet*. Also, he's only eighteen."

"I don't care. One, he doesn't act like it. And two, he doesn't act like it."

My mind is transported back to us in the Ozarks, my list of things I told him. My excuses for not being with him.

"Do you love him, Ainsley?"

"Yes. Why else would I agree to move in with him? Why else would I go through all this alone if I didn't love him so, so much?"

"Do you love your baby?"

My hand flies to my chest. "Yes! Of course!"

"Then do the right thing. You need to tell him. Like, now."

"I just told you that I'm going to tell him tomorrow."

"The offer of the carriage house stands. There's room for all three of you when Damon visits. And I'm sure he will as often as he can. But I think you and the baby will need your own space. Tell Sammy he can live in the main-floor guest suite. It has a private entrance."

"Can I see it? And can we video-call him? I called him earlier, crying and all depressed."

"Of course you can."

I hug her. "Thank you, Mom."

"Grandma," she says with a smile. "Did you know that I already have a grandma name picked out?"

"No, I didn't. When did you decide that?"

"Surprisingly, just the other day. I had lunch with my friend Ellen, and her son and his wife are expecting their first. We had a long discussion about it. I told her mine would be Niki. Even though my name is Nicole, no one has ever called me that. Do you think it's cute?"

"I think it's adorable, Mom."

"May I?" she asks, holding her hand out in the direction of my belly.

"Oh, I, um … I want Damon to be the first to feel the baby kick, if that's okay?"

Mom's grin turns down, but she says, "Of course."

And at that moment, the baby gives me a swift kick in the side.

I don't know if that was an *I agree with you for waiting* kick or an *I'm mad at you for not letting Grandma feel me* kick.

"Do you have any ultrasound photos?"

"I do, but—"

"Of course, after you show Damon," she says.

"Let's get Sammy on the phone."

"Are you okay?" Sammy asks the second he answers. "Did you go to your mom's? Did you tell her? Or did you just wallow in ice cream?"

Mom pops her face into the screen. "Hi, Sammy!"

"Nicole. How are you?" he asks.

"Well, to be honest, I'm a little shocked to learn that my daughter is pregnant and hasn't told the father. I can't believe you didn't tell me, even on the sly!"

"I wanted to, trust me, but your daughter—well, she can be stubborn sometimes."

"You are forgiven. And I'm very happy that I'm going to be a grandma."

"And *Grandma* happens to have a three-bedroom carriage house on her property that she's graciously offered. It will be perfect for me and the baby."

"And Damon, when he comes to visit them," Mom adds.

"So, you're ditching me?" Sammy asks, looking distraught.

"She's not," Mom says. "We're going to be like one big, happy family. And while you are welcome to stay in the guesthouse, I have another space that might be better suited for you." Mom turns to me and says, "Why don't I just show you both?"

She leads us around to the side of the house, just off the garage.

"This space has its own entrance," Mom says to Sammy while I pan the area to show him the beautiful, lush landscaping.

"It's gorgeous," Sammy says. "I'm sorry, Nicole, but I don't know exactly where you moved to."

"A few blocks' walk to the Country Club Plaza."

"Perfect location," he says, but he's looking at me curiously, and I can tell he's not so sure about living with my mom. "I would love to be able to walk to work."

Mom opens the door, and we find a beautifully designed guest suite. Upon entrance is a hallway with a sparkly mirror hung over an ornately carved wooden console table. Next is a kitchen, which is open to the living space. Beyond that is a set of French doors.

It's decorated in soft creams and blues with lots of gold sconces and beautiful paintings. The furniture is baroque, possibly a little bit gaudy for Sammy's taste, but then he starts squealing.

"Oh my gosh, tell me that it will be furnished and I get to live in that space as is," Sammy gushes.

"Well, that's up to you. We can have the furniture put into storage if you want to bring your own, or you can keep it how it is now." She pushes open the double doors, revealing a large bedroom suite.

"It is literally divine," he says, and when he sees the marble-clad bathroom, he looks so happy that he could cry.

"So, what do you think?" I ask him.

"I think it sounds like a fantastic idea. You are both amazing, and yes, yes, yes, I would love to live there. So, I'd be here, and Ainsley and the baby would be in the guest cottage?"

"I think Ainsley needs to talk to the father of her baby before she makes another decision," Mom says.

"For sure she does," Sammy says seriously. "But she's stubborn. It doesn't matter what I say. She refuses because she has some warped sense of trying to protect Damon even though he's a grown man and he doesn't need it."

"Look, we aren't gonna discuss this right now. I'm telling him tomorrow."

"I also think you should make the decision about where you live with him. About what job you will take."

"I'm taking the dream job! There is no discussion about that!"

"Ainsley," Sammy says, "you need to consider all possible options. Damon is going to want to take care of his baby. Bond with his baby. Live with his baby. And I'm only saying this now because you're standing there with your mother and not in the same room with me. I'm sorry."

I turn and look at my mom. "And we're paying you rent."

"Sweetheart," my mom says, "I'm not paying rent, so therefore, neither are you or Sammy. It's a big, beautiful home, and I think we should enjoy it because it's not very often that you are given a gift like this."

"One hundred percent," Sammy agrees. "Like, I can't even. Can I see the rest of the house?"

"I'll tell you what," Mom says to me. "Why don't I take the phone and give Sammy a tour while you go sit down and put your feet up? You look exhausted. Oh, and did I mention that the house comes with a chef?"

"What?" Sammy calls out. "What are you even talking about?"

"Well, Lori and Van have a chef, and he likes to walk to work, and because he lives nearby, he's going to continue to use this kitchen to make their meals. He will then drive them out to their new house, but because, in some ways, that will be inconveniencing us"—Mom laughs—"it also means that he'll cook for us too. His food is amazing."

"This just keeps getting better and better," Sammy says.

I don't sit down, but rather give my mom the phone and follow her outside.

She gives Sammy a view of the front of the house, then enters into the marble entry with its massive two-story staircase. There's a beautiful den off the front, a billiards room, and a bar as part of the entertaining space, and then we go into a grand great room with a two-story marble fireplace that looks like it was dropped in from an old French estate.

Sammy is *oohing* and *aahing* and screaming with delight over how beautiful the place is. He comments on the design elements and how he's going to find so much inspiration here.

Next stop is the designer kitchen, outfitted with every possible top-end appliance. My mom stops in front of a set of wooden doors and opens a hidden refrigerator. Inside is all sorts of food.

She looks at the containers and says to me, "How about a chicken enchilada? You've always loved those."

"That actually sounds really good," I tell her, causing her to pop it in the microwave.

While it's heating, she sets me up with a trio of warm queso, chips, and salsa—something she planned for us to snack on later. As soon as the enchilada is warm, she serves it to me, then takes Sammy on a tour of the rest of the house.

I eat the main dish quickly, realizing that I was really hungry, then snack on the rest.

About twenty minutes later, they come back. Mom excuses herself for a moment while I talk to Sammy.

"Well, what do you think? What do you think of the cottage? What do you think of this living arrangement? Like, seriously, Sammy, it's gonna be different, or it's like moving home with our parents or something."

"Yeah, rich parents. I mean, are you kidding me? A chef? Did you see the pool? The fitness room? I mean, did your uncle not take any of the furniture? Like, why is it still fully furnished?"

I laugh. "I don't know. Probably wanted new stuff for the new house."

"Well, regardless, free rent, free food. I really don't know how we would turn that down."

"Agree," I say.

"Can I say one thing that I've wanted to say for a while?" Sammy asks.

"Sure."

"I do appreciate the fact that you're trying to protect him. It's wildly romantic in a twisted sort of way."

"Thank you," I say.

"And Sammy is going to be an amazing fairy godfather."

"I know you will be." My eyes fill with tears. "And I really appreciate your support."

A new life.

Ainsley

"HEY, MOM," I say, opening our apartment door and greeting her with a hug. "I'm almost ready." I left her house really early this morning so I could get back here and get ready.

"What are you wearing?" she asks, taking in the dress I'm currently sporting.

"A dress."

"More like a tent," she says, pulling a box out from behind her back and handing it to me.

"I just—"

"I know, honey, but you're going to have pictures of this day for the rest of your life. Just go try it on."

While I'm changing in my room, I hear her and Sammy, who must finally be ready, chatting. More like gossiping probably.

I pull the dress on, look at myself in the mirror, and smile. It's the first time I've worn anything formfitting.

I actually get tears in my eyes as I cup my belly. And although I've been doing everything right with the pregnancy, I realize that I haven't really let myself accept the fact that my body is changing in a truly beautiful way. That the bump I can see is cradling a new life. My baby. Damon's baby.

Our baby.

But then the tears start sliding down my cheeks.

Because I know there's a very real possibility that he's going to hate me for this.

At the same time, I know that he's the love of my life.

But I need to face the facts.

It could end us.

Kill our trust.

And it might truly end up being just me and the baby.

I consider waiting until Christmas. Of avoiding him. Or telling him it's not his.

But the thought of that nearly breaks me.

I take a deep breath. Wipe away my tears. And stand up tall.

No matter what, today, you are going to drive your pregnant ass up to Lincoln and tell him the news.

I smile as I think about my *naked* ass and how that night started everything.

"YOU LOOK BEAUTIFUL," Mom says when I come out, wearing the dress.

"Thank you for buying it," I say sincerely.

"Literally, you're just glowing. I still can't believe my baby is going to have a baby. I'm so happy."

Sammy and I put on our royal-purple graduation gowns, and Mom helps us with our caps.

"We look amazing," Sammy says, standing in front of the hall mirror and looking at us. "Let's go get those diplomas!"

"You know they don't actually give them to you today, right?"

Mom says.

"Wait, what?" Sammy asks. "Why not? It's graduation!"

"Because final grades aren't in," I tell him. "They just give you the cover and then mail your diploma to you later."

"So, I could possibly go through all this pomp and circumstance and not *actually* graduate?"

"If you flunked a class—" Mom says.

"Oh, the horror! Not to mention the added pressure," he says, looking distressed.

"Sammy, you currently have high scores in all your classes. Even if you failed your finals, you'd still pass."

"True," he says tentatively. "I'm actually glad you told me though. I would have gone into full-on panic mode if I'd opened it and found it empty."

"Crisis averted." Mom shakes her head, looks at her watch, and nods toward the door.

WALKING ACROSS THE stage makes me more emotional than I thought it would. It's really amazing how your life—your dreams, your plans—can change. How stressful it can be when it happens, but how amazing it can turn out in the end. I'm in a relationship with the love of my life, I'm having his baby, and even though, at one point, I seriously considered giving up on college altogether, I'm graduating.

And I'm proud of myself.

SAMMY IS OFF, greeting his parents, while Mom and I navigate the crowded area.

"I'm sort of hot," I tell her, unzipping my gown.

It's a beautiful, sunny day. The temperature is a balmy—for

this time of year—fifty degrees.

"Ainsley!"

I turn toward the sound of my name. And see *him*.

My face lights up with a grin. "Damon!"

I take off running, my gown flying behind my back, making me feel so romantic, just like I did that day in the Ozarks when he surprised me with a visit. I meet him in the middle and throw my arms around him.

"I wasn't expecting you," I tell him, giving him a kiss.

It's been way too long since I've kissed him.

He takes two steps back, his eyes frantic before settling on my belly. "Looks like you actually *are* expecting."

"Oh, that," I say, my eyes getting big. When I saw him, all I thought about in that moment was getting to him. So much so that I forgot … "I'm pregnant, Damon."

"Yes, I can see that," he says coldly. "What are you, about six or seven months?"

"How would you even know that?"

"I was around when Jennifer was pregnant with my little sisters. Are you … is it mine?"

I don't answer because even though I have run this exact scenario over and over in my head a million times, I can't seem to remember anything I was going to say.

"Oh," he says, looking gutted.

"I'm thirty weeks, Damon. And, yes, it's yours. It couldn't possibly be anyone else's."

"I don't understand." His mouth drops open. "Why didn't you—why haven't you told me? How could you keep something like this from me? For so long?"

"Honestly, I did it for you," I say softly.

"I don't understand," he says again, looking equal parts sad and pissed.

I see all the people around us. "Why don't we go to my apartment so we can talk about it? Will you meet me there?" I ask him, suddenly very worried that this might be the end of us.

"Yeah," is all he says, then turns and walks away from me.

That side of you.

Damon

I WALK TO my car, my feelings everywhere—ranging from *why the fuck didn't she tell me* to shock and joy that she's having my baby.

When I put my hands on the steering wheel, I realize I'm shaking.

And I have to talk to someone.

I think about who to call, ultimately dialing my mom's number.

When she answers, I blurt out, "Ainsley is pregnant. I'm talking, like, due-in-ten-weeks pregnant. I just found out. And the only reason I found out is because I surprised her at her graduation ceremony."

"Wow," Mom says. "I'm going to be a grandmother?"

"I guess, yes, but if she didn't tell me about the baby, does that mean she doesn't want me in her life? In the baby's life? I literally don't understand. I'm pissed. Mad. Hurt. But also, like, I'm going to be a dad."

"You've been dating this whole time—like, in a relationship, right?"

"Yes, that's the crazy thing. I could see maybe if we ended things after the Ozarks, but we didn't. Do you think that's it? Do you think she thinks I'm too immature? Our age difference was something that she was concerned about at first. But I haven't heard her mention it since then. And I know she worries that, you know, I'm some hotshot football player and that I have girls flocking around me. Even though I don't."

"You don't?" Mom questions.

"I mean, some girls have expressed interest, but I'm always very clear that I'm not interested and that I'm in a relationship."

"I will admit, that was a problem for your father and me. I worried about it constantly, and it pretty much ate me alive. But you, Damon, are not just like your father. You have so much more discipline in your life. Especially at your age."

"Dad liked to party."

"He did. With Jadyn."

"They always joke that they were a bad influence on each other."

"They probably were. Overall, they were good kids. But partying isn't really what I'm referring to. It's an integral part of your being. Yes, you have your father's charm, but I think I balanced you out a bit. You come off as easygoing and carefree because you two share that naughty-looking grin, but what people don't realize is that you're quite cerebral. You think before you act." She laughs. "Well, I thought you did. But seeing as you're going to have a baby—"

"We used protection, Mom."

"Well, it must have been very *meant to be* then," she says. "What I'm saying is that maybe you need to make sure Ainsley knows that side of you."

"Should I start wearing glasses and a letterman sweater?" I tease.

"Make fun all you want, but I'm right, and you know it."

"Actually, I don't. I don't know what to do. How to feel. I should be elated. And pissed. She lied to me, Mom."

"Give her the benefit of the doubt, Damon. Don't assume anything. While I can't imagine why she didn't tell you, she obviously had some reason. And while I know that most professional athletes have to be quite committed to excel, that's not always what the public sees because it's not sexy. So, they end up seeing the splashy parts—the women, fast cars, champagne-on-yachts kind of thing."

"As opposed to the time spent in the gym? The injuries. The pain."

"Also the diversification of assets. The charities. The good so many athletes do with their gifts. It's funny though. Your dad used to tell me he was invincible and he'd never get hurt."

To that, I chuckle. "He might have been right about that because other than a couple of minor injuries that kept him out of a game or two, he didn't."

"Still, due to my own issues, I worried about everything. I was jealous of the girls who fawned over him. Even jealous of his relationship with his best friend. You know, Ainsley's mom recently told me that during Ainsley's freshman year of college, she got crushed by the boy she thought was the love of her life. She failed a semester of classes and lost her scholarship. It's what prompted her to change schools and her major."

"That Brad guy from Eureka Springs was that boy. The one who just got engaged. She told me that he'd cheated on her, but didn't tell me the rest."

"Understand that a hurt like that can make a girl … assume it will happen again. Throw in the recent trust issues with her father …"

"You think she doesn't trust me. And that's why she didn't tell me?"

"I don't know why. I'm just suggesting some possible reasons. I do believe she loves you, Damon. You can see it written all over her face whenever she's around you. So, the fact that she didn't tell you, that she went through this much of the pregnancy on her own, makes me think she had a good reason—at least in her mind. Maybe she worried about your reaction. Or she might just have been scared to tell you."

"I'm listening to all your advice, and I know I should be considering it. But right now, I'm feeling really, really upset with her."

"Can I ask you a question?" Mom says.

"Sure."

"What would you have done if she'd told you as soon as she found out?"

"I would have been surprised, but also thrilled. I would have proposed. Immediately. Gotten married. Maybe transferred schools."

For the first time in our conversation, Mom is quiet.

And it sinks in.

"Could that be why?"

"You'll have to ask her. But I would suggest not proposing just yet."

"I love babies," I say softly.

"Wait until you hold your own."

"Do you really think it's due to my age? Or that she just

doesn't think that I know what I want?"

"Let me know when you find out. And I won't mention the news to anyone. I think that should be up to the two of you."

I hang up just as I arrive at her apartment complex.

I take a deep breath, park, and get out of the car.

Fight for.
Damon

WHEN WE GET to her apartment, she sits on the couch while I pace the space in front of the television.

"Before you explain this situation," I say, "you need to know a few things. And this is going to be brutally honest. You not telling me that you're having my baby really, really hurts. And it's not fair to me. You know how important family is to me. You've seen me with my little sisters. I love kids. I love babies. I understand our relationship moved quickly. But we both confessed our love. Our wanting to be together.

"I kind of feel like I just found out you cheated on me. Regardless of what you're about to tell me, I don't know that I will be able to believe you. Because this is a betrayal, Ainsley. Of our love. Of our trust. When I told you that I fell in love with you three years ago, I meant it. When I told you at the wedding that this was going to be us someday, I meant it. I know it was only twelve days, but you know as well as I do that our love is real. Which is why you not telling me hurts so much."

I can't help it. Tears fill my eyes. Because this sucks. And hurts.

"It's telling me that you don't trust me or that you don't think I'm man enough to handle this. And I have never given you a reason for you to think those things about me, and it's not fair. So, I don't know what your plans are. I don't know where you're going to live. What you're planning to do. But know that I am going to be a part of my baby's life even if it means I have to sue you for custody."

She looks me straight in the eye and says, "I wouldn't expect anything else from you."

What she says is not what I was expecting. It shocks me. I thought I'd have to fight her on this. Fight for my baby.

"Damon, I need to explain to you why I didn't tell you. And hopefully, once you understand, you will … well, understand why I did what I did."

I run my hands down my face in frustration. I'm stressed. And I need to calm down.

I take a deep breath as she says softly, "I did it for you."

"That makes no sense."

"It's not like I did this to myself, Damon. I had some help," she says, pointing at my crotch as memories of our times together rush through my mind. The perfect bliss of it.

And I can't help but smile.

"This hasn't been easy for me."

"That was by choice," I tell her.

I want so bad to be angry at her. And I am. But she looks so beautiful and resolute.

Regardless of what my mom said, I move in front of her and drop to my knees. "Marry me."

"I want to marry you—*someday*, Damon. More than anything.

But I can't accept your proposal right now. I think we need to figure things out first. Don't you think?"

I let out a whoosh of air and nod. But I stay put.

"Family is literally everything to me," I tell her as I stare at her belly.

"But your career, your college game, your focus—those are also important. Especially this semester," she counters.

"Of course I'm passionate about football. It's a game I love and have devoted a big part of my life to, but that's not how I was raised. I was raised with balance. I know what's important in life. My family is more important than football."

"I was going to tell you first. Sammy eventually figured it out, obviously, but I never told him," she says, rubbing her belly. The belly with my baby inside it. "And I told my mom yesterday, but I always wanted to tell you first. For that moment to be between us."

"You do realize that you have already taken away so many firsts for me."

"What do you mean?" she asks.

"The first time you heard the baby's heartbeat, the first look at the baby via ultrasound, feeling those first kicks, and most importantly allowing me to talk to the baby. It needs to know that Daddy is here and that they are loved."

The emotion in my voice brings tears to her eyes.

"How do you even know about all those things?"

"Because I got to experience them with Jennifer—twice. And I shouldn't have to list all the reasons why I'll be a good dad. You should already know."

"I do know, Damon. I was going to tell you right away. I was going to tell you before your second game, but it was the wrong time."

"That's where you are dead wrong. Finding out that the love of my life is having my baby would have made any day better."

"The love of your life," she says, looking stricken before leaping off the couch and running into the bathroom.

I can hear that she's throwing up.

My butterfly.

Ainsley

AS SOON AS he said the words *love of my life*, I could feel the bile rising in my throat.

He could have used so many words to describe how he felt, and he used the ones that broke me.

I throw up, then stay in the bathroom and sob.

I don't know how I imagined this would go. But it wasn't like this.

Pretty soon, the door opens, and Damon wraps me in a hug. "I'm sorry you're sick," he states. "But you're being stupid."

"Stupid?" I ask, my claws ready to come out.

"Yes, because you are making assumptions about me. About what I want out of life."

"You have a bright future, Damon. And the reason I didn't tell you is because I wasn't going to ruin it with a scandal."

"A scandal? Having a baby isn't a scandal."

"Do you think I wanted to go through pregnancy alone? Because I did not," I say, my voice filling with the emotion I've somehow managed to hold in this whole time. "The second the line turned pink, I couldn't wait to tell you."

"Then why didn't you?"

"Because I love you."

"And that makes no sense either because if that were truly the case, you would have told me. Do you know how bad this hurts me?"

"Well, do you remember our conversation? That first time we really talked after you got to Lincoln? You were going out that night with some guys on the team."

"I remember."

"That's the night I took the test. Even though we certainly didn't plan for it, I knew you'd be excited."

"Of course I would be," he says, softening a little. "But I still don't—"

"Your coach said *no scandals, no headlines*. And I could picture them in my head. *Danny Diamond's son knocks up stepcousin at family reunion. Five-star recruit gets his twenty-two-year-old girlfriend pregnant.*"

"I wouldn't have cared about the headlines," he says.

"But your coach would have. Right?"

He sucks in a breath and considers it. Then he's kind of half nodding, half shaking his head, like he can't make his mind up. "You might be right."

He leads me back out to the living room and sits on the couch next to me.

"I still don't know how it happened," I confess. "We used condoms every time."

"I know *exactly* when it happened," he says.

"You do?"

"The golf course."

"Our first time?"

"Yeah, things went a little further than they probably should have before I put a condom on."

"I was on top of you," I say, remembering that wonderful night.

"Yeah," he says. "It was very nice."

"We need to talk about something else though," I tell him.

"We need to talk about a lot of something elses, but what are you referring to?"

"The birthday party girl."

"What birthday party girl?"

"The one who tagged you on social media. Your sister said that it was true love. But *I'm* supposed to be your true love. And you never told me about her!" I say, getting worked up again. This is all still so upsetting.

"You lost me," he says, looking at me like I'm crazy.

I whip out my phone, pull up his profile, scroll down to find it, and hold it up to his face. "See?"

He starts laughing. "I was, like, six!"

I glare at him.

He leans back and studies me. His eyes landing on my belly. "You know, sometimes, in pregnancy, women can feel—"

"If you say hormonal, you can walk right out that door forever," I say, pointing at it.

He smiles. "She doesn't compare to you. Remember how you told me that you thought you knew who your true love was, but then later you felt it for real?"

"Yes."

"Same goes for me," he says, gently pushing my bangs off my

face. "I love you, Ainsley. You're my butterfly, remember?"

I throw my arms around him. "Are you sure? You don't hate me?"

"I don't think I could ever hate you." He studies my face. "Does this have anything to do with Brad?"

I wasn't expecting that question, but I answer honestly, "Yes, and no."

"Tell me the no part first," he says.

"You know that he hurt me. And I did carry that with me. But it stopped the second you came into my life. Because I felt like I was finally, truly where I was supposed to be. With the person I was supposed to be with." I squint my eyes at him. "I just realized I never told you that he came to see me in the Ozarks."

"And why didn't you tell me?"

"I told Sammy, and I was going to tell you, but then you showed up, and I forgot all about it."

"What happened?"

"He called me the first day I got there. Told me that he missed me, thought we should get back together. That he maybe had called off the engagement—he hadn't. And then told me he was in the resort lobby and I should come see him."

"And?"

"I told him no. That I had no desire whatsoever to see him again." I roll my eyes. "I didn't want any drama in my life. I was too happy. With you."

"And the yes?" he asks.

"The yes has nothing to do with my heart. It has to do with my head. Since I can't remember what I told you about him, I'll give you the condensed version.

"We'd dated in high school. Had lots of future plans. I got a scholarship to Notre Dame. He didn't, but he followed me there. Three weeks before finals, I found out he had been cheating on me. I was devastated. Bombed all my classes. Failed. Lost my scholarship. Couldn't afford to go back.

"Notre Dame was my dream. I used to think he stole it from me. But I realize that I should have been stronger. Gotten through it.

"That's why I was so adamant about taking the dream job, even knowing that it meant we would be apart. I will not allow someone to hold that kind of power over me ever again."

"Is that really why you didn't want to fall in love with me?" he asks, taking my hand and squeezing it.

"It's why I didn't want to fall in love ever again."

"What I think is that you fell in love with a boy. What you needed was a man."

I squint my eyes at him. "I don't understand."

"A man would have been honest with you. Broken up with you if he felt the need to be with other people. Would you have reacted differently had he done that?"

I nod. "Yeah. We were young. Before we went to college, we had talked about maybe seeing other people. I was actually the one to have that conversation with him. He said no. Never. He only wanted me. And I, stupidly, believed him."

"My point. You were dating a boy. Not a man. I was raised to be a man," he says.

"I know that, Damon. But at the same time, you tried to talk me out of taking the dream job. Told me you'd take care of me."

"I said that because I wanted to be with you all the time. But I came around quickly, you have to admit."

"You did. I know you have goals for your life, but I do too.

And I am not going to let anyone screw that up for me. Even you."

"And you shouldn't. The right man would support your dreams. And you. Always."

I nod my head in agreement, but the cynic in me is thinking, *Yeah, in some fairy tale.*

He leans in, kisses my cheek sweetly, and says, "P.S. I'm the right man."

Which makes me smile. "I actually know that. And I'm really sorry you found out the way you did."

"So, when *were* you going to tell me?"

I get up and go into my room, then return with my tote bag, setting it on the coffee table in front of him. "After graduation, I was coming back here to get my bag, and then I was going to drive straight to Lincoln." I look down at my belly. "To tell you. To explain."

"That makes me feel a little better," he says. "You have tenacity, for sure. I wouldn't have been able to keep it from you. But when I think about this semester, you might be right. Knowing would have affected me. I would have obsessed over pregnancy calendars. It would've kept me up at night. And it could have possibly shifted some of my focus.

"When we were all in the Ozarks, I told Chase that I would never let my relationship interfere with my playing. That I could separate the two. He told me that I couldn't say what I would do or how I would react because I had never felt this way about a girl before." He stops and chuckles. "I've always said that shit rolls off my back because I don't care what most people think. That I only care what my family and friends think. But what he asked me next did make me wonder."

"What did he say?"

"He asked what I thought would happen if, say, you and I got in a fight, had a misunderstanding, or if you decided we were just a summer fling. How that devastation would affect me."

Feeling vulnerable.

Damon

"YOU WILL NEVER be just a summer fling, Damon. I hope you know that."

"Well, I do now," I say with a big grin. "We're having a baby together. Regardless if our romantic relationship works out, we always have to act as a family, okay?"

"Agreed," she tells me.

"Good. I do appreciate the fact that I was fully able to focus on my season, my training, and my classes." I look down, feeling vulnerable in this moment. "But it wasn't as effortless as I made it sound to you. Even though Chase was named starter quickly and I followed four games later, we still got crap from some of the older guys. When Chase started leading the team, it changed the dynamics. Some players resisted. Some were resentful. Throw in all their drama with family, girls, and partying, and I was grateful that I didn't have that in my life."

"I know my freshman year of college was definitely eye-opening about what I wanted out of life, how I handled myself on my own—which was not very well. I was all about my boyfriend, and I didn't want you to be all about me. And in some ways, it might have been a bit of a test for me. I sort of needed to know that we could be apart and together without having to worry about you cheating on me. The fact that we made it through this semester and are still together says a lot about our future. It's a big deal."

"Having a baby is a big deal," I say. "You know that the first time I laid eyes on you, I told Chase and my sister that I was going to marry you." I shake my head and smile. "But it's not all I said."

"What did you say?"

"That you were the mother of my future children."

Her eyes literally flood with tears. The emotions she must have been trying to hold back seemingly just lost the battle.

"Oh, Damon."

"Don't cry, Champ," I tell her, but I start crying again too. "I've crushed on you since I was fifteen. I'm still crushing. Actually, that's not true. I fell in love with you in the Ozarks, and we made a baby. We should be celebrating that."

I put my hand across her belly, and the baby gives me a swift kick, one Ainsley probably deserves in this moment, but I look at my hand in awe.

"I just felt our baby kick. Tell me about your pregnancy, please. Is the baby growing and developing okay?"

"Yes, everything is going well. And you should know that the baby loves to hear your voice. Has been hearing your voice. Every single time we talk."

"That makes me feel better," I say. "But I think I'll have to move back to Kansas City to be with you and the baby. I can transfer schools. I'm sure Kansas would take me. That would be the closest."

"That's a hard no, Damon. Remember when you told me we

didn't need to rush because we were soulmates? That means that we don't have to be in a hurry now. The conversation we had about how it will suck—not being together every day, but that it will allow me to get going in my career while you're in school, so that by the time you get drafted, I'll be able to work from wherever I want—still stands."

"No, it doesn't," I stress. "Because now there's a baby in the mix. *My baby.*"

"Yesterday, I went to Kansas City to look at apartments for me and Sammy. It didn't go well. I called my mom, told her on the phone that I was pregnant. And I was crying. She ended up offering to let me live in her guest cottage with the baby *and you*, whenever you are in town. We'll have space, and mostly, I'll have some extra support from both our families."

"I need to be present. With my child," I state.

"And you will be. We'll make it work. Two years will fly by. You're where you're supposed to be, Damon. Where you're going to make your mark. You wanted me to move in with you and for you to take care of me, but now, you have even more reason to want it all to happen. So you can provide for our baby."

"When's our due date?" I ask.

"You're going to love this," she says, her tears drying up as a smile spreads across her beautiful face and her eyes sparkle with excitement. "I'm due February the twenty-second."

I look upward and smile, barely being able to believe it. Double angel number. I gaze into her eyes, then roll up my sleeve and show her my new tattoo—the logo for our brand. The same tattoo my dad, Jadyn, and Phillip have.

Angel wings.

"It's an angel number. Double angel actually," I tell her in awe.

"I know. When did you get the tattoo?"

"About a month ago. I wanted to show you in person." I break out into a grin as it all really hits me. "I'm gonna be a dad."

"Yeah, you are."

"Wow. Wow," I say again, then touch her stomach gently. I bend down and speak directly to her belly. "Hi, little angel. I'm your daddy. Your mommy says that you know my voice. Is that true?"

Reason to win.

Ainsley

NOT SURPRISINGLY, WHEN Damon speaks, the baby becomes very active.

"I swear, every time we talk, this little nugget does somersaults or some kind of gymnastics inside of me."

"Well, of course, you'll be athletic," he says to my belly, his smile beaming and his eyes bright with excitement. "I also think you should know that I can't wait to be your daddy. To hold you."

He kisses my belly.

Then me.

"I love you," he says.

"I love you too. And I want to say it again. I didn't want to upset you, I promise. I just wanted you to be able to focus this semester. And you've done so incredibly. So much so that I couldn't wait until after your last game to tell you."

"Can you believe we're going to the playoffs?" he asks.

"I can actually."

He gently strokes my belly and says to the baby, "And now, I have an even bigger reason to win."

"Do you want to see the baby?" I ask him.

"Of course!"

I nod, get up, run to my room, and grab the box of baby stuff I've been saving.

"For the record, you're the first person I've allowed to feel the baby kick. And no one but me has seen these photos. I couldn't show anyone. I couldn't tell anyone. Until you knew."

He looks at the ultrasound photos in wonder. "This is amazing. Can you believe we made this? Together?"

"On a golf course, apparently," I tease. "Maybe they will be a good golfer, like their mommy."

"Look at those long legs."

"All I know is, those long legs have been kicking me in the ribs. And it hurts."

He grins about that. And he's so cute.

Literally so handsome.

Emotions overcome me again.

"What's wrong?" he says, holding my hands and gazing into my eyes.

"I knew you'd be happy about the pregnancy, but it was so hard not to tell you. I wanted to tell you so many times. When we were in our picnic spot. The first game you played in. Almost every time I saw you really. The other day when we were talking about my job, it almost slipped out. But I knew I had to tell you in person. I knew you would be mad at me. I'm so glad you aren't mad at me. I'm so glad you still love me." I hold up my arm. "Every time I wanted to tell you, I'd look at this charm bracelet. Remember when I told you that you are my first real love? And that I wanted to support you in football, life, and beyond?"

"Yeah."

"That's what I was trying to do."

"I'm a little mad," he says, "but the happiness makes up for it."

"I swear to you, I will never keep anything from you again. And although I've been going to the doctor regularly and doing everything I can to make sure our baby is healthy, I haven't done anything else. I haven't bought a single outfit or anything for the nursery. I just couldn't until you knew. Until you could be a part of it."

"Have you thought of any names yet?" he asks. "Although I will be happy either way, I've always felt like I was destined to be a girl dad."

"Really?" I say.

"Well, you know, I'm already surrounded by them."

I roll my eyes. "Sure you are, hotshot."

"I didn't mean that," he says. "I'm referring to the women in my family. I have three sisters, plus my mom and Jennifer."

"Well, you should know then that I can't wait to name our baby either."

"Do you know the baby's sex?"

"Sorta," I tell him.

"What do you mean?"

"When I had one of the ultrasounds, they asked me if I wanted to find out. I told them yes, but not to tell me. That I wanted us to find out together."

I run back into my room and come out with the envelope and hand it to him.

"The ultrasound tech was awesome," I say. "She decorated up the envelope for our big reveal."

"It's cute how she wrote *Boy or Girl* with the boy in blue marker and the girl in pink."

"Why don't you do the honors?" I say, emotion overcoming me again. Happy emotions.

He's not mad at me. He still loves me. And he's excited about the baby, just like I knew he would be.

He opens the envelope and pulls out a sheet of paper. "It's a girl! A baby girl," he says, looking misty. And happy. "I'm having a baby girl with that girl—the girl I told everyone I was destined to be with the day I met you." He bends down and kisses my belly again, whispering sweetly, "Daddy loves his baby girl."

But when she kicks him, he stands up and gazes into my eyes. "I kinda like you too." He gives me a wink before planting his lips on mine.

And when he picks me up, twirls me around, and kisses me, I don't think I've ever felt so much joy and happiness in my life.

How will it all end for Damon + Ainsley?
Find out in That Someday.

ABOUT THE AUTHOR

Jillian Dodd® is a *USA Today*, #1 Apple, and Amazon Top 5 bestselling author. Her That Boy series has been optioned for TV/Film.

She writes fun binge-able romance series with characters her readers fall in love with—from the boy next door in the That Boy series to the daughter of a famous actress in The Keatyn Chronicles to a spy who might save the world in the Spy Girl series. Her newest series include London Prep, a prep-school series about a drama filled three-week exchange, and Eastbrooke Academy, a boarding school romance series.

Jillian is married to her college sweetheart, adores writing big fat happily ever afters, wears a lot of pink, buys way too many shoes, loves to travel, and is distracted by anything covered in glitter.

Check out my books and swag at www.jilliandodd.net